THE WATCHER

Monika Jephcott-Thomas

London | New York

Published by Clink Street Publishing 2017

ISBN:s
978-1-912262-02-1 paperback
978-1-912262-03-8 ebook

To all the children in the world and their emotional well-being

Someone was watching the house.

The terraced red brick house on three floors in the suburb of Mengede in the heart of the Ruhr district. Sulphurous clouds draped the rooftop and thick soot lined the windowsills, even on the pretty, round Tiffany window in the attic.

It was the blue and red glass of the window, lit up from the inside that evening, which the watcher's eyes were fixed on. It was as if the watcher knew exactly who was in there and exactly what they were doing. Or perhaps it was just that the Tiffany window was so much more appealing than the other windows below – tall, skinny, square, humdrum – windows which made the house look gaunt.

It was time to go home. It was getting too cold to stand around on street corners. It would arouse suspicion. The watcher sneered at the house and sloped off.

Charred fragments of letters snow down over Max as he dives for cover in the icy mud. The Russians have blown the Luftwaffe plane to bits and now their infantry, clad in white, is advancing out of the mist, over the field towards him and the shell of a monastery where his field hospital cowers; where his patients lie helpless and his colleagues hide hopeless.

The floor is crunchy with shattered glass from the patients' drips. Those that can walk are already being helped to clamber out of the basement, barefoot and in their pyjamas. They limp, slip and slide across the icy ground, falling on top of one another absurdly, heading for who knows where.

Max fumbles around the remains of the basement, assessing those still in their beds, trying to reassure the monk sitting on a bench with a thick piece of the ceiling crushing his lap like a diabolical desk.

'Doctor, help me!' he cries out.

Max remains for a while, knowing the masonry is too heavy to move and even if they ever did move it the resulting reperfusion in the legs would send potassium, phosphate and urate leaking into the circulation, killing the monk before they could amputate. So he shouts reassuring words to the monk and begins clearing rubble from a pile out of which sticks a nun's legs. He soon stops. Her head is pressed flat like a flower in a book.

His fellow doctors Horst, Edgar, Lutz and Dolf are on the field with him now. Nuns who stand in for nurses and soldiers in pyjamas on crutches shiver there too. The Russians begin to fire their Tokarevs and throw grenades. Soldier after soldier, patient after patient, is shot. Two feet from Max a grenade explodes. He can feel the heat penetrate him, but he's still alive, walking across the field as if he was walking down Mengede High Street on a summer's afternoon. Nightmares are strange like that. The nuns either side of him are decapitated by more explosions, but

Max walks on. Horst is shot in the shoulder and Max runs to his brother, wrapping himself around him to protect him from further injury. But the Russian bullets find their way through Max and riddle Horst. Max walks on. Sees Lutz and Dolf on fire. He pulls Lutz to the floor and rolls him in the snow to try and douse the flames. He succeeds. Then does the same to Dolf, but as he does so Lutz spontaneously combusts again. His efforts are futile. He should be dead himself, but nothing Max does matters. He cannot be killed and he cannot save anyone else.

Captive now, they are made to march endlessly around the city.

Another shot. Another patient who cannot keep up.

And another. And another.

Max's eyes fill with tears. He is livid at the contempt this signifies his captors have for the infirm when he has made it his mission in life to mend and cure them.

'Oh God!' the soldier in front of him cries. Max can't be sure if he cried for the patients being shot or for himself as his trousers drip with urine.

All that coffee he had this morning with Jenny is having the laxative effect it was fast becoming associated with in some medical journals. He thinks about asking one of the Russians if they can stop for a break, appeal to their better nature, but then another shot rings out from behind and he realises shitting himself would be the least of his worries. But he settles on urinating, like his comrade in front, just to ease the pressure on his bowel, buy a few more hours, he hopes.

He looks at Edgar as he does it. To lock eyes with him perhaps. To keep Edgar from looking down and seeing him do it. Edgar smiles at him in the way Max had smiled at the monk crushed under the masonry.

More gunfire.

Max woke with an epileptic spasm in the attic room with the Tiffany window. Next to his wife. Drenched in his own piss.

'It's all right, darling.' Erika concealed her revulsion in a whisper, trying to both soothe her husband and not wake their daughter Netta, who was snoring gently in her little bed on the other side of the room. 'Go downstairs and have a quick wash. I'll find some spare sheets and we can get back to sleep.'

He did as he was told, silent with embarrassment, leaving half-footprints on the bedroom floor and stairs as his wet pyjamas dripped mockingly onto his feet.

She pulled her nightdress carefully over her head and used the dry half to rub down her wet leg. She rolled it into a ball and threw it by the door, finding a clean one in the drawer. Then she went downstairs to get some water to wash the mattress with.

She found him sitting in the bath, head on his knees, as it slowly filled with water. He had been back a few weeks now, but only when she saw him naked like this was she reminded just how malnourished and mistreated he had been in that labour camp on the edge of the Arctic. He would certainly never talk about it. She was at once repulsed by his appearance – his cheeks of flint, his reptile back – and yet desperately sorry for him. But most of all she felt guilty. Guilty for seeking solace in the arms of another while he was away. And guilty for thinking right now how she would rather be looking at Rodrick's muscular bulk in that bath. Guilty for the way her thighs were tingling even now with the thought of washing Rodrick as he grinned at her and grabbed at her breasts. Guilty for how difficult she found it to look at Max's skin with anything but her medical brain, with the curiosity she would usually reserve for an abnormally large sebaceous cyst on a patient's cheek.

'That's enough water,' she cooed, 'you only need a quick wash. Then you can come back to bed. Get some sleep.'

Max didn't answer. He continued to let the water run. His eyes wide, far from sleep, staring through the wall to somewhere beyond. Somewhere two thousand miles away at the dark northern edge of the world. To Gegesha, the labour camp where he'd lost good friends, been beaten, almost frozen to death, where he'd tried to heal the sick in his hospital on stilts out in the diesel coloured waters of the Barents Sea, in quarantine, away from the Russians who feared the diseases which thrived in the awful conditions they perpetuated. And yet, after four years in the camp, Gegesha had become a kind of home, albeit a perverse one. He had found a way to survive and to help others survive too. He had formed friendships with fellow prisoners and, although they could be graced with nothing like the same designation, he had formed connections of sorts with some of his captors, who favoured him for the medical attention he gave them and their families. It had all become so familiar, even the discomfort and the cold, that to change it, to leave it for something new, or return to something from the past, seemed frightening.

And, of course, there was Jenny. Jenny, who had shown him so much kindness when he had had to give her and all the other prostitutes servicing the Russian officers their regular check-up for venereal diseases. She would wash his uniform for him, a luxury many other men could only dream of, but that wasn't the reason why he looked forward to seeing her so much. Jenny was the only person he could confide in. Sure, he had Horst and Edgar too, and they were always there for each other in the way that brothers are, but the way he could talk to Jenny, and the way she talked to him, was different. It was because she was that rarest of things in wartime, a woman. And despite what others might tell him about the ways and minds of prostitutes, she was a sensitive woman. She often had a twinkle in her eye and would tease him terribly as he examined her genitals with the utmost professionalism, but despite his embarrassment he knew in his heart that she was only protecting herself from shame too with all her bravado. As soon as the examination was over and she was covered up again, they would always talk with an honesty, intimacy and concern for each other which he hadn't known since... since Erika.

And it was during those cosy conversations with Jenny that a feeling enveloped him, as if he were back in Erika's student digs, snuggled up in the threadbare armchair with her, his blanket over them; or sitting on the stairs outside her door as she stood before him swinging flirtatiously on the bannister. They had talked then of friends and books and dreams and travel and he had found the shape of her waist irresistible. He just *had* to slip his arms around it. So he did. The similar ease with which he spoke to Jenny often had him looking furtively at her petite hourglass figure and had his brain instructing his arms to encircle it. But he didn't of course. He would reprimand himself silently as he nodded at Jenny, telling himself to focus on what she was saying, and scolding himself for even noticing her figure, her incredibly slender eyebrows, her blonde hair and her beauty, which she managed to maintain admirably even in such dire conditions as the foul and cramped apartment block the Russians stuffed her and the other working girls into.

He flinched as Erika leaned over, piercing his reverie, and turned the tap off. As his body twitched he felt the scars on his scalp tighten. Scars from the beating which had confined him to his own hospital for days. Days during which he gradually became aware of someone constantly at his bedside. And when he was fully awake and lucid he realised it was Jenny. And it was then that she kissed him. Not on the cheek like she did to congratulate him on his Iron Cross all those years before, but a kiss on the lips that told him that the fear of losing him had shifted her boundaries; a fear and a shifting which he felt too, but one which sent tears streaming down his numb cheeks, because somewhere in his soul was the realisation that this was the start of something that would cause both of them pain when the time came for change.

And change came when all the prisoners were finally released. Then, from the back of the truck which shook his meatless bones as it thundered through town towards the border, he saw her standing by the roadside. And as he saw his life, the life he knew anyway, receding from view, he made one desperate attempt to cling onto a part of it and shouted:

'Mengede. I'll be in Mengede, Dortmund. Look me up!'

Much to the shock and amusement of his mischievous friend Edgar, which set the other doctor tapping out a frenetic swing beat on his long bony thighs.

He watched Erika's arms as she filled a bucket with water in the basin to wash the mattress with. Practical arms, arms which trembled slightly, and jerked about with tired industriousness. The skin of the forearm which steadied the bucket didn't seem to him as tight as it used to be, not as porcelain. He saw dark hairs on it which he didn't remember being there before. His eyes drifted away, almost repulsed... no, not repulsed, just saddened by the change. He recalled the same arm as it swung her around the bannister. Supple, strong, playful, carefree, the skin so perfect. Or perhaps that was just the lighting in the stairwell then. No it *was* so perfect. Her arm, her raven hair, what she said, the time they spent together, everything was perfect then. He would tremble in anticipation of her touch, swell with pride that she wanted to be so close to him. Of all the men she could have had in the faculty, she chose him. He felt as tall as Edgar and just as confident in her presence then. The first words she ever spoke to him, in a bar with red lights and red décor, came bubbling up through the sound of the running water.

'Every other boy here has asked me to dance tonight. Every other boy has flirted with me, except you.'

'Well,' he had said, blushing, 'I'm not really one for dancing... nor for flirting.' He jabbed his glasses further up his nose.

'Oh.'

'Not that you aren't attractive,' he had stuttered. 'I mean, I understand why all the men here would want to flirt with you, it's just that I'm not that confident, I suppose.'

'Oh really? Well, my friend Edith over there tells me you're tipped to be top of the class in all subjects this year so you can't tell me you're not confident.'

'Ah.' He raised a finger, *almost* confidently. 'Confidence in medicine is not the same as confidence in situations like this.'

'Like what? What is this?'

'This. Parties, chatting. Women.'

'Why not?'

'Well, there are hundreds of text books that tell you exactly what to do when it comes to medicine. All you have to do is memorise the facts.'

The memory of that night in the bar threatened to make him smile or cry, he wasn't sure which, so he blinked it from his mind as soon as it arrived to avoid the latter. Everything was so deliciously complicated from the moment they met. Now hunched here in the bath, incontinent and inarticulate, it just seemed complicated.

Erika heard the floorboards creak outside the bathroom. It was Karin the housekeeper. Her room was in the attic too, opposite Erika and Max's. She had heard them both descending the stairs and came to see what was going on; see if she could offer any assistance.

The door was ajar and Erika saw Karin peering in at Max slumped awkwardly in the tiny bath. Erika was speared with jealousy in that instance. Not because Karin was younger and thinner than Erika – no, the girl may have been only nineteen, but she was unhealthily thin, and her short brown hair and the dark circles round her eyes gave her the appearance of a boy rather than a female rival. It wasn't anything physical. It was the way she looked at the unseeing Max right then through the gap in the door with such sympathy. The kind of sympathy Erika found it so difficult to show. And who could blame her? This man was meant to be her brave military doctor, back from the war, undefeated by internment. The wonderful specimen she had shown photographs of to little Netta as she tried to get her off to sleep at night; to whose image they sang:

If I were a little bird and had wings, I would fly to you...

Whom she desperately wanted back – not just because she loved him, not to dampen her urges towards Rodrick even, but to help her share the unexpected and undeniable burden that being a parent was.

Erika put herself in the gap between door and frame, ostensibly to protect her husband's privacy, but actually to obscure her own lack of connection with the man in the bath.

'Is everything all right?' Karin had the voice of a mouse. 'Can I help at all?'

'It's all right, Karin,' Erika said, reminding herself and the housekeeper who was the boss here. 'We don't need you. You can go back to bed.'

To Netta it felt like flying. She wasn't really sitting cross-legged in the big basket on the front of her mother's bicycle; she was soaring over the treetops. That wasn't the clicking of a greasy chain against the chain guard; it was the vigorous sound of her little wings flapping. She wasn't a four-year-old girl from Mengede, but a beautiful blue swallow on her way back from a warm winter in Africa.

'Netta, put your arms down. A truck might come past and slice them off.'

And that wasn't her mama being a bore and a nag; it was the twittering of her fellow birds, hundreds of them, as they danced and swooped in the spring skies.

But the flight was over all too soon as they arrived at their first house-call. Frau Beltz.

Netta was in charge of the leeches. At least she was after they had gorged themselves on Frau Beltz's varicose veins and fallen with a satisfied plop onto the floor by her feet. Then Netta would pick up each one and put it back in the big glass jar they lived in. She wasn't sure what held the most morbid fascination for her down there on the floor: the leeches or the hairy elephantine calves of the patient. Up above the women were talking.

'Settling in OK, is he?'

'Oh yes, he's fine.'

'Quite an ordeal he's been through, though. Must be hard.'

'Well, no time to mope around, Frau Beltz, he's too busy working at the hospital.'

'Isn't he going to work with you at the surgery?'

'He will, yes, but all military doctors have to complete civilian experience in a local hospital first. He came straight from university into the army, you see.'

'Oh, well, I suppose keeping busy is the best thing, isn't it.'

'Yes, it is, isn't it.'

'That's if you *can* keep busy. I mean, what with the state Hitler left this country in, you two are lucky to have jobs at all.'

'Well, it was the Allies that stripped the country of its industry, Frau Beltz, but thank God that's all over now. There's no shortage of jobs for the steel workers round here, now is there? Oh! There goes the last one.'

Netta scurried across the tiles to grab the greediest black worm and before long she was flying over the treetops again with her flock twittering something over her head about a nosy old bag who should keep her opinions to herself.

On the steep hill up to the next home visit, Netta's mama had to get off the bike and push it up the hill. Netta stayed in the basket hoping she wouldn't have to get out and use her legs like a lowly human too – she didn't. It took a lot more imagination to see this wobbly plod up the hill as a dance among the clouds, but Netta was making a good go of it until a man's moo-like mumble stopped her mama in her tracks.

'Let me help you with that,' he said.

'We're just fine, thanks. We don't need your help.' Netta thought her mama sounded almost rude and she turned to see who deserved such a response.

It was Rodrick, the man who built her mama's examination table in the surgery. He was an enormous man with arms like the branches of an oak tree. She remembered thinking that, the first time she saw him when he hauled the heavy table through the front door and into the doctor's room, which her Opa had made by putting up a new wall in the middle of their living room. Opa had tried to help bring in the table, but Rodrick didn't need any help. He could do it all by himself. He was very strong. Netta quite admired this mountain of a man then, but at the same time she never liked the way her mother smiled at him, or the way she put her hand on those branches of his. However, after that first time, he only came to the house on two more occasions and on the last time he looked really unhappy as Netta peeked through the window to see her Oma turning him away at the front door.

'What are you doing here anyway,' her mama was saying. 'Following me?'

'Don't be like that. I live just down the road.' He flicked his fingers towards the village. 'Or have you forgotten that so soon.' He cleared his throat. 'I was coming out of the pharmacy there and could see you needed assistance, so I came to help. That's all.'

Netta looked from the carpenter to her mama. They both had the same look on their faces. The look Netta herself had worn on the autumn afternoon her Opa had caught her standing on tip-toe trying to sink her teeth into one of the pears dangling tantalisingly from the tree in the middle of the garden. There was no way she could deny her crime. Her little teeth marks were there in the pear for all to see, so she got a huge telling off and had to stand under the pear tree for hours and hours in tears.

Netta watched Rodrick grasp the frame of the bike in his huge knobbly fingers. She watched her mama reluctantly let go of it.

'And how are you, little princess?' Netta was surprised to find the adult was talking to her as he began to push the bike up the hill, a lot faster than her mother had been.

'I'm... I'm a bird,' Netta said and turned herself back to face the front and enjoy the flight to the top of the hill.

'A bird indeed!' the carpenter chuckled.

Netta flapped her wings and the adults were silent for a while. Until Rodrick said:

'And what about you, Erika? How are you these days?'

'Everything is fine. My husband is back.'

'Oh, I know that, but what I—'

'How do you know that?'

'Well, here we are. I think you'll be all right from here.

Nice and flat now. And I'm going that way. So, I'll see you around, no doubt.'

'I think you know as well as I do it would be better if you didn't.'

'Goodbye, little bird!'

'Bye.' Netta turned to see a rather jubilant Rodrick wave and plod off towards the village, and her mama's eyes darting around the street as if the only place they were not allowed to rest was on the receding back of the big tree man.

Erika had invited Edgar over for dinner. As Max's best friend, as his only surviving friend and colleague from the labour camp, perhaps it was Max's place to invite him, not Erika's. But that was the point. Ever since they had arrived home, the only time Max saw Edgar was in the corridors of Dortmund hospital at work. It wasn't only his wife that Max was distant from. Max hadn't socialised with anyone since he'd been back. And, on the rare occasions she had managed to get him to go out for the evening, for a meal or a drink, he always insisted on sitting with his back against a wall and spent the entire night in the restaurant scanning faces as they entered, for threat, Erika supposed, as if he were back in the ruined streets of a besieged Breslau or the damp draughty barracks of the camp where Russians circled like wolves. Given that Dortmund, like the rest of West Germany (as it had recently been named) was still occupied by Allied forces, she couldn't help feel a similar way when she saw armed British soldiers sauntering down the street.

Max's parents, Martha and Karl, whose house this was, and who had the bedroom below Karin's, loved the idea of Max's friend coming over, and consequently had food preparation *all under control* in the kitchen, whilst Karin cleaned the dining room and set seven places at the oval oak table. Erika felt almost redundant by comparison, but at least she could enjoy her in-laws' chatter as she loitered between kitchen and dining room in a pseudo- supervisory role.

'Edgar,' Martha was reiterating, 'the young man who played the organ at Max and Erika's wedding.'

'Oh, I thought that chap's name was Edward.'

'No. Edgar. He's the very talented musician. And very tall.'

'Oh, the lanky bloke! I know! Can never be serious about anything.'

'Very entertaining.'

'A bit loud.'

'Sociable.'

'Always on his own.'

'What do you mean?'

'I mean, he never brings a girl to any of these events,' Karl said, dipping a finger into the bowl in which Martha was mixing up a Silesian fruit cake.

Erika couldn't help but smile at Karl's obliviousness and Martha's blushing silence.

'It's not as if he has a face like the back end of a tram, does he?'

'Well, perhaps,' Martha hesitated as Karl dipped his finger into the bowl again, 'perhaps he's not interested in girls,' she offered before beating the cake mix with a heretofore unseen vigour.

Karl continued to speak as he sucked on his doughy finger. 'What kind of a man isn't interested in...' And he froze, his eyebrows hitting his hairline as the puck on a strongman game at the funfair strikes the bell when enough force is applied with the mallet. He slowly drew his moist finger from his lips and it seemed the fruity mixture in his mouth had turned suddenly sour.

'Delightful to meet you, Tante Bertel,' Edgar chimed, shaking the old lady's arthritic claw warmly and taking his place at the table between her, at the head, and Max, whilst Karl looked on horrified much to Erika's amusement. Well, she said to herself, it's not as if Edgar is going to start recounting to Bertel his exploits down dark alleys in Dortmund with first year med students, is it!

'Max has told me so much about you,' Edgar continued, putting his long arm easily around his best friend's slight shoulders.

'Well, we thought for a special occasion,' Martha said, 'that Bertel would like to come and join us at the table for once, instead of spending all her time stuck upstairs in her bedroom. I know you're not as steady on your feet these days, my love, but we don't want you wasting away up there, do we,' she said loudly and slowly, as one might do to the Allied soldiers who never understood a word of German.

'You're Martha's sister, is that right?' Edgar asked the old lady with great interest.

'Am I? Who's Martha?' Bertel croaked, and Martha didn't know whether to be amused by her dotty big sister or deeply hurt that she didn't recognise who was sitting right next to her.

Edgar, as was his manner generally, ploughed on regardless. 'And when Max was a boy of sixteen you were both at the theatre when this tram collided with a beer lorry in the street outside. Max said you were the first to get out there and start helping the injured. You told him to grab a ladder from beside one of the shops, wasn't that so?'

Max nodded, a hint of a smile on his lips, his eyes glazed with the memory.

'And to help you carry the injured up to the Klinik, where we both work now in fact.'

Bertel looked bewildered and a little offended by this long, loud man at her dinner table.

'You were Max's inspiration. That night made you want to become a doctor, didn't it, buddy?'

Max couldn't help but be buoyed by his Yankeephile friend's gusto. 'It certainly did,' he said, pouring Edgar a large glass of wine and another for himself. Erika noted the way his spirits had lifted since his friend's arrival and she felt her own shoulders relax in a way she hadn't for a long time.

'Carrots, sir?' Karin said, playing the part of butler, as a favour to the family, just for this evening.

'Don't mind if I do, thanks,' Edgar said, looking the housekeeper up and down in a manner which made Karl think Martha was completely wrong about his lack of interest in girls.

'From our garden,' Karl piped up, feeling more comfortable about engaging the man in conversation now. 'As are the potatoes and parsnips. Well, the parsnips are from the school plots next door, but since I'm the headmaster...' He chuckled with a benign arrogance.

'Of course you are.' Edgar slurped gratefully on his wine. 'Teaching the youth, tending to the sick, what would Mengede do without this family, eh? To the Portners!'

'The Portners!' they all chorused, even Netta right down at the end of the table opposite Karl.

'I don't know what we would have done if we didn't grow our own food,' Martha sighed. 'What with inflation since the war.'

'Well, now we have the Deutschemark things are looking up, aren't they,' Karl said somewhat dismissively, as he tended to do of any political comments from his wife.

'She should be properly dressed to serve the food,' Bertel blurted out, her eyes boring into Karin's pale face, which suddenly became flushed with colour as everyone at the table turned to look at her.

An excruciating moment unfurled itself, with only the nervous click of the serving spoon which Karin held inside the bowl of carrots to fill the silence.

'What on earth do you mean, Bertel?' Martha giggled unconvincingly.

'The maid should have her lace cap on. What's the world coming to when the servants are allowed to be so lax about their appearance?'

'Bertel, we don't have...' Martha began.

'It's OK,' Edgar announced, trying to avoid a scene or perhaps even spotting the opportunity to create one, 'Tante Bertel is of course right. What *is* the world coming to when the,' he coughed, '*servants* can't even dress appropriately?'

He rose, and grabbing the table napkin from his lap, walked over to Karin and said in a whisper all were meant to hear, 'Here's your cap, young lady. I don't know what it was doing between my legs, but don't forget to wear it in future whilst carrying out your duties. Starting now,' he said, winking at Karin in such a cordial way, she hardly hesitated in putting the table napkin on top of her head and continuing to serve the vegetables.

Bertel was satisfied, Martha and Karl could barely chew on their food, their mouths were hanging open so, and Erika was delighted to see Max and Edgar snorting with barely contained giggles like little boys at the back of the class.

Just then the doorbell rang and Karin shot a look at the clock on the wall before snatching the napkin from her head, which was now as red as the second glass of wine Max was finishing off.

'Is it all right if I'm excused now, Mrs Portner? It's a little bit later than I thought. And I think my friend is here to take me out.'

'Oh, of course,' Martha said. 'You have gone more than the extra mile for us tonight, my dear, and we shan't forget it.'

Karin did a little jig of indecision with the bowl of carrots and the erstwhile cap.

'Give those here!' Erika smiled. 'And run to the bathroom if you want to fix yourself up. I'll get the door for you.' She suddenly felt sorry for the poor girl and utterly grateful to her for the part she had just played in lifting her husband's spirits.

Until she reached the front door and found Rodrick standing behind it.

She was speechless.

He wasn't.

'Oh, so sorry to disturb you in the middle of dinner,' he said, nodding at the napkin still in her hand.

This was a scene that could never happen. Erika had no words or actions rehearsed for this because in her mind she had never allowed it to be an option. The man she'd had an affair with, while her husband was in a labour camp, turning up on the doorstep while Max was inside at the table with his best friend and his parents, who, if they hadn't suspected something was going on, knew it for sure when he'd begun pounding drunkenly on this same front door in the middle of the night, a few months ago, just hours after Erika had told the carpenter it was over between them.

'It's over. It's finished,' she'd hissed again, but this time at the disappointed faces of her in-laws as they stood on the landing listening to the fool bawling through the letter box:

'I love you, Erika. You cannot do this! You come back to me this instant! Open this door! Open this door!'

'Does that sound like something that's finished, Erika?' Karl had winced, praying that neither Tante Bertel nor little Netta, both sleeping soundly at the innocent poles of life, would be disturbed.

And now she knew what he meant.

'What the hell do you think you are doing coming—'

'Invite Karin's friend in!' Martha called from the dining room in the back of the house. 'Don't keep her waiting on the doorstep.'

And then it dawned on Erika. And if it hadn't, Rodrick was about to elucidate anyway:

'Hold your horses!' He put his hands up as if she might strike him at any minute. 'I'm not here to see *you*,' he said with a new tone of defiance, 'I'm here to take Karin out.'

'Karin?'

'Yes, Karin. She's a lovely girl, and if I'm not mistaken she's free to go out with whomever she chooses.' He grinned, then quickly swallowed the smile and added conspiratorially, 'I've always asked her to meet me away from this house, but tonight she insisted on me coming here 'cause she said she was working late, helping out with some dinner party or something.'

19

'You've been out with her before?' Erika was stunned. Stunned by the ever-shifting state of affairs over the last few seconds of her life, and stunned by her burning jealousy at the thought of Rodrick seeing another woman. And not just any other woman, but her own housekeeper. The girl who looked at her husband with a sympathy she still found so difficult to muster.

Rodrick was grinning his bovine grin again and Erika knew he was enjoying every second of this. She doubted he had resisted too strongly when Karin had insisted he come here to meet her tonight. He'd clearly hoped he'd bump into Erika here. She doubted that he was even really interested in Karin, but instead he was probably using her as a means of staying close to Erika, of making her jealous. Although it was her vanity that told her so, Rodrick's smug face corroborated the notion. And it was working.

'Erika, did you hear me?' Martha was coming down the hallway. 'Invite... Oh, it's you,' she said, pulling the face she usually reserved for sour milk.

And since Martha had no script for an occasion like this either, Erika decided the best solution was to play the director and take back control. 'It's OK. Rodrick has just come to see Karin. In fact they've been going out for some time, isn't that right, Rodrick?' But before he could answer she was ushering him inside, much to his surprise. 'As Martha said, come in and wait for Karin, she'll be out in a moment. She's been doing such a wonderful job preparing the table and serving the food tonight. She deserves a nice rest and good night out.'

And suddenly they were all in the dining room and Karl found himself unable to chew on his food yet again. Rodrick and Netta exchanged a childish wave across the room, and Edgar and Max rose to formally shake the hand of the man Erika introduced as the carpenter who'd made the examination table in the surgery and as Karin's *gentleman friend*.

'Oh,' Max said, well lubricated now, 'that is a fine piece of work, that table. I've never seen anything like it. We should get you up at the Klinik, shouldn't we, Ed? They could do with some decent equipment up there.'

'Oh, thanks very much,' Rodrick said, a little overwhelmed by this unexpected turn of events and by receiving such a cordial welcome from the man he cuckolded.

'I'm here! I'm ready!' Karin came bouncing out of the bathroom, smoothing down her hair with one hand and her dress with the other, not a moment too soon as far as both Erika and Rodrick were concerned, not to mention the cuckold's parents.

But this was the perfect opportunity, as far as Erika was concerned, to show the in-laws just how finished she was with Rodrick, that he was such a fragment of the past that she could happily send the housekeeper off with him for a romantic evening out, whilst she, unaffected, resumed her dinner party with her husband, best friend and family.

'And where are you two off to tonight?' Erika was positively beaming now.

Karin faltered, partly because she had no idea, and partly because of the lady's uncharacteristic geniality towards her. 'Well, I'm not exactly...'

Rodrick took the reins, as was his duty as the man. 'I thought we'd go to the pictures first, then perhaps have a spot of dinner at that new American restaurant in town.'

Everyone let out a suitable *Ooh* or *Ah* to denote their appreciation of the exoticness of this gesture, the greatest of which came from Edgar, who wanted a full report on the ambience, food and music played as soon as possible.

'Well, we better get going.' Rodrick gestured towards the door.

'Yes, we better.' Karin was as flushed now as when she'd had that napkin perched ridiculously on her head earlier.

And suddenly the couple were gone and Max and Edgar were talking about swing music with a volume they would never have dared to ten years ago, whilst Erika mused over how ridiculous such a waif of a girl looked next to such an oaf of a man.

'Brecht!' Bertel squawked, silencing everyone.

'I beg your pardon, darling?' her little sister ventured.

'It was Brecht we were watching that night in the theatre. When the tram crashed.' She was speaking to Max, but her eyes were fixed on Erika. '*The Threepenny Opera*, it was. The one about crooks and whores.'

Another silence ensued, decorated with the delicate ring of cutlery against crockery as Erika tried to find something to allow her to disentangle herself from the old woman's glare.

Then she found it in Netta beside her.

'Stop playing with your food and eat,' she chided lightly, 'You've hardly eaten a thing yet.'

'She might not have a clue what happened yesterday,' Martha said, kissing her sister's claw, 'but her long term memory is pristine.'

'It certainly seems to be,' Edgar said, admiring the dame, who was busy chasing a small tube of parsnip around her plate again. 'Talking of memories,' he continued with a mischievous expression, 'Do you remember the case of the exploding penis?'

Martha gave a yelp, Erika instinctively put her hands over Netta's ears and Karl told himself he knew it was only a matter of time before a man like *that* tried to drag them all into depravity.

'Oh dear, so sorry.' Edgar smiled at Netta. 'I almost forgot she was there, she's such a quiet well behaved thing.' He took a large draught of his wine. 'But really, it was the most unusual case,' he crashed on, despite the horrified looks of three of the adults at the table. 'A man in the camp at Gegesha used to urinate on the machines at the factory that made cement bags. This would cause them to mysteriously break down and the Russian electricians loved that because they got plenty of overtime out of it, fixing the machines.'

Erika should have stopped him talking about exploding penises and urination in front of her little girl, but he was talking about Gegesha and Max was nodding along with a smile on his face. At last, she thought, she was going to get some insight into her husband's life over the last four years, the life he never talked about.

'So the electricians would give our boys some bread for making the machines break down and the man kept on peeing into the machines. Until one day his luck run out, he caused an explosion and boom!' Edgar whacked the table a little too hard, Bertel looked as if she was about to arrest, but Max was laughing as much as his friend.

'It certainly made a change, didn't it?' Max's eyes were bright with the memory. 'A change from the endless cases of typhoid, yellow fever...'

'...Frostbite and lacerations.' Edgar finished the list for him and Erika's own excitement at being allowed a glimpse of that world was tinged with envy for the telepathy such a shared experience had clearly given the two men.

'Frostbite!' Max declared. 'You could never know just how cold it got up there,' he said, looking at his parents who were all ears, nodding encouragingly.

'We saw some fingers and toes go all the colours of the rainbow, didn't we, buddy?'

Max nodded.

'And try to get warm when you've got nothing in your stomach either!'

'I stashed away twenty grams of bread from my daily ration for three weeks in order to have enough to make a birthday cake for...' Max hesitated, '...for Horst.'

Martha and Karl stiffened at the name of Max's friend, whom they'd known since he was a boy; whom they'd watched grow up and grow closer to their son with every summer that passed.

'Begged the kitchen staff for a gram of sugar and put a few handfuls of berries from the forest in it.' His eyes were still shining but Erika couldn't tell if it was tears which gave them their lustre now. He was focused on the plate opposite him, still full of food. Netta's plate. 'I put candles on it. Made from spent rifle cartridges.'

And then with both hands, far harder than Edgar had, Max struck the table as he propelled himself upwards and his chair over, bellowing at his daughter, 'Your mother said don't play with your food. Now eat it, you ungrateful child!'

Netta felt sick after forcing some of that dinner into herself. She felt sick because she just wasn't hungry. And she felt sick because this skeleton stranger who had turned up out of the blue calling himself her father was shouting at her and punishing her. Only Opa and Oma and Mama (and Tante Bertel sometimes) were allowed to do that because of all the good things they did together in between the telling off. Opa sat at the piano with her, teaching her how to play music which sounded like fairies. Oma sat her on the kitchen table and taught her how to bake cakes, and allowed her to lick the bowl out afterwards. And Mama read her stories at bedtime while this man sat downstairs, his head in books about medicine and diseases. He had all the time in the world for Dr. Keinzler, but none for the Brothers Grimm.

He'd gone upstairs to bed now, after he'd gone around locking all the doors and windows and then checking them all over again, as he did every night before bed. When he finally disappeared her mama told her she could stop. She didn't have to eat all the food on her plate. Not tonight.

Edgar, the very tall man who said the word penis, had left too. Netta liked him. He was funny. And he was her father's friend. If she liked Edgar and Edgar liked her father, then perhaps one day her father would like her too. She liked it when she saw him laughing at the table tonight. He looked more like a boy then, not so much like an angry old man. She'd once asked her mother how old this newcomer was, and her mother answered, 'Thirty-two.' Netta's eyes were wide with disbelief. Just a year older than Mama! That could not be.

'He's just worried about you, darling,' Mama was saying, stroking Netta's goldilocks hair. 'We all are. You're very small for your age. You need to eat more to get big and strong.'

Netta wasn't sure if she wanted to be big and strong. She wouldn't fit in the basket on the front of her mother's bike if she was much bigger. And those times doing house calls with her were such special times. Not just because it was like flying, but because it was the only time she had her mama to herself, without *him* being around. When he was around her, Mama was too busy making sure he was OK to pay Netta any attention. When she was younger she used to sleep with her mama in the bed under the pretty coloured window. Now she had a small bed by the door on the other side of the room because there was no room for her in the big bed anymore.

He was snoring like a pig when Mama tucked her in. And not long after that her mama seemed to be asleep too. But Netta was wide awake, afraid he might get up and start shouting at her again.

She heard the floorboards grate on the landing just outside the door. Karin must be home and coming up to bed.

'Karin!' a hushed voice blew up the stairs after her.

'Yes, ma'am,' Karin squeaked.

Stairs creaked as Karin descended a few and Netta's Oma met her halfway.

'I'm sorry to say this, but you are not to see that man again,' Martha whispered.

'Rodrick?'

'Yes. He's bad news I'm afraid.'

'Oh. Really? But why?'

'I won't go into detail, but it would be very dangerous for you to go on seeing him.'

'Dangerous? What has he done?'

'So much so that if you continue to see him we cannot be held responsible for what happens to you, so we would have to let you go.'

'Let me go?'

Netta imagined Karin to be nothing more than a ghost from the way she kept echoing Oma's words.

'Yes.'

'You mean I would lose my job if I went out with him again?'

'It's quite simple. Now I don't want to hear another word about it. He's a monster. Stay away.'

More creaking and two doors clicked shut, the second some shocked and protracted moments after the first.

Behind one door, trembling with the thrill of the recent confrontation, was a mother focused on protecting her boy. Behind another, on the floor above, was a young woman weeping with confusion and loss. Behind a third, just across the hall, a girl lay in bed wide-eyed at all the scary men in her little world.

Netta was running for her life.

At least that's how it felt when you were trying to outrun the boys. And she often did. She would much rather be charging around with Peter and Josef than sitting about chatting with Mia and Inge and swapping Glanzbilder with their soppy images of kittens in dresses and angel-faced children.

Josef was the son of Herr Ritter the school caretaker, whose entire family lived in the dingy basement under the school. Peter's parents were both dead, he said. Now he had to live with his aunt – the witch who ran the sweetshop. No wonder the two of them couldn't wait to run about the woods with Netta whenever they got the chance.

They had stood on the edge of the woods, fists in tight little balls, the way they had seen Olympic athletes stand in Peter's magazine.

'First one to the canal is the champion,' he'd said.

'Last one is a rotten egg,' Josef had added.

Netta was smaller and younger than them both but there was no way she was going to be a rotten egg. Besides, this race was downhill nearly all the way, through the woods and out to the canal, which ran by her house. She was already as sure as she could be that she wouldn't be last.

'Ready, steady...' Peter had said very slowly and everyone had slid their front foot through the grass a little hoping it wouldn't be noticed.

Netta couldn't bear to wait another half a second. 'Go!' she'd squealed and shot off with the boys complaining and running at the same time.

The complaining soon stopped as Peter and Josef needed all the breath they could get to speed them between the tree trunks, over the logs and under the branches. She heard their shoes getting closer and their panting like a couple of dogs. Then a yelp and a shiver of leaves told her one of them had fallen over. She didn't dare look behind to find out which, in case she fell too. And then the ditch was before her and, with all the speed she'd gathered so far whooshing down the hill, she took off like a swallow and landed safely on the other side.

She heard Peter's *Wooo!* and hoped that meant he was impressed by her jump over the ditch. But he was probably just enjoying his own little flight. And the thud on the ground behind her as he landed told her that was so.

Her little lungs were burning, her legs were like jelly, her ears were throbbing, but she broke through the tree line ahead of the boys and the canal was only yards away.

She had done it!

But what about stopping?

Winning was so important she hadn't thought about what happened after, when your body kept going whether you wanted it to or not. When all the speed you had gathered from going downhill just kept you going straight into the water.

Peter and Josef were quick to help her out. They knew she couldn't swim yet and her falling in the canal was just desserts enough for winning. They could tease her for it endlessly, but in order to do that, they had to save her life first.

The three wet kids slapped along the towpath in the grey afternoon back to the schoolhouse where they could use the communal showers. Netta's family came here most evenings anyway to wash, as it was much bigger and better than the bathroom at home, which was so tiny you had to go in one at a time, so the wait could be forever.

The teasing started only a few yards down the path, but Netta was too proud of her win to be hurt and too interested in trying to work out who that was in the shadow of the trees by her house, staring at them as they passed.

But even the watcher was soon forgotten under a shower of liquid sunshine. Netta sat on the smooth blue tiles with the hot water pouring over her and she felt like a snowman melting. Peter had gone next door to ask Netta's Oma for

29

some dry clothes for her. He was glad her mama was too busy working in the surgery to be disturbed – she would be so much angrier about it, Peter thought, because her face always looked so serious.

After the shower, Josef had to stay in as it was nearly dinner time. Peter had to go too, so Netta had no choice but to walk home. She wasn't ready to go inside yet, so she walked the short distance to next door as if she were a snail.

It was funny how she could get so out of breath walking so slowly when she'd run all that way through the woods like an athlete. She looked at the yellow clouds above the trees as if she knew they were responsible, and that's when she could have sworn she saw someone hiding there again. She started walking faster and fixed her eyes on the front door of her house up ahead. She heard a sound of leaves, a bit like when Josef had fallen during the race earlier, then footsteps heavier than hers were on the street behind her. And she ran for the door and hammered on it with all her might.

Her mother rushed from the surgery where she was finishing her notes for the day to answer the door in case it was an emergency.

'What are you doing banging about like that?' she said to the top of her daughter's head as it rushed inside to the living room and the safety of the piano.

'There was someone out there. They were hiding in the trees. Watching me. They were watching Peter and Josef and me earlier too and just now they started chasing after me.'

'Who was watching you? Who was chasing you?' her mama huffed, peering out into the empty street before closing the door.

'Someone. I don't know. I couldn't see them.' Netta began lightly fingering the keys. Their padded bounce was reassuring.

'Well, if you couldn't see them, they couldn't have been

that close, could they?' her mama said, going back to the surgery to finish her work.

'Unless it was a ghost,' Martha said, poking her head in from the kitchen with a mischievous grin on her face, which was meant to distract and cheer up her granddaughter, but only served to frighten her further.

'Did they make a sound? Did they speak at all?' her father's voice made her jump. She hadn't even realised he was back from the Klinik already, sitting by the window, one of those blasted medical books on his lap. Yet since he was the only one who seemed to be taking her seriously she was happy to answer him.

'No. They never spoke.'

'Was it a man or a woman?'

'I'm not sure.' She wasn't being much use and she didn't want to disappoint him so she added, 'A man, I think.' Because who'd ever heard of the Bogey Woman?

'Did you get a look at what they were wearing? Normal clothes or a uniform, like a soldier?' he said, leaning forward.

This was the longest conversation she'd ever had with her father. This was the longest he had ever looked at her with such interest and concern. She didn't want to ruin it by having nothing interesting to say. 'It sounded like they... like *he* was wearing boots when he started to run after me.'

Her father leant back in his chair and looked out of the window. He had heard enough. The country was still riddled with Allied soldiers. He might have been freed from the labour camp, but who's to say they couldn't come around here and pile them all into trucks at gunpoint again? He knew all too well how cruel and fickle soldiers could be. He knew all too well now the horrors committed on all sides and the vengeful rage that those horrors fuelled.

His daughter turned back to the piano and prodded out a few forlorn notes. He looked over the top of his glasses at his frightened little girl. He got up, crossed the room and put his hands reassuringly on her shoulders. He was surprised at how big his hands looked there against her tiny form. Since he had left the monochrome world of the camp and come back to the glaring light of an infinitely diverse and well-nourished life, they had seemed skinny and frail to him. For a moment he managed to catch a welcome glimpse of himself as a protector again.

And then Karin came in, sobbing uncontrollably. He found those rejuvenated hands of his grabbing her forearms, guiding her to a chair and asking her what was wrong.

'I... we... Rodrick and I... it's over between us.'

'Oh dear,' he said, genuinely concerned for her wellbeing, but aware also of a well disguised rush of delight pumping through his veins that his pretty little housekeeper was no longer another man's concern.

The sound of a plate being pulled jubilantly from its pile in the kitchen brought Karin to her senses.

'It's nothing, really,' she said, realising the real source of her pain might be listening in in the next room only a few feet away. 'I suppose we just weren't right for each other,' she added, discerning from the anguish on Max's face that he clearly wasn't party to Martha's awful ultimatum.

'He didn't do anything to hurt you, did he?' Max asked, feeling more protective by the second.

'Oh, no, no, no. It was nothing like that.' But she knew she couldn't tell Max it was she who had finished the relationship with a curt *I just don't feel the same way about you, Rodrick.* And it was Rodrick who she'd left bewildered and quietly weeping, wringing those enormous and calloused hands of his, wondering why Erika then Karin had both lavished him with so much affection then one day turned their backs on him without warning. That she'd kept a cold composure until she'd got back to the house, then it had all come pouring out – the injustice of it all, and her guilt over what she'd done to poor Rodrick.

'Well, not to worry,' Max offered a little lamely, but he had been surrounded by nothing but men for so long it was hardly surprising. 'You're home now and you're around people that care for you.'

She looked at him, on his knees in front of her, and marvelled that there could be such a difference between mother and son.

'And don't concern yourself with work until you're ready. We'll all survive for a day or two,' he said with a consolatory chuckle.

Martha stayed out of sight in the kitchen preparing dinner, but her ears were trained on the mutterings from the living room like a seasoned intelligence operative.

Netta sat at the piano, hands resting on the keys, but she was glaring over her shoulder at the stupid girl who had stolen her father away from her just at the moment they were finally beginning to connect.

Erika stood in the hallway, unable to enter the room or go back to the surgery, stunned by the vision of her husband on his knees in front of the bloody charwoman, holding her hands as once he had Erika's on the stairs in front of their digs after the summer ball where they first kissed.

For one who had just broken up with her gentleman friend, Karin was curiously buoyant. She busied herself with the housework and, if Netta wasn't mistaken, was doing so with a hint of a song in her throat and the smudge of a smile on her lips. But then Netta was six, going on seven, so what could she be expected to know about ladies and their gentlemen friends? 'I understand only train station,' as her Oma would say when the world made no sense to her.

It was summer now, school was closed for the holidays, and Netta was in the dining room still trying to finish her lunch. Everyone else had gone, but she had to stay, her papa had grumbled, until she ate all her food. How could she possibly finish all that when she just wasn't even hungry? So she'd learnt by now how to secretly stuff some food into her cheeks and spit it out later when the coast was clear. Which is what she was doing when Karin bowled in with a satisfied sigh saying, 'I'm going to the bakery, Netta. Do you want to come? I'm going to buy a nice cake for your father.'

Netta was disturbed by this information, the latter statement, the kind of statement you hear from your mama, not from the housekeeper. But she disguised her perturbation as mere puzzlement, inducing Karin to elucidate.

'It's to say thank you to him, for being so understanding about... you know, when I was... upset the other day.'

Netta glanced at the clock on the wall and with a glee in her heart that almost shocked herself she announced, 'It shuts soon. You won't make it.'

'But it's only twenty to one, my love. You remember how to tell time I hope?'

I am not your love, Netta thought as she tongued the food deeper into her cheeks, and yes I know how to tell time!

'It shuts at one o'clock every Wednesday because Herr Brant goes to Essen to see his mother and to buy more flour,' she said carefully so none of the food fell out of its hiding place.

'Oh. Well, I better get going then, hadn't I.' The smile was fast disappearing from Karin's face, much to Netta's delight. But Karin, in her new haste, seemed to have forgotten all about Netta coming along with her and Netta, again surprised by her own feelings, found that to be quite irritating.

'I can show you a short cut, if you like.'

'A short cut?'

'I know around here better than anyone.'

'I'm sure you do, my love, but—'

'You won't make it otherwise,' Netta said, jumping up from the stool. 'I'll just go to the toilet first.'

She hurried to the toilet, ejected each horrid bolus from her mouth, flushed and rushed out to lead the way before Karin could decide to go on her own on the usual route.

The Tiffany window made cherry red and sapphire blue pools on the floor. Netta wished they were gateways to other worlds and that if she dived in her troubles would be over; wished this coughing, so hard it became retching, would stop; and wished this breathlessness would leave her so she could go back to being a little girl and not an old woman like Tante Bertel, who coughed and wheezed in the bedroom below her.

Whilst Netta looked at the floor, Erika, perched on the edge of her daughter's bed, looked out of the window at the toxic yellow clouds made orange by the glass.

The door opened and Max came in, having just arrived home from work. 'What's the matter?'

'Her cough is getting worse. Her lungs sound terrible.' She handed him her stethoscope.

He took her place on the bed and listened to Netta's chest.

She ought to have enjoyed this rare interaction, this rare concern from her father, but the way he touched her, the way he avoided looking in her face, was just the same as the way her mother handled patients downstairs in the surgery.

'And just look at how thin she's getting! It's the damned smoke from the steel works. I know it. We have to get her out of here.'

'And how are we supposed to do that?' he snapped. 'We can't afford to move. Not yet. Not while I'm still at the Klinik.'

'There's a place. Out on the coast. On the island of Sylt. A home where she can go for the rest of the summer. The sea air will do her good.'

'They might not have a place for her at this short notice,' Max said, which would force her to admit, as he suspected, that she already knew that they had.

'They have.' She flushed. 'I called them this morning. I think it's for the best, Max, don't you?'

He held the stethoscope to her back once more in order to

make himself feel like he was the one making the decision, as a husband and a father should.

'Hmm. Yes. I think it would be for the—'

The door opened and Martha shuffled in. With three adults now towering over her bed, Netta felt very small indeed.

'Martha?' Erika said, noticing her unusual pallor.

'You should both come downstairs. Right now.'

'Where's Karl? Where's my husband?' Martha babbled as they all entered the living room and found a single policeman standing by the piano and lightly fingering the keys. He whipped his hand behind his back as they came in, as if *he* was a criminal and stated:

'He went out with my colleague to the woods to make a formal identification of the body.'

'Body?' Erika said in hushed tones. 'What...? Who died?'

'Well, until Herr Portner has made the identification it would be foolhardy of me to say, but what I am more certain of is that the person in question has not so much *died* as been killed.'

'Killed?' Max's voice quivered.

Erika heard it and grabbed at his hand. She felt his whole body start to tremble and she hated this pompous police officer for setting old memories off like fireworks in Max, just when they were starting to move forward.

'We're both doctors, you know,' Erika said a little too forcefully. 'Perhaps we... or I could take a look at the body for you and determine whether there has been, you know, foul play.'

'A coroner is already on the scene, Frau...'

'Portner.'

'Ah, your daughter?' the officer said to Martha.

'Daughter-in-law,' the two women both corrected him in tandem and a little too eagerly for both their likings.

'The body was found in the canal and appears to have been struck in the face first.'

'But they could have just slipped and hit their face as they fell into the water,' Erika offered.

Officer Hummel sniffed the flowers on top of the piano. Everyone looked at him as if he was mad for doing something so leisurely at a time like this, but Officer Hummel didn't really care for flowers very much. He just did it to look as if he was investigating the environment. And he would have sniffed the piano itself, the armchair and the green tiles of the stove, the very floorboards under their feet, should that not seem particularly mad, anything to make it look as though he was onto the world and its criminal ways.

'Let's let the coroner decide exactly when the... victim was hit, shall we?' he said with a sniff in Erika's direction. A sniff which sent pollen from the flowers, until now only clinging to the edge of his nostrils, shooting up inside his nose, inducing a desperate need to sneeze.

He fought the need for all he was worth. He would hate to lose his composure now when he was doing such a good job of making them all lose theirs. And just then, his colleague appeared at the door with the older woman's husband. Karl, she'd said. Karl Portner then, he deduced. Karl was looking ghastly, as if he might keel over at any second. Max rushed over to help his papa to a chair and as he lowered himself into it, Karl let out a yelp and clutched at his wrist.

'Are you in pain, Herr Portner?' Hummel sniffed.

'Just an old injury,' Max filled in for his faint-looking father. 'It flares up now and again.'

'In the wrist, is it?' Hummel sniffed again. 'Perhaps you should let your son take a look. He's a doctor, isn't that so?'

'There's no need,' Karl barked, 'it comes and goes. Usually around stressful times, mentally or physically. And I think I can be forgiven for finding this time particularly stressful, can I not?'

'How did you injure your wrist?' Hummel persisted.

'It's just—' Max began, anxious to avoid embarrassing his father. Shooting yourself in the wrist to avoid national service in the First World War was not necessarily something you crowed about, especially when the country had just been beaten a second time.

But Karl had far more pressing things on his mind since coming back from the canal and barked, 'I shot myself in the arm, all right?'

'Oh dear!' Hummel took a step back since his nose had been getting closer and closer to the older man. 'Sorry to hear that. Not intentionally, I trust.'

A short silence ensued as no one in the room, not even Karl, felt the need to correct him on this detail.

'Well?' Martha was on tenterhooks and all this chatter about wrists was not getting them anywhere. 'Who was it? Who's been killed?'

Karl let out an enormous – Hummel thought somewhat dramatic – sigh and answered, 'It's Karin. Someone's killed Karin.'

Martha and Erika filled the room with appropriate sounds of dismay, Hummel noticed, and Max, sitting on the arm of the chair, arm around his father, whispered, 'Who on earth would want to do something like that to poor Karin?'

Erika thought she saw the first shimmering of tears forming in his eyes and it sent a hot gale howling through her ears. She so resented his reaction to the housekeeper's death and the way it signalled their mutual understanding which she was excluded from, that it made her glad the girl was... well, no longer around.

'Well, that, Dr Portner,' Hummel said, donning his octagonal hat, 'is what I intend to find out.' He thought that would be a suitably poignant line to make his exit on, leave them stewing in their own juices for a while before he brought each one of them in separately for questioning, until the old woman blurted out:

'She had just broken up with her gentleman friend. And I'm sure he wasn't happy about it.'

'Martha!' Erika mumbled, as far as you could mumble such an exclamation of indignation. She knew what her mother-in-law was doing: trying to cast the spotlight elsewhere away from this house where Karin had lived and worked. But in casting it on Rodrick, she might also be inadvertently stirring up Erika's recent indiscretions with him. Who knows what the carpenter might reveal under pressure of interrogation from the police!

Hummel stuck his hat back under his arm and nodded to his colleague to make a note. 'And what is the name of this gentleman friend?'

'Rodrick,' Martha said. 'But I don't know his surname.'

Erika, used to being one of the more knowledgeable people in a room, was bursting to inform the policeman of the missing surname, as she would want to finish a literary quote that Karl had started but couldn't finish. However, since that could possibly signpost a greater intimacy between her and the carpenter than the rest of the family, she thought it best to shut up for once.

'He's a carpenter,' Max piped up. 'Over in the village. He did some work for our surgery here.' Although he hadn't begun work in it yet, Erika was more than happy to let him call the surgery *ours* rather than hers, for now.

'And do we have an address for this carpenter?' Hummel nodded again at his scribe, imagining this is what it must feel like to be a master conductor in front of the Düsseldorf Symphony Orchestra.

'His workshop is on Mittelkamp. You can't miss it. It's such a small road. Everyone knows it.' Erika made sure to tell him such a location was common knowledge – nothing special about her knowing where to find Rodrick.

Hummel thanked them for the information, bid them all farewell and the two officers left the house.

'How's your wrist after all that scribbling?' Hummel asked his partner.

'Fine,' the junior officer replied, a little mystified.

'Well, of course it is! A wrist only hurts after doing something like... Oh, well, I don't know... punching something perhaps. Or someone.'

The Russians surround them, prodding them like cattle with the barrels of their Tokarevs.

'Get up!' a Soviet bawls at the one-legged patient on the ground, whose remaining foot is impaled with broken glass and blue from the cold.

Max dares to move to help his patient up and gets a punch in the back for his troubles.

'Get up! Get up! Get up!' the Russian screams.

The soldier in pyjamas looks up at his adversary with a knitted brow that says, 'Can't you see? That is the one thing on earth right now I cannot do for you.'

And the Russian knows it's the one thing on earth the patient can't do. It's the perfect opportunity to show the rest of these fascists what will happen to them if they disobey orders.

The Russian shoots the man in the face.

They are marched around the burning city, then piled into trucks, driven mile upon bone-shuddering mile to a train station so remote it's hard to believe a train would ever come. But it does. A cattle train. And they are herded onto it and dragged through the Siberian steppes. Day after day of unceasing and indistinguishably white and freezing plains.

Now they are pitching and rolling about on the road again, in the isolation truck. Max, Edgar and Horst. Ordered to tend to the sick and the diseased among them. The sufferers of diarrhoea, typhoid and cholera, without a single resource or medicine to do so. Licking the ice from the windows like animals just to stay hydrated.

And finally they arrive at the labour camp and all the German soldiers, all the ones who haven't died and had their bodies tossed unceremoniously from the back of a moving truck, are ordered to get down. Another disabled soldier is struggling to stand. Another bloody Ivan is screaming at him to get up.

'Get up, get up get up!'

Max's muscles twitch. He wants to help the man, but if Max is so bold as to move again he will be shot, he knows it. And then what good will he be to the rest of the unit? He tells himself over and over again: it is not cowardice, now they are prisoners of war, to stay alive. It is the best thing to do for his fellow Germans. It's the only thing he can do for Erika.

'Get up, get up, get up!' The Russian aims his gun at the German.

'Get up, get up, get up, Papa!' Netta is tugging on his pyjama sleeve. 'We're going to the seaside today!'

Max drove Netta to the seaside.

'Well, it's no good me going too,' Erika stuttered, 'I mean, I would if I could. I'd drive her myself, but I can't drive, can I, and besides I need to stay and work, the surgery will be busy that—'

Max laid a reassuring hand on her arm and she stopped rambling.

'It's just...' she tried to explain.

'It's OK,' Max whispered, finding his wife's maternal conflict so endearing, and yet being slightly envious that he didn't quite feel the same at the thought of being separated from his daughter.

It's always harder for the mother, he told himself, images of the Russian babies he'd delivered in Gegesha glinting in the caves of his memory. That physical cord may be cut – he saw himself hacking at a bloody blue umbilicus with pliers borrowed from a locksmith, used to amputate other patients' frostbitten fingers – but the spiritual bond is unbreakable.

'It's only for four weeks,' he said to his wife as Netta bounced about in the front seat, a luxury that would be denied her if her mother had insisted on coming too. 'And then she'll be back and that chest will be right as rain, eh?' He smiled a confident smile, but he wasn't totally convinced a children's home by the sea would cure all Netta's ailments.

The cases were in the boot, but Erika insisted upon checking one more time that she had put enough underwear in there, before she let Max shut it.

She kissed Netta through the window, glad her daughter looked so excited to be going and yet a little hurt that she wasn't distraught to be leaving her mama behind.

But the seaside, mama!

'Making a quick getaway, are we?' It was Hummel prowling round the car.

'I beg your pardon?' Max said, starting the engine to show he had no time to waste talking to this foolish man. Unless... 'Do you have any news about Karin? Do you know who might have killed her?'

'Nice car.' Hummel must not have heard him over the growl of the engine, 'A DKW. And brand new by the looks of it?'

'Yes. The surgery is doing well. We've both been working extremely hard. We thought it was about time we treated ourselves for once,' Erika said, with a hint of indignation at her own urge to explain herself to him.

'It just makes practical sense,' Max chipped in. 'Being out here in the suburbs.'

'You're not going away for too long, I hope?' Hummel sniffed.

'We're just going for a day at the seaside,' Netta said, squinting up at the man silhouetted against the sun outside her papa's window.

'That looked like an awful lot of luggage for a day at the—'

Hummel had to step back to avoid being hit by the car door opening with such speed. Max jumped out and growled through gritted teeth into the officer's ear, 'I am taking my daughter to a children's home to help with her health, but we haven't told her yet how long she'll have to stay as we don't want to cause her any unnecessary distress, OK?'

Hummel looked both a little scared and triumphant at the doctor's barely contained outburst. 'Ah, I see,' he said, tapping his nose and grinning at the scowling father.

Max noticed two British soldiers hanging around on the opposite side of the road. His sudden movements had grabbed their attention so he got carefully back into the car saying, 'Now, we really must be going. We have a long journey ahead. Unless you have any news for us? Unless you've made any progress.'

'Oh, we're making progress all the time, Dr Portner, but we've nothing concrete to report yet,' Hummel said, leaning in and smiling at Netta. 'Lovely upholstery. And I love the claret paintwork.'

'It's red!' Netta corrected him.

Hummel laughed and Max caught a whiff of stale beer on his breath. 'Of course it is, my dear. How could I be so silly! It's red. And what a lovely red it is!'

And with that, Max sped off almost driving over the policeman's toes.

It was Erika's turn to scowl at the officer now. After all, if he had not been irritating her husband, Max would have said a proper goodbye to her. Surely.

'You'll be the first to know,' Hummel called out to Erika as he strolled off down the street, 'if we do find out anything, doctor.'

The journey lasted for ever. It could have been days for all Netta knew: each time she woke from a nap she had no idea how long she'd been asleep. All she saw was mile upon mile of never-ending road; hours and hours of boring countryside. Where was the seaside? The sand and the waves? Her blissful bounce was now a frustrated fidget. Every glimpse of water got her hopes up only to be dashed when she realised they were just crossing over a smelly old river.

'Not much longer now,' her papa smiled, 'and then we get to go on a boat.'

At least she was with her papa. She had him all to herself now. No way could anyone steal him this time. There was nobody else around, just him and her, alone in the red car. And he was happy. He was smiling at her. He wasn't grumpy, he wasn't shouting at her, they were going to build sandcastles together on the beach. It was going to be amazing.

The port was teeming with people. It was frightening to the little girl, especially the soldiers who spoke in a funny language she didn't understand. As her papa bought the tickets to get them on the ferry she saw a sign on the dock telling anyone arriving by boat that they were entering the *Britischer Sektor*, whatever that was.

The sign was in German, English and Russian.

Max saw Netta craning her neck up to look at it and the Cyrillic he recognised there made his skin crawl. They were only going an hour across the water to the holiday island of Sylt, but suddenly Max was filled with a sense of dread, as if he was standing on the rimy edge of the Barents Sea again, looking out at the single storey wooden structure standing on stilts out in the grey water. His hospital for the four years he was a prisoner. Where he had to tend to the sick and injured with nothing but aspirin for pain and coal for diarrhoea, vascular clamps made from bits of wire fence and a piece of leather to bite on for anaesthetic.

'Come on, Papa, let's go!' Netta said, yanking him back towards the car.

He instinctively resisted. If he didn't, he felt he would never be able to return from that island. That place of isolation.

'Papa!'

His daughter's voice penetrated his misted mind and told him he was not in Gegesha anymore. There were never any little girls in Gegesha, so he couldn't possibly be there.

He blinked, looked down and saw her; smiled to smooth away the anxiety clouding her face and hurried to the car.

Once on the water he breathed in the warm salty air and toasted his face against the sun. He caught his daughter copying his movements: a big breath in, eyes scrunched up against the light. He chuckled quietly to himself. She copied this too.

The home was in a small town on the northernmost tip of the island. When they drove up to the imposing slab of a mansion, a group of gaunt children were on their way out, led by their antithesis, a gargantuan matron who seemed to be made up of a collection of spheres: a globe of a head, a very planet of a body, and two massive orbs for breasts. Even her ankles had been replaced with rondures connecting her considerable calves to her feet, which seemed to be the only slender thing about her, flattened no doubt under the weight of the solar system piled upon them.

'Ah, you must be Herr Portner?' she wheezed and, far from worrying about enlightening her with his proper title, Max was more concerned with the implications if this woman was meant to be an ambassador for the healing powers of the sea air in Sylt. 'And you must be Netta?' she said to the little girl, who had already ejected herself from the car, and was pulling on every reserve of will power she had lest she dart off towards the vast expanse of sand beckoning to her on the other side of the promenade and risk the return of the wrath of her father.

'How does she know my name?' she whispered to her papa.

'The tide is out so we were all just going out for a walk along the beach. Perhaps Netta would like to join us?'

Despite her awesome size, the lady seemed nice enough to Netta. And a whole bunch of kids to play with on the beach too! This was a pleasant surprise, but she didn't know any of them yet, so she turned to her papa to make sure he was coming too.

'Go ahead, darling,' Max said, 'I'll just get some of our things out of the car, then I'll catch you up.'

'No, I can wait for you.'

'No, go! Go on, have some fun. You've been waiting for this for ages, haven't you?' He took off his glasses and winked at the woman. 'Go with Frau...?'

'Auttenberg,' Frau Auttenberg informed him.

'Go with Frau Auttenberg...'

'Before the tide comes in and the sand is all gone again.' It was Auttenberg's turn to wink at the rather well-groomed and somewhat handsome man before her.

The thought of all that beautiful sand being swallowed up again by the sea before she'd had a chance to play on it was too much for the little girl to bear. She scampered off and some of the other waifs, who had long since had their sense of free will beaten out of them by Frau Auttenberg, forgot for a moment that this was so, infected as they were by the new ball of energy rolling past them, and they began to run towards the sand as well.

'Wait for me!' Auttenberg foghorned.

The kids came to their senses, their dull senseless senses, again, reverting to a heavy plod, which Netta, much to her own bemusement, found herself trying to emulate.

Max watched the children filing down to the sand under the surveillance of Auttenberg and felt sick. He turned away, pulled the cases from the boot and, looking at the two storey brick block in front of him, he felt as if he was looking at the long wooden mildew hut which had housed him and ten thousand other Germans in bunks with barely enough room to squeeze between them, where gaping holes let in lacerating draughts and pelting rain for four years until it became the numb norm.

Four years. His freedom taken from him for four years.

Four weeks. 'It's only for four weeks,' he'd said to Erika. But he wasn't so old as to have forgotten himself how interminable four weeks could feel when you were a child. When you were somewhere you didn't want to be.

He checked Netta in at the reception desk. Left her cases with the red-faced man there and went back out to the car.

He drove out onto the road, but had to stop. He couldn't see for the tears in his eyes. He wiped at them furiously and looked out onto the beach again. He could make out Netta's golden locks bobbing around as she ordered a boy to help her with a sand castle. In those two little humans Max saw himself and Horst as kids on the farm, playing Cowboys and Indians, and as altar boys in the cemetery using a crucifix as a ladder to get to the juiciest cherries on the branches which hung over the priest's garden wall.

Suddenly he knew how it felt to be umbilically tied to someone. And something was yanking on that bond with all its might.

Down on the sand Netta saw the bright red car easily as it zoomed by the white stucco houses on the sea front.

'Papa!' she screamed and the car came to an abrupt halt.

'Now, Netta...' Frau Auttenberg warned, but Netta had far more important things on her mind than falling into line like all the other puny idiots.

'Papa!' again she screamed, running up the beach towards the road and the stationary car.

He must have heard me, she told herself. He must have realised he had forgotten me. Silly Papa! What on earth was on his mind to make him drive off like that without...

Then the car moved off again. Faster than before and the wind filled her head with the roar of the advancing sea.

Much of the original hospital had been destroyed in the air raids, so the building in which Max and Edgar worked was brand new. Edgar seemed to luxuriate in the surroundings, which were indeed luxurious for both patients and staff compared to the execrable conditions they'd worked in in the labour camp. But Max found this clean floored, well-resourced, whitewashed place as alien as his home life. He found the doctors' and nurses' grumblings about their

49

working conditions (standard conversation for front line workers about their managers from time in memoriam) offensive, especially when any well founded comments about under-staffing were made in ignorance of the fact that, had not all the Jewish doctors been expelled by the Nazis, the place would have a full complement of staff and some of the finest doctors in Europe. And it was all he could do sometimes to restrain himself from telling a whingeing patient to buck up and think themselves lucky they were going to have anaesthetic at all.

For a brief moment at dinner at the Portners', Edgar had seen a glimmer of his old *buddy*. But the sight of his daughter's untouched plate had sent Max's shutters guillotining down again. Sometimes Edgar told himself it was just Max being his ultra-professional self whilst they were at work, but when Max politely refused every offer from Edgar of a drink after their shift, a poetry night in Bochum, or even the opera in the brand new Städtische Bühnen, he felt waves of grief wash over him, which were even more powerful than those he had felt when their friend Horst had been killed in Gegesha.

Unlike Max, Edgar had no intention of becoming a GP, so had established himself in the orthopaedics department. Max, who had to complete his civilian experience in the Klinik before moving onto the surgery with Erika, was moved around from department to department. And when his orthopaedic rotation came around, Edgar was convinced that working closely with Max again would reignite old memories and reinvigorate their friendship.

'Six of them there were. Six of our boys nailed to the table by their tongues.'

'How are we doing today...?' Edgar interrupted the grotesque tale a patient was regaling another in the ward with and checked his notes, '...Herr Leichtfuss?'

'It's Lieutenant Leichtfuss. And I'm still bloody sore. Can you give me something more for the pain?'

Edgar examined what was left of the soldier's arm, inviting Max to do the same. Leichtfuss had been in a Soviet labour camp too. His fingers had become frostbitten but he had refused to let any of the quacks, as he called the doctors among his fellow inmates, to treat him. When he was finally released a few weeks ago, the entire arm was gangrenous and had to be removed near the shoulder.

Max and Edgar exchanged the kind of telepathic looks they had done in Gegesha and it sent a thrill through the entire length of the tall doctor.

'Don't worry, *Herr* Leichtfuss,' Edgar said deliberately, 'We will order an increase in your morphine dose for now, but the site is healing well. The pain should subside soon enough.'

He scribbled on the man's chart and moved on to the next bed, leaving Leichtfuss to resume his loud reminiscences with the man opposite.

'Six of our soldiers nailed to the table by their tongues, ten hung up from meat hooks in the slaughterhouse and another fifteen thrown down the well and stoned to death. Can you believe it? Bloody barbarians those Bolshevists.'

'Dr Portner.' Edgar grabbed Max's attention back from the diabolical picture being painted behind him. 'Perhaps you wouldn't mind giving me your assessment of Herr Neuffer's arthritis?'

'I was guarding a train going to Korosten,' Leichtfusss's interlocutor chimed in, 'a cattle train packed with Ivans. Sixty or seventy men in each truck. We were transporting them to Lwow. Each time we reached a station they were herded with truncheons to the drinking troughs and back. They drank there like beasts, they were so thirsty. At every station ten of them were taken out dead: suffocated through lack of oxygen. And sometimes when the train came in, they peered out from between the slats and shouted to the civilians there, "Bread! Bread please, and God will bless you." Then they threw out their shirts and their last pairs of socks and shoes to the kids, who brought them pumpkins in return. They threw these pumpkins in through the gaps and then all you heard was a terrific din like the rearing of wild animals. They must have been killing each other in there just to get a bite of raw pumpkin.'

'You see what I mean? Bloody animals, the lot of them.' Leichtfuss whipped his remaining arm at his new friend. 'You see we're not supposed to admit it openly, but we were far too soft on our POWs. If we'd have carried it through to the hilt, made them disappear completely, our country wouldn't be in such trouble now. These half measures are always wrong.'

And then Max was no longer manipulating Herr Neuffer's wrists, but, much to Edgar's disappointment, was standing over Leichtfuss saying, 'I think you missed your friend's point there.'

'I beg your pardon?' The patient looked disgruntled at yet another interruption.

'I think what he might have been saying is: is it any wonder the Russians nailed German soldiers' tongues to the table if that's how we treated them when they were our prisoners?'

'Dr Portner...' Edgar put his hand on his colleague's shoulder.

'No, Ed! Did you ever stop to think,' Max said through gritted teeth to the soldier, 'why they treated us like they did in the labour camps?'

Leichtfuss was fuming now. 'Oh, you were in a camp too, were you? Then you should know better than anyone how brutal those bastards are.'

'Germany invaded their home. They were fighting for their lives!' His mild-mannered buddy was as close to bellowing as he ever got, his eyes moist with frustration, so Edgar used his superior height to bulldoze Max out of the ward, which now resonated with the indignant ramblings of Leichtfuss.

'Such things don't go unavenged,' Max was sobbing now in the arms of his friend, who was trying to shield him from gossiping eyes blinking up and down the corridor. 'God is punishing us for what we did to the rest of the world, Ed.'

'*You* did nothing, Max. We are not the same as that fool in there.' Edgar ushered Max further from prying eyes and ears. 'Look, remember that medical officer over at the demob centre? Let me make you an appointment to go and see him. There might be something he can do to help you?'

'Help *me*?'

'Yes, before all this gives you a nervous breakdown or something.'

'But I'm the doctor, Ed. I'm supposed to help people.' Visions of his sixteen-year-old self, standing petrified at the scene of the tram crash whilst Tante Bertel took control and ordered him to bring a ladder to use as a stretcher, throbbed through his brain. 'I can't be the one asking for help.'

'I get it.' Edgar had Max by the arms as if he might shake the sense of these words into him. 'That's the war talking. The army that teaches us we have to be big strong men. Brainwashes us into believing we always have to fight. But we're not in the army anymore, buddy. We don't have to pretend, OK?'

Max wanted to say it was the likes of Leichtfuss who should have their heads checked, not him, but he allowed himself to be persuaded by the large hands gripping his arms, the closest he was going to get to the warm embrace he really needed right then.

*

Dr. Siskin was a slight man, who wished he was stocky. A man of average height who would rather be tall. A naturally smooth faced officer who craved a handlebar moustache. But he had an enormous mahogany desk and an expensive leather chair behind which and in which he felt his shortcomings were well disguised, and as he sat listening to the doctor from Dortmund Klinik painfully pulling out his reason for being in Siskin's office today, the demob officer felt taller, stockier and hairier than ever.

Granted, Siskin was more used to examining eyes, ears and looking down throats, but this wasn't the first time in recent months an ex-POW had come to him in reasonable physical health claiming they were on the brink of a nervous breakdown. So he told Dr Max Portner the same thing he had told all the others. The same thing in fact that Siskin's father had told his son when he had cried and cried over seeing his mother run over and killed by a horse and cart outside their home:

'What are you?' As he spoke Siskin always rubbed beneath his nose with the length of his fountain pen, as if he had a little itch, to compensate for the lack of facial hair there. 'Eh? What are you, Dr Portner? A man or a mouse?'

Max left the demob centre more deflated than when he went in. But with every mile of his journey home and with every memory of Dr Siskin which lashed at his skull, his sense of defeat was transmuted into anger. He drove his car faster than usual and even sped up when pedestrians were crossing the road, enjoying the power he possessed to make them run. Once at home he asked his father about the old motorbike languishing in the garden shed.

'I think we should fix it up. It would be great for getting around from patient to patient when I take over the surgery soon.'

Karl was a little bit surprised at his son's turn of phrase. *Take over* the surgery? As far as Karl knew, Erika had no intention of stopping work. He thought they would be working together in there. And then there was the fact that they hadn't long ago splashed out on the DKW. Did they really need a second vehicle? Nevertheless he found himself saying:

'Yes, why not? We could do it together. I need a new project.' Karl beckoned his son out to the shed.

He was elated at the thought of something that would bring him closer to his son again. Since Max's return, Karl felt feckless and weak. He had fired a gun at his own wrist to avoid conscription in the First World War and hence had none of the experiences his son had had in the army, or as a prisoner. He had no common ground, no way of saying with any authority or conviction: I understand what you've been through, son. You can talk to me because I know what you've been through. And what irked him more than anything else was that Erika's father served in both wars and was at that moment still prisoner in a Siberian labour camp. When that vainglorious bastard was finally home, Karl had squirmed, he would no doubt be around swapping POW stories with Max and making snide comments, just like he did at Max and Erika's wedding, about how the country wouldn't have gone to pot if all of its men had done their duty and fought in the war. Karl's biggest fear was losing his son to Gunther Jordan, Captain of the bloody Border Guard! So he rubbed his stiff wrist with renewed vigour as he opened the shed and stood in the doorway shoulder to shoulder with Max, both of them ready to transform the rusting heap in front of them, as only real men could.

They worked on the bike all afternoon and on into the evening. Erika was envious of the time Karl was spending with Max, but Martha, as keen-eyed as ever, broke the silence as the two of them ate dinner alone, with:

'At least he seems to be cheering up a bit, eh, love?'

Max found her in bed early, after he and Karl had washed all the grease off themselves in the hot showers at the school.

She heard his satisfied exhalations as he took off his shoes. Exhalations that were meant to be noticed, commented on. But she decided to sulk and pretend to be asleep, her face to the wall. She felt the bed change shape as this new man got in. Felt his shower-hot arm, clearly pyjama-less, curl around her waist and snake up around her breast. This was the first time he had touched her like this since he had returned from the camp. She should be over the moon. The Siberian winter was gone! Summer was in full bloom. How typical, she thought, that he behaves like this when I'm grumpy – and it's him that's made me this way!

His lips and hands tried to stimulate her, move her. She refused to budge. But there was no way a real man would allow that to be the end of it. There was no way he was going to roll over and go to sleep now, not with all these unsatisfied urges rumbling and snarling inside him.

His grip on her arm, as he yanked her onto her back, was uncomfortable to say the least, his ever-increasing weight on her was awkward, his manner was rough, but she told herself to enjoy it, enjoy the return of her husband.

If only, she thought between stabs of euphoria, if only it felt like Max inside me.

'My name's Milla. It's short for Camilla. But I don't really like Camilla, so it's lucky that everyone calls me Milla really, isn't it.'

Netta had tried her hardest not to talk to any of the other kids. If she did they might think she was happy to be here, and she wasn't. She had to show them all she was not the same as them. Had to show Frau Auttenberg that she was not going to be part of this rubbish. But this Danish girl Milla just would not leave her alone. She had the bunk above Netta's. There were millions of bunks in this dorm, all lined up on each side of the room like jars of sweets were in the witch's shop, but the bunks were crammed with all the worst flavours of children instead of liquorice twists, aniseed balls, pear drops, lemon sherbets, and every other sugary treat in the whole wide world. And Netta was on the bottom bunk. At least if she was on the top, the whole bunk would not wobble like an earthquake every time Milla came down the ladder, and, if Netta was on the top, Milla wouldn't be able to come past and stick her head in Netta's face every time she got up and say, 'Morning, Netta. How are you feeling today?'

At breakfast they all had to sit at an enormous round table so big and old it reminded Netta of tales of knights and wizards and kings. It would have been great to sit there and imagine herself in medieval times had the table been anywhere else but here in this prison.

And there was all that amazing beach outside with rocks and crabs and crashing waves. Castles to be made and races to be run. But they were only allowed to go out for a walk once a day at the most, and then only under the beady eye of Frau Auttenberg or one of the other dragons.

'There you go, Netta.' A large glass of what appeared to be milk was placed in front of her. 'Drink it all up. It will make you big and strong,' Frau Auttenberg grinned. 'And you want to be big and strong, don't you?'

Why did everyone keep telling Netta that she should

be big and strong? What was so great about being big and strong? Well, strong perhaps, but big? Frau Auttenberg was as big as could be, and if that's what people meant by big and strong, then she would happily stay small and weak, thank you very much!

Netta hauled the heavy glass with both hands nearer to her. As it jerked across the uneven wooden table she feared the milk might slosh about, perhaps even spill a little, for which she would no doubt be told off. But the surface of the drink stayed remarkably steady, which told Netta it was far thicker than milk. She sniffed at it.

'Drink up, Netta! You won't be getting down from the table until it's all gone, I'm afraid.'

She took a quick sip, like a bird that fears there might be predators nearby. It was vile! Sour. A whole glass of milk that had gone off.

'It's double cream,' Milla said, who of course was sitting next to Netta.

Netta looked at Milla and then at all the other kids at the table. None of them had a great white glass of sour milk in front of them. Why was she being picked on like this?

'A whole pint of double cream!' Milla was saying and licking her lips.

'You can have it if you want.' Netta finally spoke to Milla. She had to. This was an emergency.

'Can I?' Milla's eyes lit up, not just at the offer of such a great gift, but also at the breakthrough in her relationship with the new girl.

Netta began to shove the white obelisk over to the Danish girl, but Milla stopped her with a hiss. 'Not yet. If Auttenberg sees us we'll be in for it.'

Other kids were finishing their breakfasts and being allowed to leave the table. This was keeping Frau Auttenberg's bulbous eyes rolling around in plenty of other directions, enough for Milla to put her back between the matron and Netta, grab the glass and drink the curdled contents so quickly Netta thought she couldn't possibly have a throat like normal children, but just a wide drainpipe that connected her mouth to her stomach.

The clunk Milla made when she put the glass back on the table in front of Netta caught the attention of Frau Auttenberg. Netta saw the woman sauntering over. She also saw Milla, still with her back to Auttenberg, with a thick white moustache, which was as awesome as the matron's own brown one.

Auttenberg was almost upon them now, peering over Milla's head to examine the pint glass she had left with Netta. Netta widened her eyes as if she were about to be run over by a car and pointed them as far as possible at Milla's, then at her cream moustache, which would easily give the game away.

Milla cocked her head, examining her bunk-mate's cartoon expression. She knew Netta was trying to tell her something, but she just wasn't sure what it was and why she kept staring at her mouth.

'Well, well.' Auttenberg's wheezy boom behind Milla's head jolted her enough to make the penny drop.

Her mouth! She tore at her lips with one hand just as Auttenberg came into view and she wiped the creamy mess on her dress as the woman picked up the glass and held it to the light as if she was capable of recognising the finger-prints she might find there.

'Well done, Netta. You see, it's not so bad, is it? If you keep this up, you'll be fit and healthy in no time.' And she rolled herself out to the kitchen to show off her success to the cook.

'Thank you,' Milla breathed and flopped back in her chair.

'Thank *you*,' Netta whispered and smiled at her new friend.

The bicycle was exceedingly light and so much easier to push up the hill. Erika should have been pleased about this. And indeed her skeleton and her muscles were. But every so often her lungs would suck at the air hungrily and her heart would swell painfully in her chest as a wraith of her daughter scudded across her mind. Without her little assistant, Erika had to collect the engorged leeches from the floor around Frau Beltz's thrombotic feet herself. But that wasn't the worst part of not having Netta around. The worst part, ironically, was that her little girl may come back bigger and stronger. Too big to fit in the basket on the front of her bike, too strong to *need* to sit in the basket on the front of her bike. And although she wished for her daughter's health with all of that swollen heart of hers, she knew the empty basket was a symbol of the way her daughter would one day be so much bigger and stronger, simply by virtue of her age and the natural acquiring of independence, that she wouldn't need her mama anymore. That she would one day leave the nest of her own free will.

'So sorry to hear about your housekeeper,' Frau Beltz was saying, sucking on a biscuit she had dipped in her coffee in not a dissimilar way to the worms feeding on her legs. 'Terrible business. Just terrible.'

'Oh yes. It is,' Erika said, eyeing up the leeches, willing them to finish their lunch so she could get out of here and away from this inexorable conversation.

Frau Beltz probed further. 'You heard about the carpenter from the village, no doubt?'

The mention of Rodrick – because it had to be Rodrick: no other carpenter in the vicinity was surely that gossip-worthy – made Erika flush and she gulped on her hot coffee as if the china cup could mask her face, or at least to give her an excuse for a briefly redder complexion.

'No, I didn't.'

'Well!' Frau Beltz had to put down her cup at the shocking news that her doctor was completely unaware of this turn of events – she would need all her demonstrative faculties for this one. 'This carpenter, Herr Gerlich... Well, you must have known he was seeing your housekeeper, mustn't you?' The way she poked her nose in Erika's direction reminded the doctor of that obnoxious Officer Hummel sniffing around her home.

'Oh!' Erika performed the necessary awakening. 'That carpenter. Yes I was aware of... something like that.'

'Well, turns out the police think he did it. They've had him in for questioning, the whole nine yards. But it's not surprising, is it. I've seen him about. Big old bloke. Bit dim looking. Apparently she'd finished with him and he wasn't happy about that. Raised his hand to her no doubt, clearly the type. That's probably why she broke it off. But he wasn't having any of that so he beat her up and... Well, of course you know what happened to the poor dear. And she was only a little thing, wasn't she? Wouldn't say boo to a goose, that one. Why would anybody want to lay a hand on her, eh?'

A leech hit the floor and Erika dived for it, making a great fuss about putting it back in the glass jar, so that by the time she returned to the armchair opposite her patient's, the subject may have been forgotten.

But it wasn't.

'Unless she was one of them Jew girls posing as a German. You hear a lot of that going on nowadays, don't you? One that managed to slip through the net. Because it's so hard to tell with some of them, isn't it? Come to think of it now, she could have been one of them, don't you think, doctor?'

Erika puffed out her lips and raised her eyebrows in order to demonstrate that her patient's guess was as good as hers.

Another leech dropped.

Erika hurried to pick it up. The sooner she could be out of here the better. They might have swerved from the subject of Karin's death, but now they were onto an equally distasteful subject that brought back memories of a time as a child when she was devoted to the Hitler Youth Movement; when she met Max at university and discovered the love of her life was a devoted Catholic which went against all the anti-religious and eugenic principles she had absorbed from the Movement; when that rationale resulted in some bad choices on her part, to put it mildly, the consequences of which haunted her to this day.

Frau Beltz was crashing on regardless, like a malevolent version of Edgar. 'Well, if she was she couldn't have been surprised if it caught up with her eventually. My Bert was in the Reich Labour Service and he saw how they all lined up to be executed. It was as if they knew they deserved it.'

Another leech dropped to the floor.

'He was going past on a motorcycle once and saw this great long procession of them. He stopped when he saw this pretty little one, much like your housekeeper, in a red chemise, he said – well, he was a one for the pretty girls was my Bert. I didn't mind. He always came home to me at the end of the day – anyway, where was I... oh, yes, so he stops and he asks this girl where all these people are going. A great long line of them it was, over a kilometre long, shuffling slowly towards the wood. And she says, "We're going to be shot." Well, at first he thought she was joking just coming out with it like that so matter of fact, but he followed the line up the road on his bike and sure enough at the edge of the wood they were all being stripped of their clothes – so as not to waste them, 'cause they could all be washed and mended and reused for our suffering population, see? – and then they were made to lie down in three bloody great pits. Three metres by twenty-four metres, Bert swears they were that big. And they had to lie down like sardines in a tin, he said, with their heads in the centre. Above were six men with tommy guns who put them out of their misery. What a job, eh? But those gunmen got double rations and extra pay as it was such a strain on their nerves. Well, it would be, wouldn't it?'

Another leech dropped. And another. Erika was on her knees, her head near the floor.

'Bert saw that girl in the red chemise again. Only, by the time she got to the pit, she didn't even have the red chemise anymore. They were all naked by the time they had to climb in on top of the dead ones. But first, Bert said, they sprinkled ashes and chloride of lime or something over the dead ones. I don't know, was it chloride or—'

'Chloride of lime, yes,' Erika said rather too loudly at the floor, as inert leeches rained down on her, 'it stops the decomposing bodies from smelling.'

'Well, I said to Bert that I thought that was all a bit much. I mean, you can do whatever you like to them, but not burn them, gas them, or shoot them like that. It's not their fault. They should just be imprisoned and then, after the war, ship them off somewhere. Sail them wherever you wish, I don't care where, it's just that there isn't room for them in Germany anymore, is there?'

Erika felt like she did when her friend and fellow doctor Kurt had waved one of the flyers under her nose, which the British army were sticking all over the city. At the top of the flyer were the English words REMEMBER THIS! Beneath were five photos. Appalling pictures of emaciated naked bodies piled in long rows being prodded by the barrels of German soldiers. Women picking the clothes off corpses in barbed wire cages. Men in striped pyjamas huddled in the snow in a gateway with a sign forged from iron, in German, above their heads, which read WORK SETS YOU FREE. Death and abuse on a scale even she as a doctor had never seen. And at the bottom of the page, the English words DON'T FRATERNISE!

She had told Kurt, and herself, it was all just Allied propaganda, although something inside her, which moved like one of these leeches in the jar, said otherwise. And now here was Frau Beltz and her Bert making the truth as incontrovertible as that wrought iron sign above the prisoners' shaved heads.

'Do you mind if I use your bathroom before I leave?' Erika said, her smile barely concealing her tightened jaw.

'No, of course not,' Beltz said. 'There isn't anything wrong I hope, is there, dear?' she added, although it would be a very dull day for the lady if there really was nothing wrong with the doctor – where would the drama be in that?

Without answering, Erika hurried to the bathroom and, as quietly as she could, vomited into the toilet. Perhaps her patient's horror stories from the war had tipped the gastric scales, but Erika knew it would have happened with or without Beltz's babble. Just as it had been happening every day for the past few days. Her period hadn't come this month and, although she would go through the motions – have her urine sent off to the lab to be injected into a female frog, which, if it produced eggs in the following twenty four hours would indicate a positive result – she already knew she was pregnant.

She was pregnant!

Her heart swelled and her lungs sucked at the air again, but this time it wasn't for the loss of Netta; it was elation that someone was coming to fill the hole in her life, which her growing daughter would inevitably leave. And more than that, another child would surely repair the tear in her relationship with Max, which four years apart had ripped into it. And, although it shamed her to even think it, she knew Max would be so much closer to this new child because he would watch it grow from its very first day on Earth; he would never be a stranger to it as he was to Netta.

'I thought it was the summer holidays! I do less work at school!' Netta grumbled to Milla as they stripped the sheets from the bunks and dumped them in a pile by the door. Other kids were mopping the floors in the showers and some were dusting the chairs around the knights' table in the dining room. Frau Auttenberg and the man with the red face, who Netta heard was called Herr Kahler, wandered in and out of each room the kids were working in, saying things like, 'If you want to have your dinner tonight you best get a move on,' and, 'Have you got any gumption, lad? Where did you leave your gumption?'

'What's gumption?' Netta asked her new friend.

'I don't know. Something our parents were supposed to pack for us, I think. But it looks like they all forgot.'

'Why did your parents send you here?' Netta spoke in whispers because she saw the way Frau Auttenberg flicked the ears of the boys she caught chatting at the other end of the dorm, who were stripping bunks too.

'My mama sent me here because I don't have a papa. Well, I did, because you can't make a little girl unless you have a papa and a mama, but he went away. He had to for work, Mama said. He must do a very important job because I heard Mama telling the neighbour that he went away with a secretary.'

Netta was impressed and a little jealous. Her mama was a doctor and she didn't even have a secretary. But they did have a housekeeper. Or they used to. But they didn't now, so it would be no use her bragging to Milla about that.

'And my mama has to work now, in an office, so there's no one to look after me in the holidays.'

'Oh.' Netta felt sorry for Milla. When her papa was away all those years she had Opa and Oma and even Tante Bertel to look after her when Mama was working. 'I'm just here to get better. I cough a lot because of all the smoke where we live.'

'Oh.' Milla felt sorry for Netta. She never coughed and

where she lived the air was always clean and smelled like Christmas trees.

Before the pile of dirty sheets was too big for them to carry, they hauled it downstairs to the laundry room where a woman with a nose like a beak and hands like claws grabbed them and threw them in the great copper washing tub. The crow lady, as the kids called her, grabbed the stirring stick to wash the linen with and Netta noticed how short it was; how it seemed to have been snapped in half. Milla tugged on Netta's sleeve – there were more sheets to bring down yet. But it was too late. The crow lady noticed Netta staring at the stick and squawked:

'What do you think you're looking at?'

Netta jumped, surprised to find the lady sounded as much like a crow as she looked.

'Get on with your chores or I'll break the rest of it over *your* bottom!' And she yanked the paddle from the hot water to show she meant business.

The girls scampered back up the stairs, but halfway Netta stopped and held onto Milla, not just because she felt out of breath and needed to cough, but also so she could ask Milla what on earth the crow lady meant.

'Paul caught a crab when we went to the beach last week – a big one! – and was keeping it as a pet in a box under his bunk.'

'Paul?'

'The boy with the glasses. In the bottom bunk opposite yours.'

'Oh.'

'Herr Kahler found out and dragged him out of bed in the night and smacked him on the bum with the stirring stick until it broke. Blood came through his pyjamas and everything.'

Netta was terrified. That stick was old and worn, but it was still far too thick to break on a little boy's bottom without some incredibly hard whacks.

After their chores were done they were all starving and tucked into their dinners with gusto. But Netta had barely touched her chicken when Auttenberg's voice made her freeze with her fork halfway to her open mouth.

'Is this how we sit at dinner?' Auttenberg orbited the table, prodding at some of the children's shoulders so hard that their faces nearly plunged into their food. 'Hunched over like animals at a trough?'

Auttenberg had a fist full of wire coat hangers. With pictures of the broken paddle still in her head, Netta felt her thighs start to tremble at the thought that these were what matron preferred to use to beat children's bottoms. But she didn't drag anyone from the table and begin beating them with the hangers. Instead she took one and passed one of the boy's – Henrick's – arms through it from behind and yanked it up to his shoulders, forcing them back and pulling them together.

'Now, that looks a lot straighter, doesn't it?' Auttenberg admired her handiwork. 'Doesn't it?' she honked.

'Yes, Frau Auttenberg,' the children sang in unison, and it was the saddest sounding song Netta had ever heard.

'And we wouldn't have to do this if your parents had been a bit stricter with you in the first place,' she muttered as she went around the table ensnaring each child in a coat hanger before allowing them to finish their dinner. It was the most exhausting dinner Netta had ever had. And just to top it all, Auttenberg came around at the end of the meal with a giant bottle of cod liver oil and shoved a foul tasting teaspoon between each pair of curled lips.

This was the first time Netta had ever tasted it. She was already expecting something horrible by the look of the scrunched up noses on the children that received the oil before her, but she had no idea it would be *that* horrible. Despite what her mind told her would be best to do with Frau Auttenberg and her entire system of globes bearing down on her, her mouth took charge, overruled her head, and spat the oil out onto her plate.

Many of the kids around the table slapped their hands across their mouths to hide their gasps just in case they got into trouble for making such a noise. But they needn't have worried. Auttenberg was far too shocked and appalled by the beastly sight of the spoilt little doctor's daughter spitting onto her plate. And she told the entire room so. However, she did it in such unusually quiet tones that it was the most frightening thing the young ones had ever heard, like subterranean rumblings ahead of a volcano blowing its top.

Netta was afraid she would end up like Paul, unable to sit down for days, but she just couldn't keep that awful goo in her mouth. She had no idea how the others did it, but she would be asking Milla the secret as soon as they got out of the dining room.

However, Netta didn't get out.

Everyone else was allowed to be unhooked from their coat hanger shackles and leave, but Netta had to stay. When everyone had left the room Auttenberg shoved another teaspoon of the cod liver oil at Netta, but her little opponent knew what it tasted like now so there was no way her mouth was going to be opening up. And just to make sure, her teeth clamped down like a portcullis behind her pursed lips. The spoon jabbed at those lips and cracked against her teeth like a battering ram, but although she was alone at the Round Table, Sir Netta the Noble would not be letting the dragon through.

'Fine,' Auttenberg said, 'but you will stay there all night if need be,' and she left the room.

Every half-hour that poisonous teaspoon would try and break through her defences, but Netta stood her ground. She would even dare to return the glare of the goliath above her sometimes and after three or four attempts she thought she saw something like admiration pass across Auttenberg's stony expression. It was so uncomfortable sitting on the wooden chair for hours, but eventually she fell asleep from utter exhaustion.

She was woken, as usual, at 6:30 the next morning and felt the sores where the coat hanger had cut into each armpit.

Milla's head appeared upside down over the edge of the bunk, her blues eyes burning with concern and wonder. 'How are you? What happened?'

'I'm fine.' Netta smiled. 'Nothing happened,' she boasted, the faint taste of chicken still between her unbrushed teeth, but not a hint of cod liver oil anywhere.

Milla was more in love with her new friend than ever and Netta knew it. She was proud of it; and of the way Frau Auttenberg was so quiet at breakfast that morning. Perhaps she's less used to late nights than I am, Netta thought with a wry glance at the two planets suffering constant collision in Auttenberg's skirt as she disappeared into the kitchen.

'Do you think we'll be going to the beach today?' Netta whispered to Milla.

'I hope so. If not we'll definitely be allowed into the garden. It's such a sunny day.'

The garden! Netta scoffed to herself. I can do that anytime at home. What's the point in suffering this rubbish if I—

A pint of double cream clunked down on the table in front of her.

'Drink it up, Netta! You'll be having this every day until we start to see some meat on those scrawny little bones of yours.'

A tired Netta caught the smirk on the matron's face as she walked away again and she felt like crying. Until she noticed Milla's expectant fidgeting and her cream-craving face.

If I see another child with respiratory problems…! Erika
thought as she showed the mother and a wheezing boy
out of the surgery. Perhaps we should consider moving,
all of us go and live by the sea, she sighed inwardly, a notion
which was only reinforced by the presence of the irritating
police officer hovering in her corridor the way the smoke
from the steel works did over the house.

'I'm sorry,' she said a little too cheerfully, 'but I have
another patient to see now, so I don't have the time to talk.'

'I know you have,' the officer grinned, his cap jammed
under one arm, tapping a rolled up newspaper into the
palm of his hand as he might do with his truncheon at
other times. 'It's me. I'm your next patient.'

'Er, no.' Erika's laugh was infused with a sudden
nervousness. She marched into the surgery to check her
appointments book. 'I have a Herr Hum—'

'—mel, yes,' said Hummel, who had followed her in and
closed the door behind him, 'That's me.'

Erika wilted. 'Of course.' She swallowed hard. 'Of course
it is. I should have recognised…'

She gestured to the policeman to sit down and, although
she knew by the smirk on his face that this wasn't strictly
a medical appointment, she decided to play along: it
would be the best way to demonstrate her innocence, she
thought. 'And what seems to be the matter today, Herr
Hummel.'

'Well, actually,' Hummel said, straightening, putting
down the newspaper and cap on her desk, and putting both
hands on his lumbar region, 'I seem to be getting a lot of
aches and pains in my back these days and I was wondering
if you could take a look.'

'Certainly,' she said, rubbing her hands to warm them
before touching the patient's skin. Although it was a hot
day and her hands were perfectly warm before he arrived,
she felt her extremities getting cooler with every second
she spent in the presence of this frigorific ass.

'Could you just slip off your tunic and untuck your shirt so I can take a look.'

Hummel didn't say anything, but just leered at her as he did as she asked. She was intending to feel around his spine for any signs of displacement as she would for any other patient, but she decided to just observe the area, partly because of that repellent expression and partly because she did not want him to feel her trembling hands. She got up and walked around behind him.

'Is that OK, doctor?' he said, lifting the shirt halfway up his pasty back.

The spiders of hair crawling up it from beneath the waistline of his trousers almost made her gag. It was nothing she hadn't seen on the backs of a hundred male patients before, it was just that anything on this particular human's body was likely to repulse her, just as that conceited expression had from the first moment she ever laid eyes on him.

'Doctor?'

'Yes, fine,' she said abruptly. And then after the speediest of observations, 'Well, it all seems to be in order. Nothing out of place.'

'You can tell that just by looking?' he said and she glared at the back of his head and the ridiculous line in his thinning hair left by that policeman's cap of his.

She ran her fingers down his spine quickly lest the spiders ensnare her and spin a web she could never release her hands from. 'Is it a dull pain that lingers or a sharp pain that only comes once in a while?'

'Occasionally it's sharp and brief. Other times it's dull and lingers all day.'

What a surprisingly unhelpful response, Erika said caustically to herself. And then out loud, 'I imagine it's an occupational hazard. Do you spend a lot of time at a desk?'

He was about to answer, but sized her up first as she sat down again, just in case that was a thinly veiled criticism of his policing style.

'I do spend *some* of my working day writing reports and such like.' The smug look vanished for the first time.

'Well, I would recommend a nice hot bath or a water bottle around the lumbar region there when it's lingering. Or you could just apply some menthol and methylsalicylate rub which you can pick up at the pharmacist.' She usually only described it as menthol rub to her patients, but she added the methylsalicylate in the hope that it would bamboozle him, remind him of her superiority in this room and hopefully make him sound foolish in front of the pharmacist as he tried to recall the word. 'You could ask your wife to apply it if it's easier.' She was rather pleased to notice an almost imperceptible twitch as she said this. 'Do you have a wife, Herr Hummel?'

'Er... no, I don't actually,' he said, busying himself with putting his tunic back on.

What a surprise! Erika jeered internally and sat back in her chair.

'If only I could find one as attractive as you.' The leer was back.

Erika chose to ignore his exclamation and pretended to make a note on her pad.

'And all this without the aid of make-up!' he chuckled, holding his hands up as he might in front of an exquisite painting in a gallery. 'You have no make-up on today, do you, doctor?'

'No, I don't,' she said, continuing to scribble, though she did wish she had some on now to mask her cheeks, which were beginning to flush.

'You never wear make-up to work, I take it?'

'Er... no.' She looked at him now wondering what on earth he was getting at, as he was clearly getting at something.

He picked up the paper and began to leaf through it idly and continued, 'Oh, I just mention it because you had make-up on that day I first met you in your living room there. And I assume you had been at work that day? It was a weekday after all?'

'But it was an evening, if I remember rightly.' Erika's turn to be smug. 'I was probably about to go out somewhere. With my husband.'

'Oh, I see,' he sniffed without looking up from the paper. 'It only struck me on that day particularly because I could have sworn you had a bruise just under your eye. I mean, the make-up did a really good job of covering the colour. But I suppose it was a little swollen too.'

Erika blanched and was about to splutter an excuse for the swollen eye, but she didn't need to. Hummel was too busy slapping the paper and guffawing. 'Did you see this today?' He read, *'The actress, Ida Wuest, who is now 66 years old, was recently denazified in Berlin. According to the findings of the Court, she had sometimes publicly expressed her appreciation of the Nazi movement, but the Court took the view that, as the President of the Welfare Organisation for Old Artists, "she was, like all prominent artists, compelled to make certain concessions".* Compelled to make certain concessions! What the hell is that supposed to mean? Bloody artists! *The Court was satisfied that she was no active Nazi and had lent her financial assistance to various Jewish artists.* Oh, well that's all right then, as long as she threw some cash at some Jewish artists, as if it would even make a dent in her bank balance! Don't you think, doctor?'

Erika was about to appease him with an *Mmm* or something but she couldn't get a sound let alone a word in edgeways now.

'And did you see this? *The half-monthly Youth Periodical "Der Brennpunkt" makes the following comment on Dr Adenauer's statement on the Jewish question: "It might be wrong to consider the entire German nation guilty of the murder of six million Jews. We should, however, have sufficient community feeling to realise how strongly in those days we were connected with those people who committed the crimes. They were Germans. To-day we have established a new State. One of the mortgages we took over is the death of six million Jews. We are not entitled to forget. We have to prove through our deeds that we try to right the wrongs, as far as this is possible. If the Jews of to-day are to gain confidence in the "other" Germany, it is our duty to show them our goodwill.'*

Erika felt sick and this time it was most definitely not morning sickness. What was this man trying to do to her? Was he here to accuse her of Karin's death? Or was he here to dredge up her past as a supporter of the National Socialist movement? He couldn't possibly know anything about those shady choices she made as a youth, could he?

'Our duty? Not entitled to forget?' He was banging on. '*I* never did anything that I need to forget. I never did anything but my *duty*, did you, doctor?'

'Well,' she stuttered when he finally came up for air, 'I agree with the...' She flapped a hand at the paper. 'I agree that the whole nation is not guilty, but we can all do our bit, can't we, to try and right the wrongs of the past. Yes,' she relaxed a little as a miniature epiphany tickled her, 'perhaps we all have to share responsibility as a society for the crimes committed in it, if we are to move forward as a people.'

'Hmm.' Hummel wasn't convinced, but he had found another point of interest in the *Mengede Zeitung*, which may well have been the real reason he had brought this paper with him today. 'Ah, here it is! I saw this ad in the Classifieds earlier and thought to myself, I must ask Dr Portner about it.' He lay the newspaper on her desk and tapped at the appropriate lines:

Employment
Busy professional family
(doctors and teacher), requires exp.
live-in housekeeper betw. 30-55 years
of age.
Box 854

'Is that your advertisement?' he asked.

'Yes.'

'Must be strange having to put a new advert out for a housekeeper, and so soon after your previous one... departed.'

'Well, as it says there, we are all very busy people. My father-in-law with the school, my mother-in-law with her infirm sister, my husband and I with the surgery and our daughter.' She was about to add that she had another on the way, but her pregnancy was none of his business and she had justified herself to him quite enough already.

'Yes, yes, but what I was most interested in was the age range you have in the ad: 30-55 years of age. Very specific. Why so, if you don't mind me asking?'

She absolutely did mind him bloody well asking, but was pretty sure he was no longer sitting there as her patient now, but was back in his official capacity as Officer Hummel, despite his cursory way of asking these questions. So she answered.

'Well, we don't want someone who's too old and needs looking after themselves when they should be looking after the house and our daughter.'

'Of course,' Hummel said with a dash of impatience, 'And the lower age limit?' Which Erika knew was what he was really interested in all along.

'Well, to be honest with you, officer, Karin, God rest her soul, was just a bit too young in many ways; a bit too inexperienced, naïve even.'

To be honest with you. Hummel loved and loathed that phrase. He loathed it because it was such a pointless thing to say in a conversation, unless, that is, every single other thing the speaker had said in that conversation was a lie, which it probably wasn't. More likely, Hummel believed, it was only ever the statement connected to the phrase *to be honest with you* which was to be taken with a very large pinch of salt, hence the speaker's need to preface it with a plea for credence. And that is why he loved it.

'Of course,' Hummel was leering again, 'and we don't need two attractive young ladies in one house, now do we?'

Erika was genuinely confused whether this was another creepy compliment or a suggestion of something more sinister on her part, so she opened her mouth to explain that there would surely be another patient waiting by now, but Hummel once again beat her to it.

'Anyway, I'm sure I've taken up quite enough of your time today, doctor,' he said, rising and donning his cap. 'You have to get on. And so do I. This town isn't going to police itself, now, is it?' He rolled the paper back into a truncheon shape as if he expected to be assaulted upon leaving the room.

Erika scowled at his back, which appeared to be giving him no pain whatsoever, as he left and, although to her he was undoubtedly still frigorific, she wasn't quite so sure she could describe him as an ass any longer.

Netta was happy. Yet another morning free of double cream. Milla was happy. Yet another morning full of double cream. Frau Auttenberg looked happy when she told Netta to go and see Herr Kahler, as he had a special job for her this morning. Milla looked disappointed when Frau Auttenberg told her that didn't mean her too, and she sank back into her chair watching Netta's golden hair get even more golden every time she walked through a shaft of sunshine coming in through the windows on her way out of the big dining room.

Netta found Herr Kahler in his office. 'Well, where else do you think you'll find him?' Frau Auttenberg had said when Netta had asked. He looked as red-faced as ever and his grey hair stuck up all over the place. Netta was surprised Frau Auttenberg didn't ever tell him off for not looking presentable like she did the kids every morning before breakfast. He gave her a quick look as she came in, but was more interested in whatever it was he was trying to fix with a screwdriver on his lap. It looked to Netta as if it was a very hard job and one that was making Herr Kahler redder by the second.

'Your job is to sweep the sand from the driveway this morning. There's a broom over there,' he grumbled, but, since he was too busy to point to exactly where *there* was, Netta had to look all around the room until she found it hiding behind the door.

She then waited a few seconds, which seemed like minutes, in case there were any more instructions. Nothing else came out of the man except a few grunts as he tried to twist the screwdriver, so she left her room dragging the long broom behind her like a tail – at least that's what she told herself it was, which made the whole business of sweeping sand from the driveway less of a bore.

It took a long time for a little girl with a big broom to sweep a wide driveway, but it would have taken less time had she not been distracted by the smell of seaweed and the sound of the waves munching at the beach and sight of all that beige sand just waiting to be played on. Not that it was empty. There were holiday makers dotted all about it. Their white towels laid out next to picnic baskets told Netta they were planning on staying all day. Their voices reached her on the back of the sea breeze. The excited squeaks of kids, the low pitched warnings of their parents. Kids with their parents at the beach. That was how it was supposed to be for her too, but here she was sweeping the driveway like Aschenputtel in her Brothers Grimm book while everyone else got to go to the ball. She wondered if any of the little white huts by the sea wall were empty. Perhaps she could run away from this place and stay in one of those until her parents came back for her. Then she could play on the beach whenever she wanted – as long as Frau Auttenberg or Herr Kahler weren't looking.

Eventually the job was done and she swished her tail behind her all the way back to Herr Kahler's office. He wasn't there, thankfully, so she put the broom back behind the door and hurried off to find Milla in the garden where they played for what little was left of the morning.

After lunch, Henrick, the first boy to get his arms tied up in a coat hanger the other day, walked briskly into the garden, stopped in front of Netta, pushed his glasses up his nose and said in a shaky voice, 'Herr Kahler wants to see you.'

Netta had never really spoken with Henrick before so she wasn't sure if his voice always sounded like that or if he was scared of something. But there wasn't time to think about that now. She dragged herself away from the garden and back to the office.

Herr Kahler wasn't trying to fix anything this time. He was just sitting there staring at Netta from under his thick grey eyebrows, which stuck up in greasy clumps all over the place as much as the hair on the top of his head.

'What did I tell you to do this morning?' he growled.

'Sweep the sand from the driveway,' she answered.

'And did you do that?'

'Yes I did,' she said.

'I beg your pardon?'

'Yes I did, Herr Kahler,' she added to make sure she wasn't sounding rude. She didn't want to sound rude. She was just telling the truth.

'I beg your pardon?' he repeated.

'Yes I did!' She raised her voice ever so slightly in case he was having difficulty hearing her.

'I beg your pardon, but if you had done what I'd asked you to do, why was there sand all over the driveway when I went out at lunchtime?'

Silence, except for the sound of children enjoying themselves in the garden. Netta couldn't think of anything to say.

'I'll tell you why.' The red face was getting redder again. 'Because you're a lazy, spoilt little girl, that's why.'

Netta had to tell him this wasn't true. She had to explain that she had done the job. 'No, I—'

'I beg your pardon?' he shouted, slamming his hands on the table and pushing himself up, just as her papa had done that night when the tall man who said penis came to dinner.

'I—I—I... yes, I—I'm lazy, Herr Kahler.'

'And?' He sang the word like a motorcar speeding up.

'And spoilt,' she said, but the words tasted foul in her mouth because she was sure they weren't true.

'Yes you are.' He came out from behind the desk and Netta flinched, but he passed by her and grabbed the broom from behind the door. 'Now, you'll go and do it again and you'll make sure you do it properly otherwise you'll get the slipper, do you hear?'

She took the broom, but it didn't feel like a tail anymore. It felt like it was made of lead. She went outside. The driveway was covered in sand. Her whole body drooped. But she swept it all away again, more thoroughly than she did the first time with the thought of the slipper hanging over her.

Milla found her at dinner time slumped in her chair at the round table.

'What happened?' she whispered.

'I'm too tired to even tell you,' Netta sighed.

The two girls ate their fish and cabbage that evening in the kind of silence Frau Auttenberg expected every evening. When the cod liver oil came round Netta opened her mouth obediently, as she had done ever since that long night when she had first done battle with the battle-axe. And when she was allowed to leave the dining room she spat out the oil she'd been hiding into the potted plant on the windowsill in the stairwell, which was growing much faster and looking much healthier than Netta was for its daily dose of fish oil.

But before she could begin to get undressed, Paul, the boy whose bottom had bled, came up to her and said, 'Herr Kahler wants to see you.'

Netta almost cried right there in front of Paul, but somehow she held it in and got herself back downstairs to the office. And it all sounded very familiar.

'What did I tell you to do this afternoon?' he growled.

'Sweep the sand from the driveway,' she answered.

'And did you do that?'

'Yes I did.'

'I beg your pardon?'

'Yes I did, Herr Kahler.'

'I beg your pardon?'

'Yes I—!'

'I. Beg. Your. Pardon?'

She knew what the answer was supposed to be, but she couldn't believe she hadn't done it properly this time.

She opened her mouth to speak.

'Think very carefully before you answer, young lady,' he snarled.

She couldn't hold back the tears any longer. If she told the truth she would get the slipper. If she lied and said she had been lazy again, she would get the slipper. This was so unfair!

Herr Kahler got up. He was wearing his pyjamas already with an open red dressing gown on top and red leather slippers to match.

He closed the door quietly and took Netta by the wrist.

The six kilometres back to camp seem no more than a couple to Max, intoxicated as he is on the part he's just played in the successful delivery of a Russian officer's baby. The wind that had molested him on his trudge into town this morning is gone and the atmosphere now is halcyon. Even the Northern Lights put on a brief show for him and he would stop and bow at the green dream cloud saluting him was he not flanked by two moaning Soviet guards completely ignorant of the miracles going on all around and above them that day.

Or is it that he is floating back to camp because he has just been reunited with Jenny? She might have been a prostitute, but she was his friend and confidante back in Breslau before they were all captured and shipped off to the ends of the earth. And now, having been instructed to check the health of the women who service the Russians in town, all holed up together in a rotten little apartment block, he finds Jenny among them, like an apparition. And in the second it takes him to accept that it's her in front of him, alive and well, it's all he can do not to throw his arms around her. Jenny, however, possesses none of the same boundaries when it comes to decorum and hugs him with such affection it comes as a shock to Max. He hasn't been embraced in this way, embraced by a woman since... well, since the last time he'd seen Jenny in Breslau that day in the convent, where Hitler vindictively housed all the prostitutes, when she'd congratulated him on his Iron Cross. So it takes a moment for him to allow his body to receive such a gesture, but at the welcome end of that paralysed period he melts and reciprocates with a fervour and duration that almost has *Jenny* feeling self-conscious in front of the other girls.

It seems he is on his way back from both events at the same time, which is impossible because they both happened on different days, he is sure. But dreams are strange like that. As strange as nightmares. But it doesn't matter. He doesn't care. All he knows is that his wife in the future (or is that the present?) is pregnant with their second child and he has a picture of a black Madonna in his pocket, a gift from Jenny to keep him safe. Life is good.

The guards leave him at the gatehouse and Max walks back toward the barracks alone, unaware of Volkov behind him, until the barrel of the sergeant's rifle is jammed into Max's back with unnecessary and vindictive force, shepherding him away from the barracks, away from the hospital, away from the kitchens, away from any part of the camp Max is familiar with to the row of squat wooden huts downwind of the cesspit.

'Can you explain to me, *please*, what this is all about?'

'Get in!' is the only answer as Volkov grins at one of the huts. 'Get in!' The grin is twisting. 'And if I have to tell you again you'll be shot.'

Max has to crouch to get in the doorway and once inside the windowless cage it's only shards of moonlight, slicing through the gaps in the logs that make up the roof, which show him the cell is a square, just long enough for him to lay down in either direction. There is nothing in there but a bucket in the corner for a toilet. He knows this because of the stench coming from it. The door is slammed and bolted.

Max hears the fading crunch of boots on frosted grass and he's filled with a claustrophobic panic that has him shouting, 'How long? How long do I have to stay in here? How long? *How long?*'

It was easy for Kahler to drag the sobbing girl over to the chair and put her over his lap; he was so much bigger and stronger than her. He told her to pull up her dress and pull down her knickers, in a quiet voice that was almost as shaky as Henrick's when the boy had delivered his message to her in the garden after lunch. He leant over to reach down to his feet, squashing Netta between his big hot belly and his thighs. When he straightened up he had one of his red leather slippers in his hand. He hesitated for a moment. Netta managed to quiet herself listening for a sign that it was over, that he had changed his mind, that this was just a threat, *but next time, young lady...* She furiously blinked away the tears as she hung there looking at the floorboards with just the sound of her sniffing and his breathing for the longest second of her life so far. And then the first blow came with a raging sting. He beat her and beat her. And he spoke as he did. He said a syllable with every whack on her bottom and sometimes she felt spit from his mouth landing on her skin before the burning took over:

'Now-you-will-sweep-the-sand-prop-er-ly-to-mor-row-mor-ning-o-ther-wise-you-will-get-the-slip-per-a-gain-do-you un-der-stand?'

She howled that she did understand and put her hands in the way to stop the pain, but they just got beaten too, and then he easily held them by her sides with one big heavy arm across her back while he gave her a few extra blows for putting her hands in the way, he said.

She was shivering with the pain. He was shivering with what Netta thought, as he released her, might have been pain too, but it was hard to tell through such tearful eyes. What she was sure of was that he was slumped in his chair now, head back, mouth open, panting.

'Get out.' He gulped.

She did.

She slept all night on her tummy. Every time she rolled over, her sore bottom woke her and she rolled back again. Even the blanket was too heavy on her wounds and she thanked God it was summer and it was warm enough for just a sheet.

Milla was devastated for her friend and couldn't stop watching from the corner of her eye the way Netta perched painfully on the edge of the knobbly wooden chair at breakfast. Every time Frau Auttenberg came around she'd tell Netta off for not sitting properly and stand over her until she hoisted herself back onto the chair. Milla winced on Netta's behalf and secretly gave the matron a very dirty look, but as she did so she noticed how even Auttenberg did not seem to be enjoying the sight of Netta flinching and quietly gasping as much as she expected her to.

After breakfast, Netta limped out to the driveway using the broom as a walking stick and began sweeping with a feeling of utter pointlessness. The breeze was strong and cold this morning, so at least Netta could enjoy the way it cooled the wounds which bit into her skin.

She jumped as Herr Kahler bowled out of the house, but he was only getting into his car and going off to town. He'd be back after lunch to inspect her work.

The breeze was a wind now and Netta suddenly stopped and watched the way the sand she had swept into little piles in the flowerbeds was being picked up by the wind, which was twirling and whirling and smearing it mischievously all over the driveway again. And then the truth hit her like a North Sea wave.

No wonder it looked like I hadn't swept up properly, Netta cried to herself, the wind always comes along and ruins it all by the time Herr Kahler takes a look. And I bet he knows that too! She threw down the broom, stamped her foot and went inside.

'What's the point?' she told Milla when she found her in the dorm. 'He's going to beat me anyway, so why should I even bother doing the stupid work?'

'Because,' Milla said with a terrified look on her face, 'he'll beat you twice as hard next time.'

'Well, good,' Netta said, sounding brave, but feeling petrified inside. 'Perhaps he'll beat me so hard I have to go to hospital and then I'll be free of this stinking place.'

Milla was even more terrified now, not just for Netta, but at the idea of being stuck here without her best friend.

Netta ate even less than usual at lunchtime and since Milla had wolfed hers down and was already out in the garden playing, there was no one to give her leftovers to. But before she had to worry about what Frau Auttenberg would say to that, Henrick came in with the message she was expecting.

'Herr Kahler wants to see you.'

'Does he really?' Netta said, cramming so much of the sarcasm she had absorbed from adults so far in her young life into the words that Henrick's eyes became even more magnified than usual behind his glasses.

She slouched into the office trying not to imagine how the pain would feel a second time on top of the pain that still pinched her backside and the silly script began again:

'What did I tell you to do this morning?' he growled.

'Sweep the sand from the driveway,' she grumbled, her bottom lip already quivering.

'And did you do that?'

'Yes I did.'

'I beg your pardon?'

'Yes I did, Herr Kahler.'

'I beg your pardon?'

Her stomach twisted and tightened, but she had to tell him she knew what his little game was, 'Yes I did, but the—'

'Yes you did!' he bellowed.

I did? She thought. I did. He said I did, but what about the..? He's not reaching for a slipper. He's just sitting there, elbows on the table, resting his chin on his thumbs.

He prodded that chin with those thumbs in a painful looking way and said again more quietly this time, 'Yes you did.'

He looked a little defeated for a second and Netta felt her body relax. She was safe! He couldn't give her a beating if he said himself she had done the job. Although how he could think that, when she had left the broom and the sand all over the driveway, was way beyond her imagination. But perhaps that was what he wanted to see when he told her to sweep the driveway. It made absolutely no sense whatsoever, but he was an adult and if there was something Netta was sure about, something she had learned better than any subject in school, it was that adults and their world made absolutely no sense whatsoever.

She waited to be dismissed with the same eagerness she always waited to be told she could go and play on the beach. But it didn't happen. Instead Herr Kahler was raising his voice again.

'Now then, if you could sweep up the sand properly this morning why couldn't you do it the first time I told you to do it, eh?'

She didn't know how to answer him. She was so exhausted, so tired of this game and she didn't have the energy left to guess anymore. But that was OK, because Herr Kahler knew.

'I'll tell you why, girl, shall I?' Unsurprisingly he didn't wait for her permission. 'Because you're a lazy, spoilt little girl, that's why, aren't you?'

'I...' There was no point in arguing; if that's all he needed from her to make up for the fact that she was not going to get a beating then she was more than happy to give in. 'Yes, I'm lazy, Herr Kahler.'

'And?' he sang.

'And spoilt,' she said through gritted teeth.

'Yes you are. Now get out,' he spat.

And she did, turning first not towards the garden, but to the front door where she blinked in disbelief at the sand free driveway. It wouldn't be sand free for long of course, once the wind had had its naughty way with it, but for now, just at the time when Herr Kahler was due back from town, it was and that was all that mattered. She turned back into the dark hallway and saw a figure standing in the dining room doorway watching her. As her eyes adjusted to the lack of light she recognised her friend Milla, who hadn't wolfed down her lunch to get out in the garden quicker, but had wolfed down her lunch so she could have the driveway swept just in time for Herr Kahler's return. And for the strangest of moments Netta was scared about the idea of leaving this place next week; about going back to Mengede where there wasn't a little girl she loved as much as Milla; about going back to the parents that abandoned her here, a father whom she didn't know and a mother whom she thought she knew but wasn't so sure now. For all its hatefulness and fear, the routines here were fast becoming the norm and therefore a topsy-turvy kind of safe. The little girl couldn't imagine leaving it all behind.

S omeone was watching the house.

The terraced red brick house on three floors in the suburb of Mengede in the heart of the Ruhr district. Sulphurous clouds draped the rooftop and thick soot lined the windowsills, even on the pretty, round Tiffany window in the attic.

It was the blue and red glass of the window, lit up from the inside that evening, which the watcher's eyes were fixed on. It was as if the watcher knew exactly who was in there and exactly what they were doing. Or perhaps it was just that the Tiffany window was so much more appealing than the other windows below – tall, skinny, square, humdrum – windows which made the house look gaunt.

It was time. No more standing around on street corners. The watcher shuddered and then marched towards the house.

Max was sitting by the Tiffany window, a medical journal open but unread on his lap. The late summer evening was sultry so the window was open and he could see out across the rooftops towards the quarry. The sky was aglow, not with the sun which only dipped below the horizon for a while at this time of year, but with the fires from the blast furnaces spewing their molten rivers into the legion of steel factories which dominated the district – the nights were never really dark round here, even in the dead of winter. Just as they had been along the Rhine when Edgar and Max were stationed there, where the sky was full of Christmas trees: intense cascades of light pouring down the darkness, green and red flares, incendiary sticks fizzing through the sky and landing on the timbered buildings of Rhenish towns, getting the firestorms going. The air had smelled burnt there just as it did here in Mengede, but back when Edgar and Max were fishing casualties out of the river as the French shot at them from the Maginot Line, the burning smell was the result of spent artillery shells, obliterated bridges and the bubbling flesh of grenade-blasted soldiers.

The wind changed direction at that moment and sent a sharp and rapid clanging from the factories across the rooftops and in through the window, which drilled through Max's reverie like gunfire. He started, the book hit the floor with a deep pop and Max felt himself diving for cover. He landed with his knees on the floor by the bed and his face and arms spread out on the mattress, the softness and washing soda scent of which tenderly punched him back to the present. He slowly rose up on his elbows and cradled his face in his hands. His relief at finding himself hundreds of miles and many years from the active Maginot Line made him rather amused at his landing in this way, knelt by the bedside.

'Well, while I'm here...' He smiled wryly to himself, and began to pray for an end to his mind and body's constant referencing to just a handful of years in his life. He'd had twenty-odd war free years before that on the planet, so why couldn't his soul start harking back to those times again if it needed to look back at all. He had a new baby on the way. Surely this was the time to start looking forward, surely this was the start of a change in his fortunes.

Just then there was a knock on the door and Karl poked his head in the room.

'All right, son?' he said, seeing Max getting up from behind the bed.

'Yes, fine thanks, Papa,' he said, retrieving his book from the floor and waving it at his father, 'just catching up on some of the latest medical practice.'

Karl was not quite sure how exactly Max was studying with the book closed and himself on the floor, but he had more pressing issues to concern him right at that moment. 'There's a woman downstairs. Come about the ad for a housekeeper.'

'A bit late to come calling, isn't it? And how did she know where we lived? Didn't we put a box number on the ad?'

'That's what I said, but your mother and Erika are giving her a good grilling anyway. They reckon all the other applicants have been so awful they'd be mad to send this one packing, just in case she's good, you see. So I thought you might want to come and ask a few questions too.'

'Well, I'm sure the women have got it all under—'

'Yes, but she's... how shall I put it?' Max was curious to see a glint in his father's eye that could almost be described – but surely not in Papa! – as lascivious. 'She's worth a look.'

The men bowled downstairs and crashed into the living room in a manner which would induce a reprimand from Karl should his students behave in a similar way. Martha and Erika looked up at their spouses and supplied the necessary scolding telepathically, then Martha introduced Max to the lady who was sitting in the chair with its back to the door. He came around to join the panel of women as the candidate rose to greet him.

'This is my son, Dr Portner,' Martha said with pride.

'And my husband,' Erika added with quick irritation, knowing Martha was likely to gloss over that essential bit of information.

'Max, this is J—'

'Jenny!' Max gasped.

'Ma—' Jenny was about to reciprocate his enthusiasm, but was seriously savvy when it came to working with women and knew that over familiarity with a male relation at this point could seriously jeopardise her application for the post. In the shocking split-second of surprise reunions, which seemed to punctuate her relationship with Max, she even considered pretending not to know him at all, just in case the wife became instantly jealous and then excluded her from the job on some vague pretext, but since Max had already blown that option by blurting out her name she opted for the next best thing. 'Dr Portner,' she smiled demurely and offered a hand, which Max took with a brief flicker of a sulk, hoping for the kind of hug that marked their last reunion, although even he too realised that that would most probably go down like the Hindenburg in front of his wife and mother, who had already ear-marked this down-to-earth and rather engaging woman as a top candidate for the position of housekeeper.

'You know Jenny already?' Martha asked.

'I do, yes. We met first in Breslau.' Max was finding it hard to contain his excitement.

'Oh, really?' Erika said. 'Were you a nurse?'

'Ye—' Max begun, already realising that Jenny would not have put *prostitute* on her curriculum vitae.

'No.' Jenny intercepted the lie quickly. 'Well,' she and Max exchanged a quick and nervous laugh, 'you become all things to everyone in a situation like that, don't you?'

'Do you?' Erika enquired with a polite smile draped over a twinge of suspicion.

'Yes,' Jenny sucked at her cheeks impishly and announced, 'I did a lot of the German officers—'

'Houses,' Max said, feeling beads of sweat break out instantly on his forehead.

'Yes,' Jenny smirked just as she used to in the convent when she would toy with Max, trying to embarrass him as he tried with all his might to stay professional. 'And then we were all captured and sent all over the place and wouldn't you know it, Max and I ended up in the same God-forsaken corner of Siberia where I was now employed to do the Russian officers'...' He knew her game this time and would not be drawn to finish her sentence. She knew he knew her game. That's what they loved about each other. So after a tantalising pause she added, '...houses.'

'So you were in Gegesha?' Erika, unaware of the great crevasses of history between the words, was genuinely intrigued now. Any hint of envy she'd had about this woman's relationship with Max was for now overruled by the notion that she could have a bona fide inhabitant of Max's lost world living under her roof. What conversations they could have! What stories this housekeeper could reveal to Erika, what gateways she could help her to open up into her husband's barricaded mind!

'Well, not in the camp itself, of course.' Jenny gave Erika a little patronising laugh. 'But in the village down the road where most of the Russian officers lived.'

'Oh, I see.'

Martha invited Jenny to sit down again and beckoned to her son to perch on the edge of the armchair where she sat. 'You seem to have had plenty of experience then in some quite adverse conditions.'

'I'll say!' Jenny looked around at all her interviewers and, far from being intimidated, her bright green eyes alighted on Karl and she winked.

The headmaster nearly fell backwards over the piano stool.

'Well, it has been very good to meet you.' Erika was using the words and the tone which they had all used on the previous candidates; the ones who hobbled in, clearly way over fifty-five and needing someone to look after *them*; the ones who flounced in in pigtails, clearly well below thirty without the slightest idea of what work was, let alone *this* work; the ones who, although they sat neatly within the age limits, said incredible things like, 'I don't mind dusting, but I don't do dishes.' Or, 'I'm a housekeeper of considerable calibre and experience, so I think I am best placed to determine my own hours, thank you very much.' It was as if, despite how excited Erika had been about the prospect of having another link to Max's untold story in the house, something was gnawing at the excitement and threatening to make it topple.

Max saw the sure thing wobble and did not want to lose his old confidante yet again. Karl saw the sure thing wobble and did not want to lose such a pretty addition to the household. Martha saw the sure thing wobble and was sick of doing all the chores around here herself so as Jenny began to rise they all chorused, 'Hang on!'

Jenny sank back into the chair, eyeing Erika and wondering if she would counter the rest of her family.

'Did you give us your references?' Martha said, stalling.

'Well...' Jenny hesitated.

Max, who'd been studying her like a naturalist would a rare bird, saw the uncertainty and wondered: Where the hell is she going to get references from?

'References? Pah! You can put those away.' He gestured towards Jenny as if she was reaching into her purse for them, which she wasn't. 'I can be her referee!' Max laughed a little too loudly. 'I've worked tending to patients in the very houses she's, er, kept, and I can say without a doubt,' he swallowed down images of mildewed walls and gutters filled with human faeces, 'you won't find a better housekeeper this side of the Atlantic.'

Everything was different again. Just as she was getting used to having her father around he had dumped her on the Isle of Sylt. Then just as she was getting used to that, here she was back at home torn away from her best friend Milla. But home had changed too. Now there was a new housekeeper called Jenny and her father seemed to spend even more time chatting and smiling with her than he did with Karin. And her mama told her there was a new baby growing in her tummy. She was going to have a little brother or sister by next spring.

'Isn't that wonderful?' Erika had beamed at her.

'It's rubbish,' Netta huffed to herself and stomped upstairs to go and sulk on her bed for a while.

'Who's there?' Tante Bertel's voice cracking the stale air on the first landing usually sent Netta scurrying onwards, hoping not to get dragged into helping her weird old auntie, but since Bertel seemed to be the only thing that didn't ever change around here, Netta found herself poking her head around the old lady's open door and saying:

'Hello, Tante Bertel. It's only me!'

'And who is *me*?' Bertel said, struggling to see from the bed where she was almost flat on her back.

'It's Netta,' Netta said, coming close to the bed so her great aunty could see.

'Oh,' Bertel said, studying the little girl for what seemed to Netta to be an hour. 'Well, I'm not sure a little thing like you will be much use, but I've slipped down the bed and I really need to sit up.'

'I can help,' said Netta, who hated the suggestion that she wasn't strong enough just because she was a little girl. She might have come back from the children's home as small and as thin as ever (and Milla might have put on a kilogram, mainly through drinking double cream), but she could still beat Josef and Peter at just about anything.

Bertel's sharp eyes sparkled as Netta took up the challenge and began hauling her about. Like the little girl, Bertel did not have a great appetite these days so she was not as difficult to hoist up the bed as Netta had expected her to be. Her flesh hung from her arms and neck in a way which made Netta think of the rooster in the garden. She pretended to reach across to straighten the collar of Bertel's nightdress just so she could brush her hand against that neck to see what the bluish flap of skin there felt like. In no time her great Tante was propped up against a mountain of pillows with Netta tucking the blanket around her as her mama did to her in her little bed directly above.

'That's better,' Bertel smiled. 'Now I can see everything.'

She nodded towards the three tall bay windows and Netta followed her gaze to the street below. But for Netta, hearing what was going on up above was far more interesting. She could clearly hear her papa's voice, but it was as if he was talking to himself:

'Of course I still have it. I would never lose it again, would I?'

Then came a more muffled voice. A woman's, she guessed. The words were not as clear as her father's so she asked Bertel if she was OK now, to which Bertel said, 'Yes I am, thank you, Martha,' and she left the bedroom and crept along the landing to the bottom of the stairs. Peeking through the banister she could see Jenny, arms folded, leaning in the doorway of her room talking across the tiny landing to Papa, who Netta knew must have been standing in the doorway of his room too, but she couldn't quite see him from where she was hiding.

'...look well. Much better than the last time I saw you anyway.' Jenny's smile was huge and she kept rolling her red lips inside her mouth as if she was trying to hide it, but it kept popping back out again.

'Well, that's not difficult is it?' Papa said. And then after a moment where neither of them said anything, 'You look well too.'

'It's this new life as a housekeeper, must be agreeing with me.'

Papa laughed, then said, 'Did you know?'

'Did I know what, Max?'

'Did you know that it was my house that you were coming to for a job?'

'Your father's house to be precise.'

'Well, all right.' Papa sounded a tiny bit annoyed when he said that. 'But did you know I lived here?'

'I asked around. I did some checking. And then I bleeding well hoped it was your house. Well, I wasn't going to be a bloody housekeeper for anyone else, was I?' She slapped at him playfully as she said that and Netta watched her standing there with her arm out for a while. She must be holding on to his arm or something, Netta thought.

Jenny's face looked all serious, then she let her arm flop back onto her thigh with a slap and smiled again. Netta was getting uncomfortable stuck in one position so she shifted her weight and the banister creaked.

Jenny's eyes dropped from Papa's and landed on Netta's. The housekeeper's face turned angry and Netta shrank back from the stairs telling herself that Jenny had not really seen who was there. She took a couple of slow steps on tip-toe.

'Who's there?' It was Tante Bertel again. At least Netta hoped it was and she used the noise of the voice to cover her steps as she fled back downstairs and out into the garden where she hid herself in the cold autumn mist and squelched among the over-ripe pears rotting at the base of the tree.

She managed to get to bed that night with neither her papa nor Jenny mentioning anything about it, but she couldn't get to sleep, her mind was racing with all these changes and she kept seeing Jenny's sharp face glaring at her through the shadows whenever she shut her eyes.

Then she heard the sheets shift in her parents' bed and

she knew one of them was awake. She scrunched up her eyes and kept her face to the wall. Then there was the sound of old adult joints clicking, which told her someone was trying to creep out of the room. That sound always gave them away, she thought, but we kids can slip around like cats! The door was opened and as soon as it creaked, just as Netta knew it would, the creeper froze. Then after a moment, as the silence settled again, the clicking of joints continued. But not for long. The creeper didn't go downstairs, as Netta had assumed. The creeper knocked softly on Jenny's door. And the creeper was let in.

The next morning Netta still expected Jenny or her papa to say something about her eavesdropping by the bannister yesterday, but neither of them did. Jenny just gave her the sandwiches she made for her to take to school and smiled with her red lips saying, 'There you go, my darling, now you have a good day, won't you.' And then she just stayed as she was, bent over, staring at Netta. Smiling with her mouth but not with her eyes, like a doll. And Netta was learning fast that sometimes when adults say nothing it's even worse than when they tell you off.

Netta hurried off to school, dumping the sandwiches behind the woodpile in the garden on her way out. Not because Jenny had made the sandwiches, but because that's what she always did with her sandwiches since the teachers had forbidden her from giving them to any other children at lunchtime. What choice did she have? She just wasn't that hungry and no one would listen when she told them that; they just kept making her food and kept telling her to eat it. Adults were like the British soldiers who still hung around on the streets: they spoke a different language and had no intention of learning hers.

'Whhat are you doing here?' Max smiled, genuinely happy, but knocked off balance somewhat, to see his friend sitting on the doorstep when he returned from his morning house calls.

'Well that's a nice way to greet your best buddy now, isn't it!'

'I'm sorry. I mean, I thought you'd be at work. And—and...what are you doing on the doorstep? It's cold out here, you should be inside.'

'Did you mean: you thought I'd be at work, or I should be inside? Come on, Max, what exactly did you mean by *What are you doing here?* Make up your mind!'

Max begun to stutter, grappling for an answer. Edgar laughed and grabbed his friend by the shoulders warmly, despite the temperature of his long hands, as a demonstration of the greeting he was hoping for. Max returned the half-embrace – the most cordial greeting for two men in the middle of the street without overstepping the lines of propriety – and only then did his brain manage to concoct a worthy response; a little late but he thought it worth saying anyway.

'Can't a man mean two things with one sentence?' he grinned.

Edgar instantly appreciated this and added, 'Absolutely! My entire sex life is built on that premise.'

The two men sniggered and Max ushered his lewd friend away from the house in case Erika still had patients in the surgery who might overhear him. 'Come on, let's go for a little walk along the canal then you must come in for some lunch. I assume you're not working today?'

'Oh, I am, but my shift doesn't start until three.'

'Oh, I see.'

'Well, we can't all live the GP's life of Riley, you know.' Edgar studied Max's silent response to this and knew that that wasn't quite how Max saw his life. But there was certainly a change for the better in the man and Edgar was determined to find out what the remedy was. 'Anyway, since you never come around to my place I thought Mohammed (as I'm known to some of my kinkier boyfriends) should come to the mountain.'

'Oh, I'm sorry, but you know how it is, what with working nine to five and the family.'

'Oh, here we go!' said Edgar, switching to the most irritating whine he could muster and declaring, '*You don't understand, Edgar, how hard it is to have a wife and kid.*'

Max huffed with amusement and took it on the chin, but Edgar hadn't finished and his tone became surprisingly earnest.

'You always say that, you heterosexuals, as if having a wife and kid was a curse that you didn't ask for. I assume it was your choice to marry Erika? Your choice to have Netta?'

'Of course—' Max mumbled his response because he wasn't sure he could say that unequivocally, not in the same way a child would choose lemon sherbets over raspberry drops in the confectioner's on the High Street.

'Do you not think,' Edgar continued, 'that *I* might like to have a… partner and a child one day?'

'And perhaps you will.'

'Not in my lifetime, Max, come on. It's only been a few years since we stopped sending queers to gas chambers, I don't think marriage and kids is on the cards for me any day soon, do you?'

Max put a consoling hand on his friend's back and they walked that way for a few steps until Edgar found his usual public persona again. 'Hey, I didn't come here to talk about me anyway, I came to find out how you are. Did Dr Siskin help you at all?'

'Pah!'

'Oh, that good, was he?'

Max shook his head, smiling at the towpath.

'But something's going right for you. There's a bit of that old spark back behind those little spectacles.'

Max's smiled broadened.

'There is, isn't there? Come on, out with it! Not that I don't know, of course.'

'Well...' Then Max suddenly registered Edgar's last sentence. 'You know? You've heard?'

'Of course! The hospital is a small world, as you well know. I hear everything about who comes and goes.'

'Has she been to the hospital?' Max looked concerned. 'Is there something wrong?'

'Not that I know of. I'm sure it was just routine, you know.' Edgar stopped and examined his friend. 'Who are you talking about?'

'Jenny.'

'Jenny?' Edgar had to think for a moment before the penny dropped, 'Jenny? The girl from Gegesha?'

Max nodded sheepishly.

'What about her?'

'She's living with us.'

If Edgar wore glasses like his friend, he'd be looking over the top of them right now in utter incredulity.

'She's our new housekeeper. She saw the ad in the paper. She'd come to Dortmund to find me.'

Edgar held up a hand to silence Max. 'Hold on! Just hold on there a minute, buddy! Let me get this straight. Your first housekeeper is murdered.' Edgar looked over Max's shoulder at the canal and shuddered. 'The murderer has not been found yet, by the way, so the cops are creeping all over your place, and then you go and employ a *prostitute* as your next housekeeper, but not any old prostitute, which would be bad enough, but a prostitute who has the hots for you. And now you're both living as snug as a bug in the same house as your wife and your parents?'

Max grinned.

'Are you mental?'

'What?' Max whinged disingenuously.

Edgar let out a quiet scream of concern for his friend,

but his eyes were aflame with the entertainment value inherent in the situation. 'Buddy, come on!'

'She doesn't have *the hots* for me,' Max laughed, though somewhere in the dark recesses of his ego he hoped in fact that Edgar would reaffirm the notion that she did. 'We're just friends.'

'I seem to remember her kissing you in rather more than a friendly manner when she came to see you in the hospital.'

'But that was after...' He could barely bring himself to say the name. '...Volkov had beaten me up. I was badly injured at the time, she was just being nice.'

'And she came all the way to Dortmund, hunted you down and is living under your roof, just to be a friend, just to be nice? What does Erika think of this? Don't tell me she doesn't know about you and her?'

'There's nothing to know. She knows we knew each other in Gegesha. But she thinks she was a housekeeper for the Russians there.'

Edgar's guffaw echoed beneath the bridge, despite the bridge being a long way down the towpath from where they stood. The British soldier leaning there, smoking, straightened up and looked curiously down the canal at the two Jerries deep in conversation.

'What can I say, buddy? I'd just play this one very carefully if I were you. My lord, and I thought my love life was complicated!'

They stood there in silence for a moment looking at the mists coming out of their own mouths like two more smokers before Max prompted Edgar to start walking back to the house.

'Here,' Edgar said, handing Max the paper bag he'd been holding.

'What's this?'

'A little gift for Netta. From one of those American stores in the city.'

Max pulled a white tin lunchbox from the bag. It had

cartoon baseball players, marching band musicians and baton twirlers all over it.

'I thought it might encourage her to enjoy eating a bit more, you know.'

Max wasn't sure it would do that, but he was touched by his friend's thoughtfulness and as they walked on he wished the world they lived in was one where Edgar could be a father one day. And after a few more steps of pensive silence from both men, Max looked at Edgar quizzically and said, 'What did you mean when you said you knew? Knew what my good news was, and then said something about the hospital?'

'Oh, I meant I had heard Erika was at the hospital. Seeing Dr Fischer. So naturally I thought your great news was going to be that Erika is pregnant.'

'Oh yes. That too,' Max said.

Everything was supposed to be perfect now. Max and Erika were working together. He would go out on house calls in the morning while she saw patients in the surgery. Then after they both ate lunch in the house, Erika would go out in the community while he saw patients in the surgery. The pregnancy was going smoothly, the housekeeper was competent. Max seemed more content and more talkative, but it irked Erika that most of his talking was done to Jenny or at least when Jenny was around. So Erika found herself inventing all manner of errands for Jenny to keep her out of the house as much as possible when Max was there.

'Would you pop into town and get some Henko, Jenny?' Erika held out the money for the soda to indicate the urgency, but Jenny was up to her elbows in washing up and looked amused at the idea of taking the money with soaking wet hands.

'Just leave it on the table there, Erika, I'll do it later.'

It peeved Erika that Jenny thought she could call everyone by their Christian names. It peeved her that Max didn't do anything to discourage it, but it peeved her more that Jenny always seemed to skew their intercourse so that Erika felt like the one being told what to do.

'Oh, don't worry about the washing up.' She tried to sound carefree. 'I'll finish that.'

'What's the point of having a housekeeper,' Max laughed as he packed his bag on the kitchen table, 'if you're going to do all the housekeeping? Haven't you got a surgery to set up?'

'Yes, but—'

'And I've got house calls to make so I'll see you all later.'

He was on his way out, but was happily stopped in his tracks by Jenny's enquiry, 'Who do you have the pleasure of examining first?'

Erika heard the playful innuendo and watched the way it tickled Max. 'Oh, just an old lady with arthritis, but she makes really good cakes.'

'Oh, so not that old dragon with the leeches then?'

'Max!' Erika said, still standing in the middle of the kitchen with the money in her hand.

'What?'

'You shouldn't be discussing our patients with the housekeeper,' she scolded him carefully, choosing the words *our* and *housekeeper* to demarcate her territory and remind Jenny that hers did not include Max.

Jenny shook her head at the crockery in the sink.

'But it's Jenny. It's not as if it's any old housekeeper, is it?'

'Oh?' She knew he was referring to his friendship with Jenny before her appointment, but nevertheless Erika let the question hang in the air, daring him to elaborate on any other way in which this was not any old housekeeper. 'What about the Hippocratic Oath?'

He looked blankly at her, not because he had no idea what she was talking about, but because he was starting to shut down again, the sediment taste of the alienation of his first few weeks back from Gegesha returning to his mouth.

'Confidentiality?' she bulldozed onwards. 'You do remember and respect that still, if nothing else I hope.' Even she was embarrassed by the excess of barbs on that last phrase so she massaged her pregnant belly in order to excuse her aggression, put it down to hormones, or just change the subject to her condition: perhaps she was in pain. But no sympathy came from her husband or the housekeeper. And after an excruciating crockery-knocked silence she sighed, 'Will you take this money and run along to the shop now, please?'

'I'll go when Netta's gone to school,' came the response and Erika was incredulous at this woman's effrontery.

'Why?' Max asked, more attuned to Jenny's concerns than his wife's right then.

'I have to check something first,' she said over her shoulder and then mumbled to the sink, 'Someone's got to have eyes on that child!'

Just before Erika acted on the urge to tear at the woman's fashionably short blonde hair, the sound of her daughter's little shoes on the tiles slapped her back to civility.

'Ah, and here she is! Are you all ready for school?' Jenny smiled, one wet hand on her hip, the other still in the water.

'I'll give you a lift if you want?' Max said.

Netta considered this for a second, examined her father's amiable expression, and then ran to join him at the door, keen to snap up the chance to have him to herself for a while.

'You're not taking her on the motorbike, are you?' Erika grumbled.

Netta looked up at him hopefully.

'Yes, it's not far, she'll be quite safe.'

'Yes!' Netta hissed triumphantly.

'Don't forget your sandwiches!' Jenny said, pointing to the table and the white tin lunchbox Uncle Edgar had bought her.

The sight of the box – or rather the thought of its contents – took the wind out of Netta's sails, and Erika was aware that Jenny was controlling the scene now like a puppet master. Netta grabbed the box and followed her papa out to the hallway.

'Grab your coat!' he called out. 'And I'll see you at the front.'

Erika was left in the kitchen watching the water dripping like time from the hand on Jenny's hip onto the floor.

'Now come and watch this!' Jenny said suddenly, drying her hands and ushering Erika to the back door where she indicated to her – or ordered her as Erika saw it – to be quiet and to conceal herself out of sight of the woodpile, which leant against the shed.

The two women watched as Max took the motorbike from the shed and wheeled it out to the road. They then saw Netta enter the scene, now wrapped in her blue coat, the white collar buttoned up tight against the cold, white hat like a flying saucer perched on her head. They watched her tiptoe pointlessly across the soft turf to the pear tree, where she hid unsuccessfully and opened the American lunchbox. She then scampered to the woodpile, tipped the sandwiches it contained behind the logs and walked briskly after her father, nose in the air in a terrible imitation of innocence. And that was when Jenny pounced.

'Just a minute, young lady!' she spat and grabbed the startled girl by the arm.

Netta was speechless.

'Come with me!' Jenny dragged the girl whose eyes were already streaming back to the woodpile and, changing her grip now to the back of Netta's neck, shoved her face towards the ground and the moulding pile of sandwiches the girl had been making there. 'Look at that! What a waste! Do you think I spend my time making you sandwiches every morning so you can just toss them over here?'

'Netta, what have you done?' Erika, a little slower than usual due to her ever increasing size, was now inspecting the secret dump too. 'Oh, Netta!'

Netta fought the tears furiously as she hung like a rodent in the talons of the eagle-eyed housekeeper.

'And what a waste of money! Do you think it grows on trees, do you?' Jenny yapped, shaking the girl, and Erika was about to intervene, get this stranger's hands off her daughter, if it wasn't for the next thing Jenny said: 'You think your mother has worked for all these years alone to put food on the table so you can throw it behind the woodpile?' If that tribute to Erika was supposed to ingratiate Jenny to her... it worked. 'And do you think your father now goes out to work every day so you can waste his wages like this?'

'What's going on?' Max had returned to the garden to find out what had happened to his passenger.

'She's been tossing her sandwiches out every day.' Erika flapped a despairing hand at the logs. 'No wonder she's still underweight.'

Max examined the pile of wasted food on the damp ground, but he saw himself running his finger around a wooden bowl emptied of its skilly of potato and animal fat, licking condensation from the window of a Russian truck, scavenging cranberries and pine needles from the forest floor. He grabbed a chopped branch from the woodpile, grabbed his daughter from the clutches of the housekeeper and whacked at her bottom with all the ferocity that Sergeant Volkov had once whacked at his head with a bunch of keys, the keys which kept him locked away from the world for four whole famished years. He heard the squeals of pain and didn't know whether they came from him, the bruised bleeding ball of himself on the floor of the labour camp office, or from his daughter.

'OK enough, Max! That'll do!'

Despite the pain and the uncontrollable sobbing, Netta could just about register surprise and resentment that the voice of reason here, her liberator right then, was not her mother but Jenny. She had pulled him away from the girl, who now fled into the house, and Max would have followed her, had Jenny not stood in his way and shouted:

'Calm down, Max! Leave it now! I think she got the message.'

'Calm down?' Max seethed. 'Calm down? You of all people should know,' he said as if everyone present had been able to see the maelstrom of thoughts and memories which had raged inside him for the last minute or so. 'You were there.' He fought the tears just as his daughter had and with an equal lack of success. 'You know what it was like.'

'Yes I was there,' Jenny yelled, and Erika felt as if she was watching her younger self argue with a younger Max when they were students in Freiburg outside a bar where they'd had a disagreement. She could hardly remember what the argument was about now, and it didn't matter, the point was she wanted it to be *her* arguing with Max now, she wanted it to be him arguing with her, instead of the way it was: her watching from the side-lines like a ghost as someone else did the living with him. 'Yes I was there,' Jenny said, 'but *she* wasn't.'

Erika hoped Jenny was referring to her, trying to bring her into the debate, just as she'd desired. Once again the housekeeper was saying all the right things, Erika thought. Until she enlightened them all.

'*Netta* wasn't in Gegesha, was she, Max? So how the hell is she supposed to know what you went through? How the hell is she supposed to know what changed for you in there?'

Erika was silently screaming now at the glass wall she felt she was stuck behind. Screaming at Max to see the sense in what Jenny was saying. But in a desperate flood of selfishness, she wanted him not to see it for Netta's sake, but to see it and apply it to *her*, to Erika, his wife, the love of his life.

Max hung his head for a moment. Nodded it. Shook it. Wiped at his eyes aggressively. Then hurried from the garden, leaving the ladies to listen to the motorbike roar in a way that Max only dreamed he could.

Martha eased herself into the wing-back chair with a great sigh of weariness. Netta, who was practising the piano, found it overdramatic. All adults did it; even her mother had started doing it recently. But they couldn't all be that tired all the time, could they? After a pause in which Netta thought Martha was waiting for someone to respond to her little show – either her Opa who was engrossed in the newspaper, or her mama who had just returned from a house call and was finishing her notes here in the living room whilst her papa finished up in the surgery – no response came so Martha herself spoke.

'Did you see the article in there about that carpenter?'

'Mmm?' Karl kept his eyes on the piece he was reading about the confiscation of German patents by the Allies, but he found it difficult to take in the words now anticipating a lengthy interruption by his wife.

'It says he's been released.'

Erika stopped writing and looked up, and Martha was content to have at least her attention.

'He has a *watertight alibi*, that's the way they put it. He was with his sister the night of the murder. And the sister's neighbour even saw them that night too. Watertight alibi! Rather a conscienceless sister and a liar for a neighbour.'

Martha was a little defeated that her news had still failed to lift Karl's eyes from the paper, but Erika was certainly affected by the news. Not surprisingly, thought Martha with an icy glance at her unfaithful daughter-in-law. She just hoped that Erika's now heaving chest was the result of fear of this killer being on the loose again and not some amorous anticipation of his return to the community.

Netta listened to her Oma's frightening news as she played. She knew she wasn't supposed to be listening, she knew the adults thought she couldn't hear or understand, especially if she was in another room. But that was just another of those strange adult things – did they think she had anything more exciting to do at home than listen to the sordid secrets of grown-ups?

The sound of the surgery door shutting gave Erika's chest even greater cause to heave. Max was done for the day. He marched through the living room and into the kitchen.

'Well, at last!' Martha said. 'Perhaps we can all have some dinner now.'

The sound of a glass being filled from the tap and Max stomped back through the living room with it, heading upstairs and calling back over his shoulder, 'I'm not hungry, I have some study to do. You go ahead without me.'

'But we waited. My God,' Martha wailed and finally Karl had put the paper down and watched as Erika followed his son up to their room.

'Who's there?' Tante Bertel called out as Erika passed over the first landing, but this was no time to get drawn into Bertel's palaver.

'It's me, Erika,' she called out. 'I'll be right back to help you, Tante, just give me a minute please.'

Erika paused on the tiny landing between her bedroom door and Jenny's. She wondered if the housekeeper was in there and tried desperately to remember where she'd last seen her. Was she in the kitchen? Was she out for the night? She hated the thought that the conversation she was about to attempt would be overheard by anyone, let alone *her*.

She listened for a moment. Satisfied herself Jenny had gone out and went into her own room to find Max sat by the Tiffany window staring out through the translucent glass, no hint of any studying going on. She had an overwhelming urge to find a hammer, nails and wood and board up that blasted window, so he had to look somewhere else for a change. Look into the room. Look at her. He didn't even turn to look when she came in, but she knew damn well he knew she was there and why.

'Max. About this morning. With Netta. And the sandwiches.' She hated his silence and the way it teased

111

each additional phrase from her. Of course she was talking about Netta and the sandwiches! What else happened this morning of greater note? She forged on. She had to talk about things with him now in a way they weren't really used to doing. But she was not going to let the housekeeper have a more articulate and expressive relationship with her husband than she had. 'I know it's been really difficult for you since you got back. I know that you went through some terrible things and that your mind is—'

'Please do not presume to tell me what's going on in my own mind!' he snapped, eyes still on the window. 'You do not know what's going on in my head.'

'So tell me!' she cried. 'Let me in! I'm your wife and I want to know.' She refrained from adding *as Jenny does,* but hurried over to the bed and perched on the nearside, a sea of blankets between her and where he sat. 'I want to help you.'

Those last words seemed to prick him. She saw him flinch and knew she was onto something. She knew he always thought of himself as the helper, the curer, not the victim or the casualty.

'You can't help me. Even the demob officer thinks...' He picked up a medical book.

She hurled herself across the bed to stop him opening it and disappearing into it. 'Even the demob officer thinks what?' she implored him to respond, hand on his book as if it were a Bible.

He knew she wasn't going anywhere till he gave her something, but it couldn't be the answer to that question, so instead he said, 'You do not want to hear about my time in Gegesha. I mean, I do not want to burden you with such horrible stories. There are Allied soldiers crawling all over this country still. If I told you what went on in those camps you'd be afraid to leave the house, and that's no way to live.'

'We live in an occupied state, not a labour camp. I promise it won't upset me to hear—'

'Look, it's bad enough one of us having nightmares. We don't need two of us at it. And besides,' he sat up suddenly, realising he held the trump card, 'you've got the baby to think about now, you can't be getting unnecessarily anxious.'

'But you not talking to me *is* making me unnecessarily anxious, you foolish man!'

He shrivelled again.

'My father is still in one of those labour camps, Max.'

He twitched at the mention of her overbearing father. Or was his reaction something more sympathetic than that? Was it the awful notion of a man still stuck in one of those Siberian hell holes?

'And he has been sentenced to twenty-five years there. Twenty-five years!' She was bawling now. 'My God, you were there for four and this is what you're like. What the hell have I got to look forward to when *he* is finally released? I... I... Anxious? I'm terrified, darling.'

He was about to turn on her, missing her point entirely, focusing on what he saw as her belittling his stretch in the camp. 'My God, you were *only* there for four years.' That's what he heard, but that, of course, was what she was very careful not to have said. But he didn't get a chance because at that moment there was a commotion on the stairs and the door burst open.

Hummel strode across the room pursued by Martha and Karl and, licking his lips where he could already taste the flavour of a celebratory beer, he announced, 'Dr Portner, I am arresting you on suspicion of the murder of Karin Kranz.'

'**P**lease don't take him away. Please don't put those things on him. Can't you just talk to him here? We can straighten all this out in no time.' Erika was distraught. The wall that Max had built between them would only get higher, she was sure, if his liberty was taken from him again. But Hummel was not interested in discussing anything here. He was leading Max to the door slaloming round each of the prisoner's bewildered parents as he went, saying over his shoulder to his young colleague, 'Amsel, I would start your search in this room if I were you.'

'Right you are,' Amsel said and began opening drawers.

'What are you doing?' Erika tried to stop Officer Amsel delving into her underwear as her body strained to follow Hummel and her husband downstairs.

'Stay and watch this fellow!' Karl found his voice and his headmaster's authority at last. 'I'll go down to the station with Max.'

Erika and Martha did what they were told and, as Amsel pulled Max's suitcase from under the bed, Netta ran in and clung to her mother's legs. 'What's happening, Mama? Why is the policeman taking Papa away?'

'Don't worry.' Erika crouched and squeezed Netta so hard it almost hurt the little girl. 'There's just been a big mistake. He'll be home in a little while when it's all been straightened out.'

But Netta had heard that phrase *he'll be home in a little while* many times before, as she had lain in the big bed with her mama looking at photos of the smart, strong, gentle looking man Mama told her was her father, so naturally she thought now that she wouldn't be seeing him again for another four years. And if it wasn't for her mama and Oma, from whom she was taking her lead on crying, she couldn't be sure she would really be that upset about it.

Amsel sat back on his haunches, satisfied with his find. It was a picture, a very faded, curled, stained image of the baby Jesus held by a black Madonna. And on the back just fifteen words, but enough, he congratulated himself, to sentence the suspect to at least as many years behind bars.

My dear brave Max,
May you never lose me again!
With admiration always
from Jenny. X x

There was something bizarrely anaesthetising about being shackled and locked in a cell. It should have filled him with terror. It should have been the greatest trigger yet to those awful flashbacks which had become part of his life as a free man. But being incarcerated in this way was perhaps the most recognisable thing that had happened to Max since his return to suburban life. His existence in this little room was in many ways less terrifying than the world beyond, where there were so many more unknown and ever-changing exterior agents which could intrude on his fragile being.

But Hummel, every time he peeked through the grate and saw the prisoner sitting stoically on the cot, took Max's demeanour as even more evidence of his guilt.

Since time in the cell was not causing the suspect to crack up and start spewing confessions, Hummel had him brought into the interview room, as sparsely furnished as the cell, where they sat opposite each other like chess players – at least that's how Hummel liked to think of it. And since he was, of course, playing white pieces he made the first move.

'So tell me about Karin Kranz, Dr Portner.'

'Officer, I think there has been a terrible—'

'Mistake? Accident?' Hummel couldn't resist making great sweeps across the board with his major pieces already. 'Was it an accident? Perhaps it was and you can let me know that and then perhaps it will make the judge look more favourably on you when it comes to sentencing.'

'Was what an accident?'

'You killing Karin Kranz.'

'Why are you accusing me of her murder?'

'Well, it appears you had a very good reason for wanting to get rid of Karin.'

'Did I?'

'OK, let's talk about your new housekeeper. Jenny Blau.' Hummel noticed the change in Max's colour and rejoiced in what he saw as himself lining up black pieces all over the board to be taken. 'Your advertisement in the *Zeitung* asked for an experienced housekeeper. Is Jenny experienced?'

'I—I—I—'

'Oh she's experienced all right,' Hummel leered, 'but not in the domestic sense, eh, Doctor? You see I had been interviewing some of your patients in relation to my investigation into Karin's murder. After all, patients come and go from your house all the time. One of them could be the murderer, couldn't they?'

Max nodded with genuine interest, as he had never thought of this possibility before.

'And I came across a patient called Frau Beltz. You know her?'

'Of course.'

'Yes, rather unforgettable, isn't she!' Hummel said wryly. 'Hard to stop her talking in fact, which is a gift for an investigating officer. Sometimes.' He blinked the spectre of Frau Beltz from his eyes. 'And she told me she'd taken on a new housekeeper recently, just like you did. And her new housekeeper is called Isabel. Isabel Dreher. Ring a bell, Doctor?'

Isabel Dreher. Dreher, no, thought Max. But Isabel... The hiss of that name did blow the dust from an abandoned memory; a memory of the apartment crowded with girls where Jenny lived in the town near the labour camp; a memory of him going there to check the girls for sexually transmitted diseases; a memory of one of the girls clearly being jealous of the friendship he had with Jenny and trying to make him feel awkward with prying personal questions whenever he visited; a memory of a bitch.

'No, not really,' he answered.

'No, not really.' Hummel chewed on that phrase. Like *to be honest with you*, it was one of those phrases he loved and loathed. He loathed it because it spoke of an imprecision, a wishy-washy nature in the speaker – because surely either something is or it isn't, isn't it. But he loved it because *no, not really* also meant that the speaker, nine times out of ten at least, meant yes. 'Well, let me help you out, Doctor. Isabel, much like her new employer, has a big mouth and she told Frau Beltz that she and Jenny know each other. That they travelled here together, in fact, to Dortmund after all the Russians they worked for dispersed when the labour camp you were a prisoner of war in closed. Jenny was a prostitute, Isabel said, and I daresay Isabel was too, although she claims she only knew Jenny "to speak to", not as a colleague. She claims she was a housekeeper up there in Siberia. Which I imagine Jenny does too. But why come all the way to Dortmund to find work as a housekeeper, I asked dear Frau Beltz? And do you know what she said? She said because Jenny was coming to look for you, Doctor.'

'Yes, it is true I knew Jenny in Siberia. It is true she was a prostitute. She was my patient, actually. They all were. I had to check them over for diseases regularly before the Russians would go near them. We got on well. We became friends. And now she wants to start a new life, a decent life. And she knew I would be happy to help her if I could.'

'Friends, eh?' Hummel said, reaching in his pocket and pulling out the picture of the black Madonna. 'Does this sound like the kind of message a friend writes to another? Because to me it sounds more like the kind of message a lover would write to another. *My dear brave Max. May you never lose me again.*' It was all Hummel could do not to shout out *Check!*

'The reason it says that,' Max said with some irritation, 'is because I lost the picture once and she found it and gave it back to me. You see, it's the picture that is saying don't lose me again, not Jenny.' Although it was the truth, his excuse sounded lame even to Max.

'So your wife knows that Jenny was a prostitute?'

'No, of course not. Jenny is trying to forget her past—'

'Your wife knows about this picture, then?'

'Yes,' Max lied. He wasn't sure why he lied for the first time now, but it was the worst time to do so.

'Well, that's funny because when my colleague pulled it out of your suitcase, your wife took a look at the inscription and went berserk, apparently.'

Max blanched and was speechless.

'You might be better off doing fifteen years than going back to her right now, eh, Doctor.' Hummel laughed and admired the picture for a moment before going on. 'So I put it to you that in order to get your lover under the same roof as yourself, the only way was to concoct this story about her being a housekeeper, but of course you needed to get the other housekeeper out of the way first, didn't you.'

The absurdity of the suggestion caused Max to sit forward and raise his voice for the first time. 'If what you say is the case, then why on earth would I not just sack Karin? It would be very easy for me to do that. A lot easier than murdering her anyway.'

'Perhaps you did try sacking her,' Hummel immediately countered, unfazed. 'Perhaps she didn't just roll over as you expected her to. Perhaps she didn't like it and refused to be sacked for no good reason. And then perhaps you argued about it and the argument, shall we say, got out of control.'

'That's...'

'Yes, Doctor?'

'That's ridiculous.'

'Well how about you tell—'

The door flew open just then and Max got a glimpse of his father waiting anxiously outside before a tiny hurricane blew through the room depositing its briefcase with a slap on the table between Max and Hummel, sending all the policeman's carefully positioned chess pieces scattering across the room.

'Who the hell let you in?' Hummel barked.

'I let me in,' said the little dust devil, 'since you were so rude as not to invite me in the first place.' And then the uninvited one stuck out the hand of a Lilliputian to Max and introduced himself. 'Jansen Jäger at your service, Dr Portner. Your father Karl and I are old friends and when he told me about your plight I came as fast as I could, knowing how Officer Hummel here has a tendency to crash on regardless of the correct and legal procedures, isn't that right, Officer?'

It was Hummel's turn to be speechless whilst Max marvelled at the short, thin lawyer with the high-pitched voice who in every way was diminutive except in his manner: the most welcome of storms, which razed everything built on flimsy foundations to the ground.

'What's your line, Hummel?' Hummel opened his mouth to answer but Jäger immediately turned to Max and asked the same question. 'What's he saying your motive is?'

'Well,' Max began quickly lest he lose the attention of his lawyer as quickly as the policeman did, 'he reckons I killed our previous housekeeper—'

'Karin Kranz, yes.' Jäger nodded and Max was impressed that he already knew her name.

'Yes, and he says I did it so as to make way for Jenny, our new housekeeper, who is a friend of mine from the war.'

'Absurd.' Jäger said the word so quickly it sounded like one syllable.

'That's what I said!' Max said triumphantly.

'Unless there's more to your relationship with this Jenny.'

And suddenly Max deflated again as it felt as if Jäger was switching sides.

'Ah,' Hummel piped up. 'Perhaps it would have been good to have you here earlier after—'

'Shut up, Hummel, before I make you step outside, which of course I am well within my rights to do.'

Now Hummel looked as if he might vomit at any moment.

'Well?' Jäger snapped in Max's face whilst remaining absolutely erect, which was quite a feat since he was still standing up and Max was sitting.

'Well, Jenny and I are nothing more than friends, but she used to be a prostitute and I neglected to tell my family that.'

'For obvious reasons,' Jäger said with just a hint of a reduction in the winds that constituted his aura. 'And where's this evidence you took from my client's belongings?' He clicked his fingers at Hummel.

Hummel produced the picture of the Madonna again from his pocket, carefully pointing out the inscription on the reverse.

Jäger scanned the words in an instant then with the briefest leap of his eyebrows he turned over to view the image. 'God fearing woman is she, this Jenny?'

'I think so,' Max said as Hummel simultaneously huffed with derision.

'Clearly, if she is handing out pictures like this.' He tossed the exhibit back at Hummel as if it were a piece of rubbish. 'So why wouldn't you sack her if you wanted her out of the way?'

'I said that too,' Max said, 'And besides I didn't want her out of the way. I had no idea that I would ever see Jenny again after I left the labour camp. No idea she even knew where I lived. The officer is claiming that I tried to sack her and she wouldn't accept it, that we got into an argument and it got out of control.'

The air pressure in the room changed and Jäger lit up like a miniature summer storm cloud on hearing this. 'Karin Kranz? Karl told me all about Karin Kranz on our way here. Karin Kranz – and I have no doubt we could get numerous testimonies to corroborate this from upstanding members of the local community – would not say boo to a goose. She was just about the most timid thing you could ever come across. She was the kind of girl, was she not, that if you told her she was sacked, would have a good cry and gather her things at once without so much as asking why, let alone arguing the toss with you about it.'

'That's exactly the kind of person she was,' Max said, in awe of the lawyer.

'Her body was found in the canal, was it not?'

'Yes,' Hummel said, 'but she had been hit in the face first.'

'So she was hit in the face. A blow to the face doesn't usually kill someone, even someone as timid as Karin Kranz, does it, Hummel?'

Hummel knew where Jäger was heading.

'So accusing my client of murder when she may well have been alive, albeit with a black eye, before she *fell* into the canal, is rather a rash action, don't you think?'

Hummel was already on his feet. 'Get out. Both of you.'

Jäger ushered a bewildered Max from the room ahead of the policeman, who called after them, 'And you better get me a hundred testimonies to prove Kranz's demeanour, because you can bet I'll have a thousand to prove his.'

'What happened?' Karl said, trying to keep up with the whirlwind and his client.

'The bloke is clutching at straws,' Jäger said from the corner of his mouth as the three men sped along the cold dark street.

'How do you know?' Max asked with giggle of relief.

'Because he let you go. I wouldn't have let you go based on what you just told me.'

They woke to the first truly trenchant frosts of the season. The temperature plummeted and everything looked monochrome. Netta, Peter and Josef, when they looked outside, would be like all the children in Mengede that day: excited. Erika, like all the adults in her household, felt she was looking at her own insides spread out across the country.

She was so glad to have him back that she had let Max off the hook at first and hadn't broached the subject of the Black Madonna, but today, with its biting stinging blankness, seemed the perfect time.

She sat up in bed. She knew he was awake though he was facing the other way. She knew Netta was not, as she was flat on her back, mouth wide open, not unlike a cadaver she'd once had to study, except for the reassuring rise and fall of her little chest.

'She has to go,' she said quietly.

Nothing, but perhaps the tightening of his shoulders.

'Max. She cannot stay here after what's happened.'

'There's nothing going on between us,' he said into his pillow with a bored groan as if they'd had this conversation a thousand times already. And they had. But only in their own cacophonous minds. 'The picture was a good luck gift. I lost it. She found it. Hence the inscription when she gave it back to me in Gegesha.'

'But... the gossip that will go around. The gossip that is already going around.'

'Frau Beltz can sort out her own damn varicose veins from now on.'

'I can't have her here.'

'If we send her away the gossips will love that even more. That will look like an admission of guilt. And we have nothing to be guilty about.'

Erika felt herself shrink a little as her own indiscretion with Rodrick came bubbling up from the depths again. She needed to find something even more morally questionable to counter Max with. And she found it.

'But what about this rumour that she's a...' She glanced over at her daughter again, now rolled onto her side facing the wall.

'A prostitute?' Max rolled onto his back, feeling at last he owed his wife the sight of his remorseful face, on this point at least. 'She was.' Erika twitched and he carried on quickly before he lost her. 'I had to check all the... women's health. It was my job. Jenny was nicer than most of them. You know that. She has a great character.'

Erika couldn't argue with that. She found Jenny beguiling, attractive, and she hated herself for it.

'And now she wants to change her ways, make a fresh start. It wouldn't be Christian of me to turn her away.'

In her student days Erika would have seen this reference to his religion as an excuse, but, since her own conversion and since she knew how passionate and devout a Catholic Max was, this only made his reasoning for keeping Jenny stronger. Irritating, but stronger nonetheless.

'We're the only chance she's got of getting on in life. She couldn't have got into another house without references, without experience. And you can't deny she's great at the job.'

Here Erika saw a chink in the argument and struck. 'But you lied to me about her past. You lied to all of us about her. Surely it would have been the Christian thing to do to tell the truth and ask for us all to support her. You lied, and so why should I believe you when you say nothing happened between you and her?'

He thought for a moment he would tell her about the kiss. The kiss she gave *him* when he was at his lowest ebb, when he had been physically battered by that vicious sergeant and was lying in a bed in his own camp hospital, reeling and hallucinating. He could have told Erika that he wanted to return that kiss, that it stirred something in him, that he thought about a future with Jenny when he wasn't sure there would be a future with Erika. He had no idea he would ever get away from Gegesha and when his best friend, his 'brother' Horst received a letter from his wife Eva telling him she was going to marry another man because she couldn't go on alone, not knowing if he would ever return, was it any wonder Max began to question the future? If he had told her all these things right then, if he had been able to untangle each thought and lay them out on the bed smoothly and cleanly for her to examine, she, with her own misdemeanours in mind, could have done nothing but empathise and embrace him. But his tangle of thoughts clogged the channel between his mind and his mouth and all he could see was Erika translating the kiss into evidence of adultery, and all he could manage was, 'I don't know why you should believe me. Ask Jenny,' he offered.

As if I would lower myself to discuss this with her, Erika sneered internally.

'She has to stay,' he asserted.

Because she's a great housekeeper? Because it is our Christian duty? Erika needed him to just add something like that onto that terrible imperative. Anything to stop the unspoken words *because life is so much easier for me with her here* tapping at the Tiffany window as fingers of freezing yellow fog did then.

But nothing came.

In his effort to spare her feelings again, the unspoken words were deafening and gouged at her chilly ears.

And with her eyes scrunched shut in imitation of sleep, Netta begun to imagine ways of getting rid of this nasty housekeeper that was coming between her mama and papa, just as she had dreamt up fantastical stories about Karin's demise.

It was the weekend and he went for a walk in the bleached polluted countryside to escape the unbreathable air of home. His feet crunched to a halt on the edge of the towpath and he found himself diverting up through the forest and out onto the open fields beyond. The frozen clods of earth were hard to negotiate but he relished the pain they induced in his ankles. Pain which he could tell himself was a kind of self-flagellation for the misery he knew he was causing his wife, when more likely the physical pain was triggering an opiate numbing within to block out the more excruciating mental pain there.

He walked faster to try and generate some heat. This time of year always did and always would remind him of his time in the camp inside the Arctic Circle. His body would never know temperatures as low again, but it shuddered in anticipation of them every winter. The vast expanse of farmland before him here reminded him of the endless Siberian steppes which had lain between him and home. Steppes which Horst had tried to flee across when he'd received that letter from Eva saying she was going to marry another man. If he could only get back to her, he had told Max, everything would be fine. This other man was merely a practical solution to a dire predicament, he'd said. But Max hadn't thought for a minute his brother would actually try and escape the camp and make his own way back to Germany. Horst was a hulk of a man, even after a long time in the labour camp; strong but not fast, so he was hunted down by the guards quickly and shot, so Volkov claims, because he tried to attack the Russian sergeant. Max had never known a grief like it. He had never lost a parent, a spouse, a child even, but he had lost his real brother Sepp when they were both teenagers, and that blow had only been lessened by the presence of Horst in his life and Horst's typically and wonderfully homely and unadorned offer: 'I know it is not the same, but would you be my adopted brother, brother?'

Max blinked rapidly at the dirty white sky, trying to mop the welling tears back inside himself so he didn't have to bring his hands from the warmth of his pockets to wipe at his face. The distant sound of a scream soon had him focusing on the few trees at the bottom of the field he stood in; trees which huddled around the pond, unsuccessfully shielding the goings-on there with their naked winter skeletons. The scream came again and a smudge of dark blue followed by two brown ones passed quickly across the frozen surface of the pond. Three children playing on the ice. And as he got closer he saw the three were Peter, Josef and Netta. Each daring the others to slide further and further out, all of them skating about with a joyful obliviousness to the cold. Max knew it was his duty to go and tell them off for playing in such a dangerous place, but his feet planted themselves in the cracked earth behind the thickest tree and he watched their abandon with an amused envy.

'I bet you can't beat me to the other side,' Netta challenged both the boys and, as they all shot off across the ice, Max found himself admiring her fearlessness and felt he was watching Erika back at University in Freiburg, the only girl in their little circle of friends – Erika, Max, Edgar, Horst and Kurt – and one of only a handful of female medical students in the entire department. She'd always had to be the most determined amongst them, aggressive even, to be heard over the clamour of male mulishness. And now it seemed that characteristic was to be found in her daughter – through genetics, if you listened to Erika, through God's will if you listened to Max, or perhaps through sheer coincidence in a world with so many more billions of ever-changing people than there are behavioural traits.

And then he saw her fall right onto her face. He watched her head rebound from the unforgiving ice as Peter and Josef's eyes were fixed on the winning line. He saw her clutch at her nose and saw how bright the red blood looked against the white solid surface of the pond. And then he was there, scooping her howling body up and carrying her back to the trees as Peter and Josef looked on, petrified of the scolding they expected from the doctor when he was finished with his patient. He pinched her nose and held her head back and before long the wailing and bleeding both subsided.

'I'm sorry, Papa,' she pleaded, as he examined her face, 'I'm sorry.'

He wasn't just examining her nose, but her expression too and the fear he saw there. It saddened him, but didn't surprise him after his behaviour in the garden when he'd discovered her sandwich dump, so a conscious softening of his own stony features and a rub on the arm of her dark blue coat was the best way he could think of right then to tell her not to be frightened of him. And then, when he came back to assessing her physical state, he realised one or two more reassuring rubs of the arm would be necessary, at least, as he delivered the news.

'Netta, it looks like you've broken your nose,' he said with a consoling smile.

'Ow,' was her shivery response.

'So the best thing to do is for me to put it straight before it stays in that crooked shape forever. You don't want it to stay all broken like that forever, do you?'

She shook her head as hard as her pounding face would allow her and tried to feel about her nose for the crookedness her papa had described. Her little gloved fingers were repelled by the alien shape they found there and so she quickly surrendered to her father's grasp as Peter and Josef looked on with morbid fascination. He did it quickly. It felt as if she was being punched in the face by the ice yet again. She screamed, but it was a brief scream, clipped by the easing sensation that everything was back in its proper place.

'Jump on,' he said, offering his daughter his back. 'We need to get home so I can fix you up a little more.'

Netta hesitated – at the idea of such close proximity to her papa or at the idea of more treatment to her bruised face, Max couldn't tell.

'It won't hurt,' he said, hoping the statement would serve to remedy both possibilities.

And after a last glance at her two open-mouthed chums, she climbed gingerly onto her papa's back and he set off across the fields for home.

Martha made a welcome fuss of Netta as Max sat her on the kitchen table.

'What's happened?' Erika came into the room and begun scanning her daughter's broken face with the double intensity of a mother and a doctor.

'I was playing on the frozen pond and I fell on the ice.'

'Oh, how many times have—'

'It was broken. I've reset it.' Netta appreciated her papa interrupting the reprimand, 'Do you have any tampons?'

Erika looked momentarily stunned as her already suspicious mind (when it came to Max and other women's private parts) started making all sorts of bizarre connections. But then the penny dropped and she hurried off to find some.

'What's a tampon, Papa?' Netta asked.

'Well, I—I—I don't think...' Martha began and Max just enjoyed watching his mother squirm until Erika returned and he simply said:

'These are tampons, Netta. And they are really good,' he said, inserting one up each of her nostrils, 'for mending a broken nose.'

'Oh,' said Netta.

'Oh,' Martha blushed.

'Oh,' Erika breathed.

'Have a look!' Max said, picking up his daughter and holding her up to the mirror over the mantelpiece in the living room.

Netta giggled at the sight of her two new tusks and the

smiley man in the mirror, whose strong grip on her waist felt so secure she tried to make it last by pulling faces and encouraging him to do the same.

'Oh,' her mama huffed again, with more intensity this time.

'What is it, Erika?' Netta heard her Oma say.

'It's coming,' Mama groaned. 'The baby's coming!'

And suddenly her papa was letting go of Netta again all too soon, as he lowered her abruptly to the floor and hurried away with Mama in the red car to the hospital to bring his brand new child into the world in a way he had never done with Netta.

There was a sign on the farmer's gate which said *no trespassing*. But Netta and her friends often ignored it. She wondered, if she could put the same sign on her life, whether it would be ignored too. Perhaps, she thought, God was punishing her for ignoring the farmer's sign. Because there seemed to be nothing but trespassers in her home. Trespassing on her life with her parents. If it wasn't Karin, it was Jenny. And now she had Emmy to deal with too.

Emmy had kept Netta's parents away from her in hospital for fourteen whole days. At first they had told her it would be just for a week, but Emmy's lungs were as bad as Netta's and she wasn't strong enough to leave – or so they told her. Her Oma and Opa sometimes went to the hospital too, but since children weren't allowed to visit, Netta was left behind at home with Tante Bertel and Jenny.

'If children aren't allowed,' Netta would pout to herself, 'then how come Emmy gets to stay in hospital all this time? They must be lying,' she'd grizzle, 'just trying to leave me out as always!'

So she'd stomp off to the piano and bang on the low black notes until Jenny, who seemed to be even more impatient with Netta than ever for some reason, would come from the other room hissing:

'Do you think I need to hear that racket while I'm stuck here slaving away on my own?'

'Sorry,' Netta would mutter.

But it was too late. It was always too late. Jenny would grab her by the wrist and yank her along to the cellar where Tante Bertel's chickens lived. Then she would shove her in there, in the stinking dark, and leave her there for hours. Usually until she heard Oma or Opa coming home. Then Jenny would whip Netta out of the cellar and tell her to go upstairs and get herself cleaned up.

'And if I hear you whingeing about this to your grand-parents, I'll put you back in there all night next time, got it?'

Finally her parents came home. But then Netta felt they hardly ever looked at her, unless it was to show off their new daughter. 'What do you think of your new little sister?' they'd say, as if Netta was somehow responsible for this trespasser too. 'Isn't she beautiful?' they'd say, as if a wrinkly pink ball that shits and pukes all the time could be beautiful!

Everyone put on silly high-pitched voices when they talked to Emmy and then switched to their usual tired growls when they spoke to Netta, or each other. Netta thought there was a time, long ago, when the adults had used squeaky voices to talk to her too, but those days had obviously gone. Perhaps that was because she was an adult too now. But that couldn't be possible at the age of seven and three quarters, could it? She didn't want it to be true. She still wanted to play and have fun. But most of the things that were said to her now were things like: 'Look after Emmy while I sort out the nappies, Netta!' Or, 'Hold your sister while I get the milk, Netta!' She even had to take Emmy out for a walk in the pram after a hard day at school because her parents were busy in the surgery and Jenny was busy with the house and Oma was busy with Tante Bertel and Opa was still at the school. Peter and Josef would come running by asking her to play with them, but she'd just shrug at them and point out the great big stupid pram, which was no good for running through the woods with.

'Pay attention, Netta!' her teacher would say across the classroom as she saw Netta drifting off, her head propped up on one weak and tired forearm.

She wanted to tell the teachers that she had been kept up all night by the crying of the baby, and that she wouldn't even be able to sneak in a nap when she got home from school because she'd have to look after Emmy then until her parents were finished with their work. But she didn't. She didn't think they'd believe her. No one ever believed her when she had a story to tell.

When her mama told her they were sending Netta back

to the children's home on Sylt next summer, it was the last straw. She cried and cried and couldn't hold in her thoughts any longer.

'I can't go back there! It's so horrible there!'

'But it's only for a few weeks again.'

'A few weeks *again*! That's forever!'

'You're still having trouble with your chest and you're still terribly thin for your age, darling. The sea air will do you good.'

'You don't want me anymore, do you? You only want Emmy! You're trying to get rid of me. You're going to leave me there forever this time, I know it.'

Through her tears she saw her mama look despairingly at her papa, saw her hand Emmy to him and come hurrying across the room to wrap her in her bosom.

'Of course we still want you, silly. Whatever gave you that idea?'

But Netta could not be consoled, until she heard her papa say in one of those adult mumbles that kids are not supposed to hear even though they are sitting right under the nose of the adult who's mumbling it, 'Well, what if we all go up to Sylt for a few weeks? We could all do with the break. And I think Emmy's lungs would benefit from getting away from this place too.'

'Really?' Netta felt the surprise in her mama's voice, which vibrated against her little head still nestled between her swollen boobs.

'Yes. Look how often we've been up and down to the hospital with her already,' Papa said, but even Netta had a feeling that wasn't the part Mama was so happy about.

And Netta was even more sure about that feeling when she saw Jenny standing in the kitchen doorway, rubbing at a plate with a tea towel, her face twisted in just the same way Netta's had been when she had watched Peter and Josef running off into the woods as she was left pushing that stupid pram.

Erika sat next to Max in the front of the DKW with all the excitement Netta had done the day the little girl had gone unwittingly to the children's home for the first time. She was going away with her family. *Her* family. Her husband and two children. Not with her in-laws as well, or the housekeeper, but just the family that she had always wanted before the war came and ransacked her life.

As the car drove out of the village she thought she saw Rodrick's brawny back disappear into the pharmacy. She blinked away the tiny urge to look further, to see if it really was him. She tried to clear her throat of the sediment of desire that would inevitably be there forever and turned to look at her baby instead, sitting doll-like on the back seat next to her big sister.

'How's it going back there?' she beamed.

'Fine, Mama.' Netta spoke for both of them, since Emmy was still a few months from her first words.

Erika was happy to see her own excitement reflected in Netta's, reined in though it was by the little girl's irritation at having to look after her sister in the back when she should be riding up front with Papa as before and by the dormant bug of doubt curled up in her gut that this was all a scheme to abandon her to the merciless clutches of Frau Auttenberg and Herr Kahler again.

As Erika cooed at her, Emmy's face contorted and she coughed up some phlegm. Erika's face dropped as she reached over to mop at her baby's mouth with a hand-kerchief and glare out of the back window at Mengede receding into the distance with its eternal clouds of sulphur and its eternal phantoms of the past.

As they drove out of the relatively cocooned little suburb and up through the country, Erika was shocked and a little shaken to see so many British and American soldiers still hanging around on the streets and rumbling by in great loutish lorries. It made her nervous. God knows, she thought, what it does to Max.

She put a hand lightly on his right arm and felt it stiffen – just a little startled because he was so focused on the road, she told herself, and he corroborated this by smiling at her and adjusting his glasses with his left hand, allowing her hand to remain as long as she liked.

'I'll go and get the tickets for the ferry,' he said as they parked near the checkpoint. 'Why don't you stretch your legs for a bit?'

So she scooped up Emmy and did just that.

'Netta, don't go far!' she called to her inquisitive daughter, who was already darting up the quayside, but quickly Erika turned her face away from Netta and into the warm breeze allowing herself to feel cleansed by it, rejuvenated by it.

Erika did not know much English so the words of the British soldier who came to stand by her side at the railings meant little, but she had a good idea what his intentions were. He smiled at Emmy, complimented her, she guessed, then he offered Erika a cigarette. She shook her head politely.

'Nein?' he said at the limit of his German. 'Nein?' he repeated, leaning on the railings now and looking her up and down through the smoke curling up from the tip of his own cigarette.

She used to consider herself reasonably attractive. The long dark hair, the high cheekbones, they hadn't gone away, but her confidence in her body had waned somewhat after the birth of each child, so it did her self-esteem no end of good to be getting this attention from a foreign soldier. And it did it even greater good when she felt the unusually possessive hand of her husband clamp itself around her waist and saw him throw an intrepid scowl at the soldier as he guided her back to the car.

*

135

Netta played on the beach every day. She was in heaven. Which was funny because hell was only next door. Their bed and breakfast was right next to the children's home and after a few days of playing on the beach in uninterrupted sunshine, Netta felt the skies cloud over and she looked up from her sandcastle to see there were in fact no clouds, but an eclipse of Biblical proportions. It was Frau Auttenberg standing over her.

'Well, well, fancy seeing you here, Netta.'

Netta searched around desperately for her parents who were flopped nearby on a picnic blanket and replied, 'I'm with my parents. We're staying over there.' She pointed at the B&B so there was no chance the matron might consider her a waif that needed taking in, strapping up and correcting this time.

'And who is this?' Auttenberg bared her yellowing teeth at Emmy who was planted nearby, her doughy legs completely covered by the unwanted sand from the moat around Netta's castle.

'Emmy,' Netta said.

'A new little sister?' Auttenberg said, licking her lips.

Netta nodded but Auttenberg was smiling now at her papa who was squinting across the bright sand at whoever it was talking to his daughters.

'Nice to see you again, doctor,' she called out, 'I was just saying how well Netta is looking.'

No she wasn't, thought Netta, examining the woman's clothes. She was all in black. She had never worn black before. She still looked like an enormous sack of globes, but now she looked like a solar system where the fiery centre had finally exhausted itself and gone out.

'The sea air really does her good, doesn't it?' she was saying to Papa.

'I hope so,' he answered.

'Well, if you ever need our services again, we'd be more than happy to have her back.'

'Lovely,' Papa said.

And after an awkward silence which the waves filled in, she said, 'Well, come on children, on with our walk.'

That was when she rolled on and Netta finally noticed the line of kids trailing behind her. She looked up at it as it passed, a little proud of not being stuck in it, a little embarrassed at not being part of it. And then she saw Milla and she jumped up and quietly hugged her friend so that Auttenberg up ahead would not hear.

'You're here!' Milla whispered.

'You too!'

'Where are you staying?'

'Over there.' She pointed with great excitement until she saw Milla's shoulders droop.

'Not with us?' Milla moaned.

Netta shook her head and sucked on her lips.

The waves filled the silence again.

'But I'll be here every day, so when they do let you out—'

'They never let us out. It's worse than last time. She says she doesn't have enough adults to look after us outside.' Milla thought this next bit of news was best breathed between cupped hands straight into Netta's ear. 'Because Herr Kahler died.'

Netta's eyes grew wide at the news and she looked over her shoulder at the black clothes of Auttenberg. She looked back at her incarcerated friend. She thought for a second that if Herr Kahler was gone, it might not be so bad staying there for a while. For Milla. With Milla. She could ask her parents. She looked at them, her papa snoozing with his head in her mama's lap. She looked at the bright sand, blue sky, the unchained space.

'Camilla!' Auttenberg's familiar foghorn.

'I'll be here every day. I'll see you whenever you come out.'

Milla smiled weakly and scampered off.

Netta waved limply and went half-heartedly back to her

sandcastle, oblivious of her papa who had watched the two little girls' interaction through one secret eye with anxious fascination and an aching in his heart.

Max felt a happiness on the island which surprised him and scared him. The only time he thought about Jenny was as he watched Milla and Netta part and then it was just to think how little he had thought about her in the last few days. He looked out across the wide beach between the holiday makers and the sea; a rich blue and very still. Nothing like the sea on which his hospital stood in Gegesha; a charcoal, choppy wilderness that slapped at the stilts underneath the hospital. His body shivered, as if trying to expel the image and remind him that it was tourists' legs he was seeing in the water now, not wooden stilts; and it was the jetty where the pedal boat rides started over there and not the wooden bridge which led to the slippery floor of his building where maggots abandoned the corpses and black fingers were chopped off with pliers. Where after years of trying to work by the light of makeshift candles constructed from spent rifle cartridges with a piece of cotton for a wick, they finally got electricity. Where, by the ever fluctuating intensity of light that electricity brought, he once turned from staring out over the grey sea to see Bubi, his young Polish helper, dash across the bridge and into the hospital, his voice cracked with grief, one of their wonderful new light bulbs dangling like a noose above his head, as he uttered one word: 'Horst.'

Erika felt tears bubble up inside her as she watched her sleeping husband twitching and weeping in her lap.

'No, no, no,' she whispered to herself and to him.

She had thought this was all behind them. She was sure it couldn't happen here anyway, on this idyllic family holiday. Her face burned as if she had had too much sun already, but it was in fact with sadness for him, pity for herself, embarrassment should anyone notice her whimpering man, and irritation that a perfect picture was being torn to shreds again.

'Shh, shh,' she said, stroking his hair with trembling fingers and all the tenderness she could muster. 'You're safe. You're safe here. You're safe with me. There's no war here. It's over. Shh, shh.' She imitated the sea. 'There's no more war. Shh, shh.'

She repeated it over and over, but with images of Rodrick clamouring for access to her brain, images of Jenny reclining in the back of her mind, images of Karin's body floating behind her eyes and images of Allied soldiers crawling all over her country, she knew she would have to chant this mantra innumerable times before even she believed it, let alone convinced her fractured husband that it was true. And just then, as if the universe decided to throw her another obstacle, she became aware of the sound of a seal. She turned to look for the animal and for her daughters so she could show them this entertaining creature, but there was no seal. Incredibly the sound was coming from the little body of Emmy, who was coughing so hard she was retching, blue features now drawn on her red face, watery eyes bulging as she looked helplessly across the beach for help from where she was buried up to her waist in sand, Netta nowhere to be seen.

'Emmy!' Erika screamed as Max and she hurtled across the beach. Then, both on their knees, he clawed away the sand from her legs before Erika scooped her up, cradling her and forgetting every bit of medical training she had ever had.

'What's happening to her? What's going on?' she pleaded to Max who was trying to listen to her chest and see into her mouth.

Emmy was fighting for every snatch of that healthy sea air she could get and still making the terrible honk of a seal.

'Hear that sound?' he said to Erika as curious holiday makers began to crowd round.

'Croup?' she offered.

He nodded. 'Run ahead,' he said, grabbing his daughter. 'Turn on the hot water in the bathroom, full on and let it run.'

She did as she was told and glanced back to see Max hot on her heels with an exhausted Emmy flopping about in his arms.

'And see if they have a kettle in reception. Put that on in the bathroom too,' he called out.

She nodded furiously, crashed into the B&B, shrieked at a startled bell boy until he went to find a kettle then rushed upstairs and turned on the tap. Max, despite his little load, was there in no time.

'Sit there!' he said, indicating the toilet lid and passing Emmy to her.

'She's cyanotic, Max,' she called out as he disappeared into the bedroom and began tearing the white sheets from the bed.

'But she's still coughing, isn't she?' he shouted as the bell boy arrived with the kettle.

'Yes,' Erika said, knowing that it was when she stopped coughing, stopped fighting for her breath, that it was really time to worry.

Max came back into the room and arranged one of the

sheets like a tent over Emmy with Erika's head as the tent pole. He snatched the kettle from the boy and plugged it in, aiming its spout into the tent, which quickly added to the steam filling the room from the hot tap.

This sauna tent was oppressive and yet strangely calming to Erika, who responded like a bird in a covered cage. On the outside, Max paced back and forth looking at the bizarre sight of his wife and daughter shrouded in the white sheet like ghosts and he prayed it was no premonition.

Five minutes elapsed and the hot water from the tap ran cold. But Max refilled the kettle and switched it on again.

'We should take her to the hospital,' Erika's disembodied voice said.

'Just a few more minutes,' Max said, chewing on his thumbnail.

'It could be too late then.'

'What do the hospitals do? What have they ever done every time we've been back and forth with her, eh? They terrify her and have no answers. No, just give it time,' he said, listening through the sheet at Emmy's breathing, which had now lost its raucous sound. 'How does she look?'

There was a long pause, then, 'Better.'

A little bolt of triumph rushed through Max and sent him springing upright. He nodded at the boy, who had been standing petrified with his mouth wide open all this time, his signal to scurry back downstairs and tell the proprietor the incredible events he'd just been a pivotal part of.

'Let's take her to the hospital anyway,' Erika said.

'OK, but we should stay in the bathroom with the steam for a lot longer first, just to make sure her lungs are really clear.'

He heard Erika sigh and knew she was itching to find the hospital now, but he was galvanised by his little victory and stood firm.

'Mama, mama!' Netta's anxious voice pierced his musings from the other side of the bathroom door and he went through to the bedroom to find her, a little reluctant moon of distress in the system of Auttenberg which engulfed her.

'She was playing with my group when you disappeared and some of the tourists on the beach told us you had rushed back here and that your baby had been taken ill. Is everything all right now?'

'I think so, yes,' Max sighed. 'Thanks for looking after her.'

'Always a pleasure,' Auttenberg said, finally relinquishing her grip on the child's shoulders.

'What's wrong with Emmy?' Netta approached her papa, who sat on the bed wearily.

'Her cough got very bad. We're not sure why, but she seems to be—'

'Max!' Erika's cry was like a huge dose of Benzedrine to him and he was on his feet again and full of energy. He burst back into the bathroom to see the sheet on the floor and Erika offering up Emmy for his inspection.

'She's all stiff. I think she's got a raging fever too.'

'It's probably just the heat from the steam,' he said with a hint of irritation as Erika barged past him into the cooler bedroom, moping at her daughter's brow with her sleeve.

'No, I think she's burning up, Max, and look at her!'

Max tried to manipulate her neck. It was rigid.

'I told you we should have gone to the hospital,' she shouted.

He wanted to shout at her back and perhaps he would have if Frau Auttenberg had not been loitering still. Instead he scooped up Emmy and ran down to the car calling out over his shoulder, 'Fraulein, would you mind awfully looking after Netta for a little longer? We'll be back as soon as we can.'

'Of course not,' Auttenberg called back.

'No!' Netta wailed, convinced this was the start of another four week abandonment. She tried to follow her parents, but the matron, with all the authority now invested in her by the doctor, clamped the little girl between some of her orbs and they watched the red car speed away from them again, just as it had done last summer.

'The drip is in, doctor.'

'Thank you, nurse,' Doctor Bähr said, keeping his gaze fixed on the infant's face through his half-moon spectacles.

'Meningitis,' Max said over Bähr's shoulder into the doctor's ear, which was fringed with the only hair he had left on his head.

'I thought you said it was croup?' Erika said from the other side of the bed.

'If it's tubercular meningitis you could test for it with PPD, can't you? I've read about great results in America and Canada,' Max said to the old man's pate which shone in the glare of the examination lamp.

'Are you in the medical field, sir?' Bähr said without looking up.

'We're both general practitioners.'

'Oh.' Bähr grimaced. 'Nevertheless, you must both know it could just as likely be a bad case of the 'flu. The symptoms are very similar to meningitis.'

'Blood pressure is dropping, doctor.'

'Emmy, Emmy,' Bähr said loudly, rubbing at the girl's sternum with his knuckles. 'Wake up! Wake up now.'

'What about a spinal tap then?' Erika asked.

'Well, let's just see how she responds to these antibiotics first. Then we may need to consider that, yes.'

'Consider it now!' Max barked.

With slow and condescending eyelids Bähr looked up at Max for the first time over the top of his spectacles, paused, and then turned his attention back to the patient.

'Darling, Emmy,' Erika moaned, 'come on, wake up and breathe for Mama now.'

'Oh this is ridiculous!' Max said to the air. 'What if they're not the right antibiotics and we're just standing here like loons waiting for her to respond to them?'

'We can do the tap,' Bähr said, straightening up and folding his arms, 'but we won't get the results for a couple of days anyway.'

'A couple of days!' Erika gasped.

'Young lady,' Bähr said, 'you clearly do not have a lot of experience, but even you should know that that is usual practice. Besides, this is a small hospital with limited resources.' He mumbled his next words as if they were meant for his ears only, but clearly they were not, 'And, here as anywhere else, there is still a shortage of good doctors and laboratory technicians since the Nazis got rid of all the Jewish ones.'

His words pricked Erika and she resented the sense of guilt they injected into her.

'How about,' he continued, 'you just concentrate on being mother right now and leave the medical decisions to me?'

'Doctor,' the nurse said and all three doctors turned to see her knitted brow as she read the thermometer she had just pulled from Emmy's mouth.

'Forget your resources and your "usual practice" and your experience,' Max seethed, slapping at his trousers and pacing about the room, 'Just look at what's here in front of you and make a decision for God's sake! There's no time to wait for evidence and responses. She's getting worse, what more do you need to know?'

'I can't find a pulse now, doctor.'

Erika smothered a shriek with both of her hands as Bähr grabbed Emmy's wrist, fingered her neck, listened to her chest, then began compressions. Erika watched through bulging eyes as her baby's fragile rib cage was pounded again and again by Bähr's blunt fingers.

'Oh, God!' cried Max. If only I had brought her in sooner, he thought, beating himself internally with every passive pump of his daughter's chest.

'Oh, God!' Erika sobbed. I believe, I believe, she cried to herself, I have faith in you, she said to the heavens as

Max's rant to the doctor took on a whole new meaning for her. I'm sorry I didn't always believe, but I got there in the end, didn't I? Max showed me and now I have faith. Don't punish Emmy for my own sins! Please, don't punish her because of me!

She rushed over to Max and gripped his hand as she'd once done under a blanket when they were wedged into the old armchair in her student digs together. Then, as now, she had taken a deep breath, as deep a breath as her rib cage would allow her to, squeezed there between him and the fraying upholstery, and had said, 'Your faith is so important to you, Max, I know that. But so is my belief that there is no need for religion in the new Germany.'

Then, as now, they had both stared in silence for a moment across the room to the gap under the door.

'We are students of medicine,' she'd continued, 'students of science. We already know that physics and chemistry is what makes the world go round, not superstition.'

She felt him twitch then beneath the blanket and wished she had used a slightly less abrasive word, yet in that same moment she'd wanted to slap him for putting his life in the hands of those who believed a work of fiction, which described simply impossible events, to be true. That was simply stupid!

But here she was now faced with the loss of her baby, with physics and chemistry stretched to their limits, and she could tell herself she was just regurgitating the code of her religious parents instilled in her along with table manners and good grammar, but her compulsion to pray for some supernatural being's help now seemed to come from her very viscera, as if it had been planted there when that same being shaped it from a mystical clay many years before.

'I think you both know how this works, at least,' Dr Bäher said many minutes later with a stunning coldness, the immense cruelty of which only dawned on the parents when they relived this moment a thousand times over the next few months. 'I've been working on the child for long enough now. Her heart refuses to beat again. So I'm going to stop. Time of death... Oh,' he exclaimed quietly, as if the roundness of the time gave him some kind of satisfaction, '1800 hours precisely.'

Netta's dream world turned to bubbles which roared in her ears as she broke the surface of sleep, then in the long slow heart beat between dreaming and waking she felt the sheets around her fingers and realised they were not the bobbly flannel sheets of her little bed at home, which were as nice to stroke as a cat – but that was OK because she was on holiday, wasn't she? However, before the heart beat was up, she realised what she felt was not the starched white sheets of the B&B either, but the limp grey ones of the bunks in the children's home, boiled to death in that big copper tub and stirred resentfully by the taloned hands of the crow lady gripping that worn out paddle once broken across Paul's backside. Netta blinked at the darkness above her and the mattress which hung there like a coffin lid gave her more clues. She was on the bottom bunk again, but did that mean..? She scrambled out of bed and stood on tip toe to try and see the face of the child in the bunk above. No Milla. Of course! Netta had only arrived after dinner yesterday and was given the first empty bunk on the end of a row of full ones. Milla had been here for weeks before and was somewhere in the middle of that row with a new bunk mate, and even a new best friend for all Netta knew. She felt sick. She knew Mama and Papa were going to do this to her again. She knew this family holiday to the beach was just their horrible plan to trick her into coming to this place again. She looked out of the window. The sky was a perfect blue, the waves twinkled as if it was raining sunshine and the driveway was covered in a thin layer of sand.

Unlike the B&B, this place never had hot water in the showers, so after what felt like a breath-taking pelting with lumps of ice, during which Frau Auttenberg stood in the doorway, reminding Netta of the stone that was rolled in front of the tomb where Jesus was buried, the children dressed hurriedly and scampered downstairs for breakfast. Finally, on the stairs Netta caught up with Milla.

'Milla,' she hissed remembering Frau Auttenberg's preference for quiet inside the house.

'Netta! You're back!' Milla squealed, her hand over her mouth to muffle the noise.

At the round table Milla sat down next to another girl, a big girl with one very thick eyebrow which stretched across both eyes. She was sitting on Milla's right, which is where Netta always used to sit. But there was still a place on her left, which a little boy was heading for, so Netta ran with the kind of speed she usually saved for races against Peter and Josef and slipped into the chair first, much to the boy's embarrassment, who now had to float around the table with all the places being rapidly filled, until he came to the two places no one wanted – either side of Flea-bag Fleur. He and an unlucky little girl took those places, sitting on the edge of their seats and turning their noses up at the smell of Fleur to show the rest of the table that they were not sitting there because they wanted to, but because they had no choice.

'How long are you staying?' Milla whispered as they tongued their salty porridge.

'I don't know,' Netta said. 'Forever I suppose, for all my parents care.'

'Who are you?' the girl with one eyebrow said stroppily.

'Oh, Trudi, this is Netta. She stayed here last summer. Netta, this is Trudi.'

'Hi,' Netta squeaked, fascinated and a little scared of this enormous girl and her enormous black eyebrow. She wondered, a little jealously, just how friendly Milla could be with someone like this, but felt better at the thought that there was no way Trudi needed a pint of double cream every morning, so she would have nothing to give to Milla, nothing to make Milla's eyes light up, unlike Netta would.

And yet after the porridge the glass of cream didn't come. But her papa did.

As he walked into the dining room Netta's instinct was

to jump up and hug him, but she made herself stay in her seat and scowled at him instead to punish him for leaving her here. Besides, she had no idea what he was here for now. Just to drop off more of her things, probably, and tell her he'd be back in four weeks. She scowled even harder and crossed her arms tightly punching the air out of her little lungs as she did so.

'Come on, darling,' her papa said quietly, crouching down by her chair, 'We're going home. You're coming with me and Mama now.'

'I'm not staying here anymore?' she said, her scowl melting.

She turned to look at him and noticed his eyes were bloodshot. He tried to smile and stood up.

'Come on, go and grab your things. Don't leave anything behind now.'

Don't leave anything behind! She liked the sound of that. If they were going to leave her here again soon it wouldn't matter if she forgot something, would it? So she was definitely not coming back if he wanted her to make sure she brought everything with her this time.

She looked at Milla's disappointed face and told herself it was OK, because Milla had Trudi now, so she didn't have to feel bad about running upstairs, stuffing her things back into her valise and hurtling back down again lest her papa was gone again by the time she did.

'I'll see you on the beach perhaps,' she smiled at Milla.

Milla nodded. And her papa ushered her out into the light, leaving the black-clothed Auttenberg on the doorstep looking even more snuffed out than ever.

'Take care now, Dr Portner,' she honked, 'and you, Netta.'

Netta looked over her shoulder at the matron and was surprised to see her face looking soft, sad even. But her attention was soon diverted by the sand on the driveway which she joyfully shuffled her shoes through, just like she would leaves in the wood in a month or two.

Then her papa's words came blowing back through her head: 'Come on, darling. We're going *home*,' he had said. Not, 'We're going back to the B&B.'

'Are we going home?' she asked.

'Yes.'

But that meant no more holiday, no more playing on the beach. Why was it over so soon? She began to whine, but immediately her papa stopped her by saying, 'But we're going to go to the beach one more time. Right now!'

'Yay!' she shouted and ran off ahead of him across the promenade and down onto the sand.

'Netta,' he called out and she turned to see what he wanted. Be careful, don't do this, don't go there, don't do that!

He hesitated. Then, 'It's OK,' he shouted and sat down on a bench waving her off to play.

She was so happy to be free again she didn't stop to think where Emmy or her mama were, she just knew everything must be fine again otherwise she'd still be stuck in that horrible home. Occasionally she'd look up the beach to make sure papa was still there and there he would be, still sat on the bench, but sitting a little bit like a doll, a bit floppy and looking out to sea. One of these times, he caught her staring at him and waved her over.

'Yes, papa?' she said, out of breath from racing to him right from the water where she'd been paddling.

'Come and sit down for a minute,' he said patting the bench, 'I have something to tell you.'

She did as she was told, a little reluctantly because she'd rather be paddling some more and because it felt weird being asked to sit down with her papa like this. *I have something to tell you.* The words could mean a nice surprise, but the way he said them and the look on his face told her it wasn't that.

Their eyes met and he snatched his gaze away back to the ocean again. He took a deep breath of that healthy sea air and let it out in a long and massive sigh. 'Netta,' he said, his voice quivering, 'Emmy wasn't well yesterday, was she?'

'No,' Netta said, following his gaze out to sea. 'Is she all right now?'

'Oh.' He sang the word in a shiver. Netta hadn't heard him use such a high pitch since she last heard him cooing over her little sister and that might have been yesterday, but it seemed an awfully long time ago now. 'Well, you see, no... she isn't... I mean, she was very sick. And she got sicker and sicker and we tried to help her, but Mama and Papa couldn't so we took her to the hospital and the doctors and nurses there, well...' She looked out of the corner of her eye at him and saw his eyes were full of tears and he was biting his lip with a trembling jaw.

She rolled her eyes back out to sea and pushed her hands under her thighs. She knew something bad was coming. She knew her papa was sad, but she had no idea how to help him. It was usually she who was crying and he who did the comforting, just like when she had broken her nose on the ice last winter.

'They did everything they could to help her too, but then Emmy's heart stopped beating. And they couldn't get it started again. And they did everything they could to get it started again, but,' he spat out that last word as he tried to hold a great sob back. Then he took in a huge breath again and let the words tumble out in the air as he breathed it all out, as if they might be disguised in the whoosh, as if it was the only way he could get them out. 'But she died, Netta. Your little sister Emmy has died.'

Everything went quiet then. Even the gentle roar of the waves seemed to stop as Netta took in the facts. And just as when her parents told her anything she didn't quite understand, she had questions. And asking questions now seemed like a better idea than ever because it also meant she didn't have to think of what to say to a grown man who was crying like a child.

'But you and Mama are doctors too. Why couldn't you help Emmy? Why couldn't you get her heart beating again?'

'We... oh, Netta, we are doctors and we should have been able to help her, you're right,' he said, his voice cracking and swooping from high to low, 'but we couldn't. No one could.'

Netta looked down at her toes which were still dripping with water, and with every drop that fell to the ground and soaked in leaving a dark stain on the concrete, the meaning of what her papa was saying did the same to her. He was sobbing uncontrollably now and, just as she would cry when she was younger not because her knee hurt when she fell, but because she saw her mother's face warped in horror and heard her gasp as she hit the ground, she knew it was time to cry herself now. She knew Emmy was dead. And that meant she would never ever see her little sister again, just when she was getting used to having her around. And she knew that if Emmy could die, then Netta could die just as easily. And that everyone would die sooner or later, including her papa and her mama, her Opa and Oma and what would she do then?

She felt her papa's hand rubbing her back. 'It's OK, it's OK.'

'No it's not because...' She could barely speak, her body was convulsing now with the thought of losing everyone.

'Sometimes it is God's will. And although it seems unfair, God has decided that Emmy must go and be with Him now.'

'But I thought God was good. Why would he do a thing like that to us if he is good? He might take Oma and Opa and Mama and you too and then I'll be—'

'Well, Emmy's in heaven now and yes we will all die one day, but you know the great thing is we will all see each other again in heaven then. And heaven is such a wonderful place and we can stay there forever and ever, darling.'

Netta thought about this for a moment. She wondered if there would be a beach and sea in heaven. She hoped so.

And then the thought of Emmy being all alone on a beach like this for years and years until Oma or Opa or Papa or Mama got there sent her into fits of grief again and she knew that what her papa was saying could not be true. It wasn't OK and her papa was actually very angry at her for making them all come here to the island.

'It's my fault!' she cried.

'Of course it's not your fault,' he said, taking his hand from her back and leaning on his knees so he could look straight into her face. 'How is it your fault?'

'Because,' she whined, looking into his eyes which were more bloodshot than ever now, 'if I hadn't complained so much about coming back to Sylt then you would never have decided to bring everyone along. And if the whole family hadn't come, then Emmy would still be safely at home right now instead of getting sick by whatever it was that made her sick here, wouldn't she?'

She looked at her feet again. There was no sea water left to drip onto the concrete. The drips now came from the end of her nose.

Her papa studied her and what she had just said for a moment, then he straightened up slowly and put a trembling hand out to rub her back again. But the hand lingered there in the space between them for a while before returning to his lap to wring the other as he silently wept and chewed on his lip till it bled.

Netta leaned on the red car, her palms flat on the window squashing her nose and lips against the cool glass. She was looking in at the strange sight of the car with no passenger seat in front.

'Why are you taking the seat out?' she'd asked her papa as he lay on the driveway of the B&B with his tool kit, his head under the seat making straining noises.

'We need to make some room,' he had said, then Netta thought she heard him swear, but she might have got that wrong because it was difficult to hear him with his face under the seat like that and, besides, Papa never swore.

'But why do we need to make some room?'

'Because...' There was the sound of metal scraping against metal and she was almost positive he swore that time. 'We just do, all right?' he snapped so Netta knew it was time to be quiet.

Then they had driven to a house on the other side of the island, the side without the long sandy beach – Papa driving and Netta and her mama in the back seats, the only seats left. This was where Netta was leaning against the window whilst her parents talked to a man stood in the narrow doorway, dressed in grey striped trousers and a black waistcoat. In the reflection from the glass Netta could see the sign above the door. She turned around so she could read the three names on it with what Netta guessed were their jobs underneath: *Builder, Joiner* and *Undertaker.* She knew what a builder and a joiner were, but she wasn't so sure about the third job. The house was ramshackle, with small dirty windows and lots of tiles missing from the roof above the sign. Netta thought that, just like Frau Auttenberg and her breathless fat body, this place was not a good advert for at least two of the services it was supposed to deliver. Perhaps this whole island was cursed, she thought; after all, this was supposed to be where you came to have a holiday and feel great and look what had happened to her sister!

'I have to reiterate,' the man was saying to her parents, 'that it is illegal to transport a body in your own vehicle.'

'I appreciate that,' her papa replied, 'but we have no choice all the way out here.'

'We just want to get her home as quickly as possible,' her mama sighed.

The man shrugged and went inside. Her parents followed and Netta went back to pressing her nose and lips up against the glass. She was wondering what her lips looked like from the other side, whether they looked like the mouths of the leeches she used to collect from around the feet of Frau Beltz, when she heard he father say sharply:

'Move out of the way, Netta!' He and the man in the stripy trousers were bringing a white box out to the car. Her mama opened the car door for them and they lowered it gently into the space where the passenger seat used to be.

'What's that?' Netta asked.

Ignoring her, her Papa went around to the boot while her mama said softly, laying a hand on Netta's hair, 'It's your sister's coffin, darling.'

Papa pulled the picnic blanket from the boot, the one they had used on the beach all last week, and covered the coffin with it.

'If she goes to sleep on top the guards at the checkpoint are not likely to bother her or worry about what's underneath, don't you think?' Netta's father said to the man in the black waistcoat, who, although he looked kind and smiled reassuringly, did a lot of shrugging.

'OK, Netta,' her mother said, ushering her towards the car, 'Your special job on this journey is to lie down on the blanket there and just go to sleep.'

'But I'm not very sleepy, Ma—'

'You just try and go to sleep and stay like that until we wake you up, OK?' Her mama's voice was shaky and her eyes watery, just like her father's were the other day when he picked her up from the home, so she did as she was told, as it was much easier than knowing what to do or say when an adult was crying.

Despite the thick blanket, it was quite uncomfortable lying on top of the hard coffin and she soon found it was best to lie on her front with her arms wrapped around it to stop her from slipping off as the car bumped her and the coffin around on the uneven roads. With her face pressed against it and her body wrapped around it, she felt something inside the coffin knocking against the lid with every bump in the road.

'It's your sister's coffin, darling,' her mama had told her, but only as the rattling and knocking continued did Netta start to realise that it wasn't just her sister's coffin, but that her sister was actually inside it. As the thought dawned of that little dead body being bumped around just an inch or two below her face, Netta wanted to cry out. Her face was soon soaked and itchy with tears, but she couldn't let go of the coffin to wipe it for fear of falling off. Her weak little lungs pumped her chest up and down against the lid as she sobbed silently mile after mile, but she knew she could not complain. She knew she would be in even more trouble if she did. It was her fault – she told herself to remember that – her fault that Emmy had died and this was her punishment. And she would take her punishment like a good girl so that her parents, especially her papa, didn't hate her anymore after this. When they got home and this awful journey was over, everything would go back to normal. Better than normal. Her papa would love her and look after her all the time, just like he did when he took care of her broken nose last winter.

With her face to the window she heard her mama in the back seat chanting the rosary over and over. She felt the car shudder as it drove onto the ferry and then for half an hour or so the bumping and the knocking thankfully stopped as they floated on the water, heading for the mainland and the checkpoint where the policemen and the foreign soldiers waited.

The port served a number of German islands as well as Scandinavia so the traffic there was always high and inevitably there were queues at the checkpoint. Erika looked over Max's shoulder and through the windscreen she counted about ten cars ahead of them. Some of them were waved through immediately, hardly seeming to stop, others had German policemen leaning in their windows and armed British soldiers prowling around them. Now only five cars away Erika and Max watched as a soldier signalled to a policeman who in turn instructed the driver to get out of his car and open the boot. The driver, a small man whose face glistened with sweat in the heat of the day, obeyed, but dropped his keys as he fiddled with the lock. He bent down to pick them up and Erika drew a sharp breath as the soldier behind him raised his gun. The man retrieved his keys and unlocked the boot. The two policemen rifled through the contents with little regard for its original neatness. Satisfied, the policeman sauntered away and the soldier lowered his gun, leaving the sweating man to make a brief attempt to restore order to his belongings before deciding that it was best just to get going and worry about his packing many miles further down the road.

Erika looked over at Netta sleeping on the blanket, her face to the door. She winced at the sight of the gruesome bed her daughter lay on, then noticed Netta's breathing which seemed to be fast and shallow. She put a hand gently on her forehead. Her temperature was fine. She felt the car edge forward and her attention was back on the road and the checkpoint now only two cars away.

She examined the policemen as well as she could from that distance. Looking for signs of a pleasant, forgiving demeanour. But their uniforms, identical to Officer Hummel's, had her imagining all sorts of probing questions and a terrible scene in front of all these people.

'Perhaps we should turn around,' she mumbled to Max.

'Let's turn around. Get back on the ferry, go back to Sylt, make an arrangement with the undertaker there, like he suggested.'

'We can't turn around. We're stuck in this queue now,' Max said irritably. 'Besides, even if we could, just imagine the attention that would draw upon us. No, Erika, we're going through with this now.' He looked over his shoulder at her. 'Try not to look so frightened. Look happy... well, not too happy. Innocent, but not too innocent. Look them in the eyes, but don't stare them out.'

The car edged forward again and Erika looked at the back of her husband's head with a nauseous wonder. How did he know how to act in this situation? Why was he talking like a seasoned criminal? And then the missing years between them reared their ugly head again. She could only imagine the kind of mistreatment and fear that had led him to learn things like this.

The car before them was waved through without so much as a glance inside from the guards. How the hell did they decide who was deserving of delay and who was worthy of waving through, Erika sneered to herself.

A policeman indicated to Max to stop. Erika felt her lightly tanned skin turn white again. He leaned in the open window.

'Where are you coming from, sir?'

'From Sylt. We've just been on holiday.'

'Very nice,' he said looking with some curiosity at the girl asleep on the blanket and the woman huddled in the back.

'I think all that playing on the beach has worn this one out,' Max said, nodding at his daughter and grinning rather excessively at the policeman.

Erika, who had been trying to look happy but not too happy, innocent but not too innocent, flicking her gaze back and forth from the prying policeman to the nails on one of her hands sunk painfully into the palm of the other, now let her eyes drift over to the subject of her husband's conversation and was met by the amused face of a British soldier pressed up against the window just above Netta's head.

Erika could barely conceal the way her body flinched, but she kept her eyes fixed on his without trying not to stare him out as Max had warned.

'How long did you spend in Sylt?' the policeman asked Max.

'Oh, just a week,' he answered. 'We're both doctors, you see, and we have to get back to work.'

'Both of you doctors?'

'Mmm.'

'Well, well!' the policeman said with more than a hint of sarcasm. 'And where are you *both* doctors?'

'In Dortmund. We are general practitioners. We have our own surgery there.'

Erika was still focused on the soldier whose face was just inches from the coffin. His face looked familiar. And he looked at her as if they were old friends.

'Impressive,' the policeman continued, 'Papers please?'

As Max produced some identification, Erika realised that this was the same soldier who had offered her a cigarette on the quayside last week as they waited for the ferry to Sylt. The same soldier who had tried to flirt with her with his hopeless German vocabulary. He indicated to her to wind down the window near Netta's head. She gave a brief smile of acquiescence as she reached for the handle, her heart palpitating, as if trying to break out of her chest so it could restrain her hand. But then the window was down and the soldier was leaning in, saying:

'Guten Tag. Again.' He winked at Erika. Held out a packet of cigarettes to her. She shook her head politely, so he let his hands droop in mock disappointment and began eyeing Netta and her sleeping arrangements instead. Erika watched his hand, the one without the cigarettes in, come to life again and reach for the picnic blanket. And suddenly her hand was upon his hand, firmly, then seductively smoothing his fingers with hers as she moved her hand away to alight on the cigarette packet. His now wide eyes followed her slender fingers as they slowly pulled out a cigarette and placed it enticingly between pouting lips. Then she gave him a sheepish grin and he scrambled around in his breast pocket, proudly pulling out a brass Zippo lighter. He lit her cigarette. She took a short draw on it. Longer would have been more alluring, she knew that, but it was all she could do not to choke on the repulsive smoke entering her lungs. It was all she could do not to cry right then as she thought of her baby, lying under the nose of the soldier, dead, she believed, from her own infant battle with the smoke of Mengede.

She saw the soldier's attention shift to the policeman at Max's window. She saw him nod discreetly at the officer and lean back from the car, still gripping the window frame. He looked as if he wanted to say something to Erika before this enigmatic lady drove out of his life forever, but he didn't have the vocabulary, in English or German.

She became aware of the DKW engine revving and the soldier and the checkpoint and the harbour town sliding out of view as Max accelerated away into the safety of the German countryside. She found herself coughing violently, then, before she threw the cigarette out of the window in disgust, she took one last drag on it, as the first one hit her brain with surprisingly analgesic results.

Netta sat at the piano. She wanted to play something to blot out the gurgling sounds of her Oma's grief, but as soon as she played the first chord her father came and slammed down the lid, almost chopping off her fingers in the process. The horrible journey home was over but the sadness hadn't ended. Her papa was still angry, and everyone else still upset. Even Jenny was crying and Netta noticed her papa rubbing Jenny's back just as he had done to Netta on the bench at the beach that morning.

They had put the white coffin on the table in the living room and opened the lid so Netta could finally see Emmy instead of just imagining this ghoulish version of her little sister underneath her for all those hours it took to get home. In fact, Emmy looked like an angel. In a white dress, her little hands folded across her chest, in that white coffin, she looked as if she were sleeping. She looked well, not dead. Netta thought she might wake up at any moment. Netta prayed she would wake up soon and stop all this pain and anger that filled the house like smoke. So when everyone had gone to bed and she could hear her father snoring and the soft huffs of her mother's restless sleep, she crept out of her bed and opened the bedroom door. She didn't open it wide, because she knew it made a squeak when it was halfway open. She only needed a tiny gap to squeeze through and then she was on the little landing facing Jenny's door. She thought of her father rubbing Jenny's back and pulled a face as if there were a bad smell coming from Jenny's room. She leaned forward to make sure Jenny's door got the full brunt of her sneer, but in doing so she forgot about the floorboard just in front of it which let out a spooky meow as she trod on it.

She froze. Listened for signs of stirring from both rooms. Then deciding it was safe to continue she slipped down the stairs with renewed concentration, carefully avoiding the parts she knew creaked.

The next obstacle on her quest was crossing the great

expanse of landing outside Tante Bertel's door. The door was always left ajar so her great aunt could be heard if she called out for assistance, but that meant Bertel could always hear when somebody was walking past too. However, since it was the middle of the night and the long low grunting sound coming from her room told Netta she was fast asleep, she tip-toed quickly across the landing, past Tante Bertel's open door and past the firmly shut door of her grandparents, down the second staircase and into the living room.

There in the centre of the room was the open coffin, which seemed to be glowing, so white it was against the surrounding gloom. Netta stood for a while just staring at it. Staring at her baby sister's face, looking so peaceful, so healthy. Netta wasn't afraid, even here in the dark. After all, she had spent mile after terrible mile lying on top of that coffin with all sorts of horrible imaginings clattering around her mind. So she approached the table and put her hand on Emmy's hands. They were cold. She touched her sister's forehead, just as Mama did to them both when she thought they were ill, just as Mama had done to Netta that morning when she thought Netta was sleeping as they had approached the checkpoint. Netta remembered the smell of smoke from the soldier's breath who'd leaned right over her. She could see right up his nose when she peeked out of her scrunched up eyes to see where that stink was coming from. Emmy's forehead and cheeks and lips were cold too. But she looked so alive. Netta knew it was just a matter of warming her up again and her little sister would come back to life. And then the smog of sadness that filled the house would fade away. She pulled the coffin a little closer to the edge of the table so it was easier to reach, then Netta gathered the baby up in her arms. It was hard to do. She still had to stand on tip-toe to get a good grip, but when she had a safe hold of her she went and sat on one of the armchairs and, holding her close to her body so that Emmy would feel the warmth of her big sister, Netta began to rock gently. Ever so quietly, so as not to wake the adults, she sang the song she and her mother used to sing at bedtime to her papa who had been taken away by the Russians.

'If I were a little bird and had wings
I would fly to you,
But because it cannot be
We are waiting here for you.'
And then she added a new line to the song:
'Come back, Emmy, come back, come back,
Come back, Emmy, come back, come back.'

She sat and rocked her little sister all night. She desperately wanted to fall asleep herself, but she knew she had to keep going, keep holding her tight and keep her moving so she would warm up and wake up again.

The rising sun made the living room glow red and blue just like the Tiffany window did in the attic room at all times of the day. When Netta noticed this, she knew it was time to stop, unless she wanted to be found by one of the adults, who would surely get the wrong idea, just like they always did about anything she tried to do or say. Her bottom lip began to tremble with exhaustion and a sense of failure. She shuffled off the armchair and on numb legs carried her sister back to the table, giving her a kiss on the forehead before she lifted her back into the coffin.

'Don't cry,' she whispered, noticing the tear on Emmy's cheek and wiping it off gently. 'Papa said we'll see you again soon.'

Netta rubbed at her own watery eyes, the real source of Emmy's tear, and hurried to the door, pulling it open and immediately bumping into the legs of the person lurking out in the hallway.

'What the hell do you think you're doing, little lady?'

Netta gasped at the twisted red lips that swooped down at her from the shadows.

'What kind of child are you? Messing with a dead baby's body!'

'I—I—I was just trying to—'

'You were just playing with it,' Jenny spat, 'like it was a bloody doll or something, but that's not a doll, is it?' She grabbed Netta by the arm and shook her. 'That's your little sister, you foolish little girl. Your parents are in mourning, for God's sake, what do you think they would say if they heard you were messing around with their precious baby's body like that?'

'Please don't tell them, I—'

'Don't tell them?' she cackled, dragging Netta back into the living room as floorboards creaked and the mumbling of waking voices was heard overhead. 'Don't you think they would notice their little baby has been meddled with? Look at the state of her now! Her hands have been moved, the coffin's been moved, the dress is all ruffled. Do you think I'm going to let your mother blame me for that? Coz she'd love that, she would. And so would you, I bet. No, I'm going to tell them all right and you're going to be locked in the basement until I do.'

'No!' Netta tried to resist. The stinking dark basement petrified her, but Jenny yanked her down the corridor and pushed her so hard into it that Netta even heard the housekeeper blurt out something in sympathy for the way she crashed down the small staircase to the mildewed floor.

'Let me out! Let me out!' Netta howled over and over until she heard voices above in the kitchen, then she listened. Oma and Opa. And Jenny filling their heads with lies, thought Netta. She waited for one of her grandparents to come and let her out as she snivelled, nursing the grazed hands which broke her fall.

They did not come.

Something shifted in the blackness behind her and she began to cry uncontrollably. 'When can I come out? How long do I have to stay in here? How long? How long?'

Max's dream world turned to bubbles which roared in his ears as he broke the surface of sleep. His eyes snapped open. Then in the long slow heart beat between dreaming and waking he felt the sheets around his fingers and realised it was not the unforgiving canvas of a military cot he was sleeping on, not the limbs from a soldier dismembered by a grenade which lay next to him, but the intact body of his sleeping wife. And just as he began to exhale with relief, the air stuck in his throat as his equally mournful reality came rushing into him like mustard gas.

Emmy was dead.

He sat up. He thought about lying down again, wondered if his body could be bothered to go through the motions of living today, but the distant commotion reaching his ears from way below in the kitchen compelled him to stand up, pull on his dressing gown and slump downstairs, groggy as if with a hangover.

He had to go through the living room to get to the kitchen and the sight of the coffin there on the table was an icy slap to his face. He'd almost forgotten that it was there; that *she* was there; his baby. He stared at the body in the little coffin, began to register the changes in her posture, her dress, the position of the coffin on the edge of the table, but his attention was drawn to the raised voices in the kitchen and the muffled wailing of a girl beyond.

'I want to come out. How long do I have to stay here? Please, let me out! I can't stand it in here.'

He took a step towards the kitchen and heard his mother. 'Well, I suppose it won't hurt her to stay in there a little bit longer.'

He heard Jenny. 'She needs to know she can't get away with things like that. I mean, that's just awful, isn't it? And it's not the first time she's done something really silly. She's always disobeying us.'

He heard his father. 'Well, perhaps they have been a

bit remiss when it comes to disciplining her, but we must remember they have both had a lot on their plates what with Max being away for so long and...'

He heard Netta. 'Let me out! Please! Mama, Mama! How long? How long do I have to stay in here? How long? *How long?*'

He heard Sergeant Volkov. 'Get in! Solitary confinement. That was the punishment stated for sloppy medical practice, was it not?'

He heard himself. 'Look, let's just go back to the hospital and I can show you the figures, you can count the patients for yourself if you like. I am sure that there are less than nine percent sick.'

He heard Volkov again, felt the jabbing of a gun in his back. 'Get in! And if I have to tell you again you'll be shot.'

He felt the damp floor of his two-metre-square cell. He heard himself. 'How long? How long do I have to stay in here? How long? *How long?*'

He heard his mother. 'Well I suppose it won't hurt her to stay in there a little bit longer.'

But it will! He ground the thought between his teeth. It *will* hurt her to stay in there a bit longer! He felt the need to stretch, to unfurl himself in the way that cell back in Gegesha had stopped him from doing. He looked at his daughter in the coffin. He heard his daughter in the basement. He barged into the kitchen, making the three guards there jump, slammed back the bolt on the basement door calling out into the darkness below, 'Come on, Emmy, come on, darling. It's OK, you can come out now.'

His daughter scampered up the stairs and grabbed the hand he held out for her with her own stinging mucky one. He led her out of the kitchen glaring at Karl and Martha and Jenny as he went. Martha was about to say something, perhaps about the fact that he had just called Netta Emmy, but Karl's hand on her arm silenced her. Max led Netta through to the living room, but the sight of Emmy in the coffin stopped him in his tracks – as if he had forgotten she was there again.

He stood holding Netta's hand for a moment; a moment which felt stretched, as in a nightmare, to both of them. Then without taking his eyes from the corpse he muttered, 'Go on. Go and get cleaned up. Go and get dressed.'

Netta gratefully did as she was told.

He moved falteringly to the coffin and with the fingers of an old man began to straighten Emmy's dress and rearrange her hands.

Karl went to work as usual. He tried to stay home but the others wouldn't have it. They could close the surgery for a few days – there was always the hospital or the other GPs in the area for patients to go to if it was an emergency. But all those children missing out on their education if Karl didn't open the school, Erika and Max wouldn't hear of it. And if Karl was honest with himself, he was glad to get out of the house and occupy himself with something other than the sight of his grandchild lying in that coffin on the living room table.

The primary school was relatively small and his few colleagues offered their condolences, which he smiled politely at before deftly changing the subject to the new term's timetable or asking Herr Ritter the caretaker about the progress of repairs on the roof.

He sat in his office and marked some books, but his mind kept wandering bizarrely, he thought at first, to the motorbike in the shed next door. But, he soon realised, it was fixing up this motorbike with Max that had given him a way to connect with the stranger who had returned from the Siberian labour camp. They had enjoyed this time together just as they used to enjoy playing the piano together when Max was a boy, or listening to the crystal radio set – the first such set in the whole street – tuned in to the Landenberg station. Back then Karl would help both his sons, Max and Sepp, build the carts they would then hitch to the horses on their grandmother's farm and gallop along the fields with them at breakneck speeds. Martha would frown at this dangerous sport, just like she did at the motorbike, but that only told Karl he was doing the right manly things with his boys. And then in '43, at the age of eighteen, his boy barely a man, Sepp was killed on the Russian front only days after arriving there. Max had lost his brother and Karl had lost a child. He shook out his aching wrist and went back to his marking, shaking his head too at the irony – the only thing he could truly say he understood about the man who came back from Gegesha now was what he was feeling today at the loss of his child.

'That old war wound playing up again, is it, Herr Portner?'

Karl looked up at the doorway where Officer Hummel leaned, arms folded, as if he thought he was an American film star or something, Karl scoffed inwardly.

'I beg your pardon?' Karl said with barely concealed irritation.

'The wrist.' Hummel nodded at Karl's disability and sauntered into the room.

'Oh, yes. Nothing to worry about though.' Karl gave a brief smile and turned back to his books to give the uninvited guest a hint that he was too busy for a chat.

'Remind me how you got that injury again?' Hummel had seemed to have missed the hint and sat himself down on the other side of Karl's desk.

Karl let his pen fall on the page in front of him with a slap, sat back and after eyeing the intruder for a moment said slowly and deliberately, 'I shot myself in the arm.'

Hummel sucked at the air in sympathy, 'Ooh, nasty. An accident you said?'

Karl studied Hummel and resented the way it felt as if Hummel was the headmaster and he was a child on the other side of the desk being told off for some naïve misdemeanour. No one outside the family knew he shot himself to avoid military service. It was too dangerous when he did it to let anyone know that his hatred of Imperial policies drove him to it. And yet here was Hummel interrogating him as if he already knew the truth. And so what if he told the truth now? The Empire was long gone, the Nazis were long gone, he didn't need to live in fear anymore. And if Hummel did somehow know the truth, Karl lying about it would just make Hummel more suspicious of him generally. But he was sure Hummel couldn't know. Martha and Max would never have said anything. And even Erika... he knew they were not the best of friends since her indiscretion with the carpenter, but... And then there was the fact that Hummel, being Hummel, was probably a National Socialist in his time. Knowledge of the strength of Karl's political leanings would probably make this policeman more suspicious of him than lying about his injury would. And so Karl opened his mouth and heard himself growl:

'How can I help you today, Officer?'

Hummel sniffed smugly and replied, 'Well, I just came to pay my respects really. I heard about your granddaughter. Terrible, terrible.'

Karl reddened with anger. Hummel's tone was so devoid of sincerity and Karl despised him for it.

'You must feel cursed or something in that house,' he continued with astounding insensitivity. 'First Fraulein Kranz and now little Emmy?' He waited for an answer, as if anyone would dignify such a question with one. 'I really wouldn't know what to do with myself if I were you.'

'Well, that's just it, isn't it?' Karl said eventually, trying desperately to contain his wrath. 'You really don't know what to do, do you?'

'Mmm?'

'It's been a year.'

'I'm sorry?'

'A year since Karin was killed. And still the culprit has not been found. Don't you think perhaps it's time to draft in a detective from outside Mengede, you know, someone with more expertise in these matters? Someone who actually knows what they're doing? Someone who can get the job done?'

Karl saw Hummel shrink from the swipe and picked up his pen to resume his marking, his position as headmaster regained. The scolded child on the other side of the desk got up quietly and shuffled sheepishly back to school.

K arl and Max secured the lid and everyone sat around the room looking furtively at each other, hoping someone else would know how this worked, what to do and when to do it.

Netta sat with her legs dangling from the armchair, just as she did a few nights ago, the memory of the weight of Emmy in her arms and on her lap pressing on her black dress. Bertel in the wing-back chair looked resplendent in a dress trimmed with black lace, a string of pearls around her neck and a black bonnet over her long silver hair. Erika, despite the late summer weather, was buttoned up tightly in a long black coat as if she were trying to hide as much of herself from the world as possible. Jenny stood by the mantelpiece trying discreetly to check her make-up and hair in the mirror. She and Isabel had gone shopping especially to buy new outfits for the occasion and Jenny was determined to look like the actress Linda Christian at the funeral of Ivor Novello, which she'd seen on the news at the cinema a few months before.

Karl and Martha were painfully aware of how this worked, what to do and when to do it, and, as Martha straightened his tie, Karl grimaced as if she were strangling him and said, 'Are you ready, son?'

Max nodded and turned to Erika. 'Are you sure you're up to this?'

'No,' she said, her eyes focused on nothing. 'Are you?'

Karl helped Max carry the coffin out to the street, where Edgar, Karl's lawyer friend Jäger, Herr Ritter, his wife, and their three sons including Netta's friend Josef waited uncomfortably in the hazy sunshine. In her trembling hands Erika took one end of the coffin from Karl. The weight of it seemed to press the tears from her. Edgar stretched out a long arm and squeezed Max's shoulder in an eloquent silence which seemed to wring the tears from him too. And then the quietly weeping couple started the longest walk of their lives through the town to the cemetery, an entourage of mourners behind whose legs, apart from Bertel's, were aching to walk faster, whose minds were aching with thoughts of their own mortality.

As they passed down the street, other friends and acquaintances left their houses and joined the troop. Isabel trotted over to Jenny bursting with gossip, which would have to be contained for now as her employer Frau Beltz hobbled beside them.

Outside the church two British soldiers doffed their berets respectfully. Inside even more people were waiting and Erika didn't know whether to feel proud of such a turnout or ashamed that all these people were gawping at her grief.

'Both doctors,' she thought she heard whispered from somewhere in the congregation, 'and still she died.'

'First the housekeeper and now this,' she thought she heard mumbled from behind a book of psalms. 'Who's next, I wonder?'

After the service Father Egger led the mourners out to the cemetery where other onlookers waited – those who wanted to pay their respects but didn't feel quite part of the family and its circle of friends enough to invite themselves into the church. The large figure of Rodrick skulking by the trees was unmistakable to Erika, and a stern-faced woman clutching an infant stirred a memory in her which she couldn't quite pin down in the maelstrom of her despair. Hummel loitering by the gates, his nose in the air, added to her nausea.

As much as he wanted to take in every last image of his daughter's coffin before it was lowered out of sight forever, Max's attention was diverted by the sight of the altar boys in their bright white cassocks. He saw himself and Horst in the very same costumes in this very same cemetery, twenty years before, attending funerals with a younger Father Egger. He winced at the way the grief of the mourners then meant so little to him, his young mind occupied with just how he and Horst could use the crucifix as a ladder after the burial to climb the wall of the priest's garden and plunder the sweet fruit from the cherry trees there. He examined the boys' cassocks for signs of red stains, the kind of stains he and Horst had made as they carelessly munched on their bounty, the kind of stains that had earned him and Horst a wallop from Father Egger. His innards smiled at the memory of Horst, red stains on white cassocks. The image morphed into blood stains on a doctor's coat and he jumped noticeably as if someone had fired a rifle close to his head. He blinked away the image and found his eyes resting on Horst's wife, Eva, the stern-faced woman clutching the infant. And as Father Egger asked the mourners to pray, all Max could recite was the letter she had written to Horst while they were rotting in Gegesha.

Dear Husband,

This is the last letter I am writing to you because on June 24ᵗʰ I am going to marry another man. Then I don't have to work any longer. I have already been working for three years since you've been away from home. All the other men come home for leave, only you POWs never come. Nobody knows how long it will take until you come home. That's why I am going to have a new husband. I will give the child to the orphanage. I have to. I cannot stomach this life any longer. There is no way to survive with these few pfennig benefits. At work they have a big mouth when it comes to the women. But now I don't need to go there anymore, ~~my new~~ the other man is going to work for me. All wives whose husbands are POWs will do the same thing and they will all get rid of the children. Three years of work is too much for a woman and 20 Mark for benefit and 10 Mark child benefit is not enough. You cannot live on that. Everything is so expensive now. One pound of bacon costs 8 Mark, a shirt 9 Mark.

Your wife.

With every word he remembered, with the recollection of the jaw-clenching, teeth-grinding face of his best friend as he read it, Max's anger grew. As the mourners slowly dispersed, he marched between the graves towards Eva, who hitched the infant further up into her arms like a shield as she saw him approach.

'Max?' he heard Erika's confused voice somewhere in the distance.

'Max!' Edgar called out, but he marched on oblivious of their concern.

'What are you doing here?' he snarled at Eva.

'Hello, Max,' she said wearily.

'I said what—'

'I'm here to pay my respects, that's all.'

'Pay your respects to a little girl you never knew?'

'I would have liked to have known her.'

'Why?'

'Because she's your daughter and we used to be friends.'

'Yes, we used to be friends, before you stabbed my brother in the back.'

'I didn't stab him in the back, Max, I didn't know if he was alive or dead. I didn't know if he was ever coming back, I had to do something.'

'Perhaps this conversation is for another time,' Edgar said over Max's shoulder as those mourners who had not already left began to turn and watch this unexpected after-show, Isabel, Beltz and Jenny making sure they had front row seats.

'Yes, perhaps,' Eva agreed, taking a step to leave.

'No, no,' Max put up his hands to stop her. 'Now is the perfect time. A funeral. What could be more appropriate?'

Eva sighed, but made no attempt to leave, as if she thought this was punishment she deserved.

'You see, that letter of yours killed Horst. Quite literally. It destroyed him to hear you giving up on him like that.'

'Times were hard, Max.'

'Times were hard?' He cackled in a way that chilled Erika as she stood helpless grasping Edgar's arm, watching the stranger return. 'Twenty Mark for benefit and ten Mark child benefit, wasn't it? A pound of bacon for eight Mark, a shirt for nine? My God, woman, how tough that must have been, while your husband lorded it up in the same filthy rags he'd worn every day for three years with nothing but black bread and watery broth to eat every single day.'

'How was I to know that? He never wrote back to tell me.'

'He wrote. He wrote letters all the damn time, but the vicious guards that made our life a misery never sent them on and they never let him see your letters until that last one.'

'Max, can we go back to the house,' Erika said weakly. 'Everyone's waiting.'

Everyone's watching, she had wanted to say, as she looked round to see Jenny and Isabel and Beltz, among others, their eyes shining with the drama before them as if it were coming from a cinema screen.

'And how was I to know that?'

'You could have had faith.'

Eva scoffed at such an insubstantial commodity. 'How many loaves of bread and pounds of bacon will faith get you these days, Max?'

'*She* managed it.' Erika was almost pleasantly stunned to see Max's finger pointed at her. But then she saw Rodrick shift about in the shadows and she blushed at the thought of Max making her the nonpareil of fidelity.

'Well, no offence, Erika, but you're a doctor. I had to work in a bloody factory. It was hell.'

'You have no idea what hell is,' Max seethed. 'But I can tell you Horst did. He lived in it for three years. And then he tried to escape. He ran for it because he thought if he could just get back here to you, you would forget about that other man. They killed him for trying to escape.'

175

'And I'm sorry—'

'*You* killed him.' Max jabbed his finger at Eva now. 'If you hadn't written that letter he would be here right now, right here supporting me on this day when I need him more than ever.'

Erika felt Edgar, her big tall rock, shrink as the news that he wasn't friend enough for Max hit home. She tightened her grip on his arm, for her own benefit as well as his.

'I lost a husband too,' Eva shrieked, unable to take the punishment any more.

'You got yourself a new one,' Max jeered, 'and a new child by the looks of it too.' He gestured at the little boy in Eva's arms who shrank from the horrible man's touch and began to bawl in an effort to outdo the rowing adults. 'So where's Lisa? Still in the orphanage?'

Eva blushed, jiggling the child about on her hip in an attempt to quieten him down.

'So, you can afford to have a child by another man, but Horst's little girl gets thrown on the scrap heap along with his memory, is that it?'

'Another family took her,' Eva mumbled, 'before I got back on my feet again.'

'Before you got back on your feet again,' he mocked. 'Before you found yourself another man to bleed dry, more like.'

'Do you not think, Max,' Eva said with an exhausted urgency, 'that if Horst had come back, that I would have ever so much as looked at another man?'

Max had known Eva for almost as long as he'd known Horst and he couldn't argue with that.

'Do you not think,' she continued, 'that if I had Horst back, like Erika had you, that I wouldn't drop everything to be with him again? He was the love of my life, you know that. But he's not here anymore. He's gone forever. And I wish every day that he wasn't. I wish I was as lucky as you, Max,' she spat, jerking her head in the direction of his wife.

Max turned to look at the prize Eva envied and instead saw Jenny standing with her friend, who was leaning against a gravestone, agape, and his own hypocrisy hit him in the face with all the grazing coldness a shovel full of earth would, should he be lying in his daughter's grave right now as the gravediggers got to work. After an excruciating silence mocked by the cawing of the crows in the trees, he eventually muttered to the earth.

'I'm sorry.'

Eva didn't believe the words were directed at her. Erika prayed they were for her. Edgar pretended they were for him. And Jenny was sure that they would somehow affect her new life negatively in the days to come.

As for Netta...

Netta was positive that the words weren't for her, because no one had said a word to her all day, apart from *brush your hair properly*, and *don't get that dress dirty.*

No one had even looked at her apart from Josef who'd looked back and smiled at her nervously as they began the long walk from the house. She was the last one then and she was the last one now as everyone trudged back through the town to have coffee and sandwiches at the house. She wondered, if she just stayed here in the graveyard, if anyone would even notice she wasn't there as they all sat round nibbling bits of cake and saying the kind of pointless things adults do when they don't feel comfortable with silence. She looked around at the gaping grave of her sister, the ancient tombstones going a mouldy green, the gathering crows on the gate, and she hurried off behind Father Egger who was talking to the policeman Netta remembered from the first time she and her papa ever went to the island. The silly old policeman didn't even know their car was red. He had called it some colour that no one had ever heard of: clarinet or something.

'You've known the Portners for some time then, Father?' the policeman was saying.

'Yes indeed. Max used to be one of my altar boys when he was young.'

'Do you know what that was all about just now?'

'I do.'

'Care to enlighten me, Father?'

'Are we just having a chat or is this official police business now?'

'I hope we can just keep this unofficial, Father. But that's up to you.'

There was a pause in the conversation and Netta was mesmerised by the priest's cassock swishing about him as he walked, until he said, 'Horst was Max's best friend ever since they were children. He was an altar boy too. They were thick as thieves. A mischievous pair, but devoted to each other. A rarity to see in young boys these days, don't you think?'

'Mmm.'

'They both became doctors and were both captured by the Russians in Breslau. Both taken to a labour camp in Siberia where Horst was killed when he tried to escape. He was trying to get back home to Eva, the woman Max was upset with, because she had written him a letter saying she couldn't wait for him any longer. Ironically, all the prisoners were freed less than a year after that. Max lost his best friend, his brother and he blames Eva for it. I didn't realise that or the extent of his resentment until today. But of course the man has just buried his baby, I think we can all forgive him for letting off a little steam, don't you?'

'Of course.'

Netta watched as the policeman took off his hat and tucked it under his arm. She was curious to see his bald patch which matched the priest's, except the priest's was trimmed with grey hair and the officer's trimmed with a light brown. Like two eggs walking down the street, she giggled to herself.

'But what about the family in general. What kind of family are they?'

'Pillars of the community,' Father Egger said quickly. 'Karl is an esteemed teacher, Martha too before she retired. Max and Erika doctors—'

'Yes, yes, but I'm not talking about what they do for a living, Father, I'm more concerned with the kind of personalities and temperaments involved.'

'You mean, are they the kind of people that would kill their housekeeper? I assume that's what we're talking about, Officer? Still, after all these months.'

Netta watched the policeman scratch at his head just like she did when she couldn't work out a sum in Maths, which was often.

'I mean are they the kind of people that would kill *anyone?*'

'I do hope you're not referring to the death of little Emmy too?'

The policeman shrugged.

'Did you not see the distress both those parents were under? Did you see the face of a murderer carrying that tiny coffin today?'

'I'm not accusing either of them.'

'Well, the child died when they were on holiday on the Isle of Sylt. Martha and Karl were not there, nor was their new housekeeper... unless you're accusing young Netta?'

Netta felt as if someone had opened two holes in her feet and all the blood had drained out of her body in a flash. She held back a little so she could be sure the men had not noticed her, but kept close enough to hear more of their conversation.

'No, no,' the policeman was grumbling.

'Look, Officer, if you really want to know what I think, I think you're looking in the wrong place if you're looking for a murderer among the Portners.'

'Really?'

'Yes. Since the occupation of Germany there have been countless reports of Allied soldiers raping young women.'

'Most of them completely unsubstantiated,' the policeman said. 'The rest committed by the Soviets in the East.'

'Are you saying the British and American soldiers have never committed such crimes on this side?'

'Well, I've never heard about it.'

'Really? Now that does disturb me,' the priest sighed, 'because a number of women have reported such crimes to me.'

'Well, they should report it to the police, not the clergy, with all due respect, Father.'

'With all due respect, Officer Hummel, the women probably feel uncomfortable enough reporting it to me, let alone a male police officer like yourself.' The policeman didn't speak for a moment, just sniffed a few times, so the priest went on, 'And I have, of course, passed on the reports of these terrible crimes to the police and yet you say you've never heard of such reports.'

'Well,' he scratched his head, harder this time, 'I am not the only policeman in Mengede, Father. We are a small force, but not *that* small.'

'Well, given what I have heard from women around here, and from my colleagues in other parishes around Dortmund and beyond, the abuse of German women by British and American soldiers is significant. And I'm afraid it wouldn't surprise me in the least if the person you seek for the murder of Karin Kranz wore the uniform of the British army.'

Netta frowned as she tried to make sense of what she heard. She remembered running home, frightened, convinced someone was following her and convinced that that someone was wearing boots like a soldier would... Oh, no! She hushed herself. She wasn't sure that the person following her had boots on at all. She had only said that to her papa because he suggested it and because he looked worried and she wanted to keep him interested in her and worried about her for a little bit longer that evening. Before Karin came in snivelling and ruined it all.

Erika's soul was shattered and the sharp pieces weighed so heavily on her chest she could barely take a decent breath. She longed to be on the Isle of Sylt again. Before Emmy became ill. Just the four of them under a sky so blue it seemed unreal, her heart so light she felt she could float up into the arm-spreading space around them. Yet here she was in a room too small for all these people drably dressed, the sky outside the colour of corrosion.

She sat holding a coffee she would never drink, Edgar by her side, a protective hand on her back and she wished that hand was Max's. But he was standing by the door, his eyes fixed on Jenny, who was clearly aware of this and was shifting about into various poses as she pretended to be engrossed in conversation with Isabel by the mantelpiece. One hand kept tapping vainly at her hat and tugging at the neckline on her dress, she even pouted her red lips in his direction.

Once a whore, always a whore, Erika thought, resenting her own bitterness, then instantly transferring that resentment to Max for giving her something to be resentful for.

Father Egger arrived then, the white of his cassock a welcome swathe of brightness among the sombre costumes, and gave her something else to focus on – being polite. She made to put down her cup and rise to greet him, but Martha was there first.

'Welcome, Father,' she fussed and Erika was glad of it. 'Please come and sit down.' Martha looked around for a seat that wasn't taken. All were full, so Herr Ritter shooed Josef from his chair near Erika to make way for the priest. 'There you go, take a seat there.'

Far from being indignant at this ousting, Josef seized the opportunity to go outside and play with Netta, who had arrived just behind Egger and loitered at the door as if she was unsure whether she was invited to this gathering or not.

'Can I get you something to drink?' Martha asked the priest. 'A coffee or something a little stronger perhaps.'

'Ooh, well now.' Father Egger's eyes lit up and he used this opportunity to try and lighten the mood in the room. 'What do you have in mind when you say something a little stronger, Martha?'

'We have some wine or perhaps a cognac.' Karl took over, glad of something to talk about other than how the day had gone so far.

'Ah, a cognac would be delightful, if it's not too much trouble.' He grinned a grin which gave everyone in the room permission to laugh a polite, but relieving laugh.

'And who are you now?' Bertel said from the other side of the room, propped up in the wing-back chair.

'Oh, Bertel,' Martha tutted and fluttered embarrassed eyes at the priest, 'you know who this is, it's Father Egger from the church, remember?'

'Of course I remember,' Bertel croaked, 'I wasn't talking about him, was I? I was talking to you, girl.' She focused her sharp eyes unequivocally on Erika.

Erika looked about the room awkwardly for a moment, hoping Martha would come to her rescue as she did to the priest's, but since Martha thought selecting sandwiches for Father Egger was more important, she answered the senile old aunt for herself. 'Bertel, I'm Erika,' she smiled, then realised she'd just been given the perfect opportunity to remind that hussy by the mantelpiece just who she was. 'Erika, Max's wife,' she announced slowly, deliberately.

Bertel tutted now and sighed with irritation. 'I know you're Erika! Why does everybody always treat me like I'm stupid or something? I wasn't asking what your name is, I was asking you who you are now.'

'I don't understand,' Erika said shakily, her broken soul unable to deal with the least aggression, even from Bertel, today.

'Well,' Bertel waved her clawed hands about as she spoke,

enthroned in that chair, clad in black, her witch-coloured hair coming loose, appearing to Erika like a diabolical antithesis to the priest she sat opposite, 'when someone loses their parents they become an orphan. When someone loses a husband they become a widow. When they lose a wife they become a widower. But when you lose a child what are you? Is there a name for that? I was just wondering, because I can't think of the name for that.'

Isabel pulled a face as if she had just been punched in the stomach, but her eyes shone with delight as she grasped Jenny's arm. Erika *felt* as if she had been punched in the stomach and for the first time Max took his eyes off Jenny and watched his wife trying to politely swallow the fishbone of a notion Bertel had just fed her.

'Father, can I interest you in a ham sandwich?' Martha said tactfully.

'So you're the caretaker,' Edgar asked Herr Ritter in an attempt to divert attention from his friend.

Bertel was right, Erika winced, there was no word for what she was now. Because it was an unnatural state of being. No one should live to see their children die. It was supposed to be the other way round. She had read of cultures in Africa where, when a parent dies, the children throw a party and celebrate that the natural order of things has prevailed. She tried to put her cup down quietly but it crashed onto the table as she hurried out to the kitchen, past Max who still lingered in the doorway, feeling the need to vomit. The last time she felt that way was in Frau Beltz's bathroom when she had morning sickness, pregnant with Emmy, and the memory of her joy then made her pain now seem all the more vicious.

She held onto the sink for a moment then felt two long hands rubbing her shoulders.

'Hey. Don't listen to that dotty old bag,' Edgar said.

'I want to die,' she cried.

'Ah, don't say that!'

'If I die I can go and be with Emmy right now. I shouldn't be here without her, that's not the way it should be. Bertel's right.'

In the doorway Max had his back to the kitchen and his eyes trained on Jenny, as they had been almost constantly since they returned from the church. But he was listening to everything, and Erika's words cut him then as much has Bertel's had a minute before, and as much as Eva's had in the cemetery earlier. The thought of Erika wanting to die, the thought of her dying, the thought of losing her, was the last nudge that Max needed. He couldn't bring Emmy back, he couldn't stop the bad dreams, the moods, the flashbacks and the turbulent nights, but there was one thing that was killing his wife which he could do something about and he'd been examining it ever since they'd got back to the house this afternoon, and he could see just how shallow and manipulative and vain it was now and how he had made himself a fool for it ever since it had swanned back into his life and he had dropped everything for her beauty... no, not her beauty, her physical form, which he knew as a doctor, was nothing more than flesh stretched over bone, flesh that deteriorates with time, he thought, throwing a glance at Bertel, bone that breaks, he thought, glancing at his father's wrist as he poured more cognac for the priest. Stood there next to the callous Isabel, he saw Jenny more than ever as a simple parasite and the woman he had his back to as a complex, intelligent, independent, strong and soulful human being – his match.

As he stared at her, Jenny smiled at him through pursed lips, which parted seductively as he crossed the room towards her.

'You have to go,' he said quietly.

'I'm sorry, darling?'

'I want you to leave this house. We don't need your services anymore.'

Jenny's eyes darted desperately about his face looking for the joke. 'What are you saying?'

185

'Are you kicking her out?' Isabel yapped.

Max looked at Isabel as he had looked at his first gangrenous limb as a student and she shut up.

'I'm not doing this to my family anymore,' he whispered. 'I'm sorry.'

'You're sorry?' Jenny raised her voice, silencing any other murmured conversation in the room.

'Just go, please,' Max said through gritted teeth now. 'Don't make me throw you out.'

'*Now* you want to throw me out? But... I was all right to have around when you needed a chat, a laugh, when you needed a shoulder to cry on.' She desperately wanted to say *when you came crawling into my bedroom.* The shock waves that would ripple through this room would be fabulous. It was true, he had come to her bedroom one night after a particularly harrowing nightmare. He had managed not to wake Erika and went to Jenny in tears. He felt he *could* cry in front of Jenny, because she knew what he had to cry about. He didn't have to be the man Dr Siskin demanded of him, that he demanded of himself in front of his wife and child. In front of Jenny he could be the mouse. However, he might have come crawling to her bedroom, but he never crawled into her bed. When he was empty of tears that night sitting on the edge of her bed, he simply went back to his own.

Max saw the flash in her eyes as she contemplated all this, as she weighed up whether to drop a vengeful grenade or not, so he grabbed her by the arm, yanking her out of the room so quickly she couldn't get another word out until she was on the doorstep.

'What the hell, Max!'

'I kept you on as long as I could. Everyone else would have had you out a long time ago. This situation is ridiculous. It's selfish.'

'There's nothing wrong with being selfish, Max. Did you not learn anything in Gegesha? Look after number one, that's what I say. You think *she'll* ever understand what we went through up there?'

'She does nothing but try to understand,' he fumed, at himself as much as Jenny.

'Are you all right, love?' Isabel was there bristling, eager for a fight.

'Yeah, I'm all right,' she sneered at Max and took a few steps away from the house before she stopped and looked suddenly forlorn. 'What about my things?'

'I'll leave them outside later. Come and get them tonight, but if you don't mind, I'm in the middle of a wake right now.'

He saw her wither. 'Of course,' she whimpered. 'I'm so sorry about Emmy.'

He closed the door.

'Come on, Jenny, love,' Isabel tugged at her sleeve, 'let's get out of here.'

Jenny looked up at the house and the Tiffany window, just as she'd done the day she first knocked at the door, and as her eyes fell to earth again she saw Josef and Netta sitting on the steps of the school watching her. Netta could barely contain her excitement and, after some deliberation, decided it was safe to stick out her tongue at the housekeeper, who, as ever, allowed herself to be led down the road by her friend.

And so things were changing again. Netta wondered why her heart jumped whenever changed happened, even the good changes, like Jenny leaving and her mama being happier, as if the good changes were as frightening as the bad – like going to secondary school.

Josef didn't pass the exams to get into the same school as Netta – that was one rotten thing about secondary school. The other rotten thing was, unlike primary school, her new school was not next door to home, and it took an hour and a half to get there on the tram. Peter and the others that Netta knew from Mengede, who went to the same school, travelled there by train and it only took them ten minutes. But they all looked like stretched versions of their primary school selves now and Netta, still underweight and short for her age, couldn't reach the door handle on the train, so the tram was her only option. And the school was not run by her Opa, unlike her primary school. This one was run by nuns. Nuns like Schwester Hildegarda – and that was the very worst thing about secondary school.

'Pay attention, Anetta!' Schwester Hildegarda would gobble across the classroom when she noticed Netta staring into space as yet another equation stumped her. Schwester Hildegarda's words always sounded like the shrill gobbling of a turkey to Netta. Not just because of the sound, but because they came from a wrinkly red face strapped up in the big black and white plumage of a nun's habit.

The nun waddled over to Netta and stood over her, her biro raised as if it were a rolled up newspaper ready to swat a fly.

'If x plus 2x is thirty-three, what is x?'

'Er...' Netta said, delaying the inevitable.

'How on earth did you ever pass the entrance exam for this school if you can't even master simple algebra like that?' Schwester Hildegarda scoffed and whacked Netta on the head with the biro. 'Hurry up!'

'Erm,' Netta said through clenched teeth as her scalp stung with the blow.

'Oh come on!' Hildegarda whipped at Netta's head again and this time the clasp of the pen became entangled in her golden locks. 'Ugh!' the teacher said as if Netta was not only rubbish at Maths but rubbish at getting her head whacked by a biro too, and she yanked at the pen to free it. It didn't come away immediately. Netta yelped and slammed a hand on her head which burned with a pain that made her feel sick, but Schwester Hildegarda yanked again and then the pen came away along with a handful of Netta's hair.

Netta saw Peter's worried face looking back at her as if through a fish bowl as her eyes filled with tears, while the nun picked the hair from the clasp as if it was nothing more than fluff on her habit, saying:

'You'd better snap out of that stupor, young lady, if you want to amount to anything in this life. Now, Barbara, if x plus 2x is thirty-three, what is x?'

'Are you all right?' Peter asked at break time.

'I'm fine,' Netta sighed, 'but what's going on over there?'

Peter followed Netta to the playground wall where a small crowd of first years had gathered. The smell reached them before they reached the crowd – the warm, sweet, stomach-growling smell of the bakery which stood next door to the school. Even Netta was hungry at the sight of all those fresh doughnuts piled high in the shop window. Now why couldn't they feed us doughnuts back in the children's home on the island every day, Netta wondered. I would be as big and strong as that old battle-axe Auttenberg had wanted me to be if she had served up those instead of mouldy milk after every breakfast.

'Don't be stupid, they'd never let us out to go and buy some,' one of the girls was saying.

'Well, someone should bunk over the wall and get them for everyone,' said another.

'Yeah, right! And who'd dare to do that?'

'I will,' Netta said.

'Netta!' Peter said with fear and excitement tickling his face.

'But the deal is you all have to give me a little more than the price of a doughnut so I can get one for myself.'

'Ah that's not fair,' a boy said.

'Then get them yourself,' Netta said, hoping they wouldn't. She liked the idea of getting a doughnut for free. And if she made a habit of it, she thought, she might grow big enough to reach the train door handle in no time and then she wouldn't have to go all that way on the stinking tram every day.

'Yeah, that's fair,' said the girl who came up with the idea of bunking over the wall in the first place. 'That's her payment for taking the risk. She'll be the one who gets done if she's spotted, no one else.'

The boy thought about this for a moment with pursed lips then said, 'Oh all right then,' and dug around in his pocket for the necessary coins.

Netta collected up the money from everyone feeling like a rich and successful businessman then, with a foot on Peter's cupped hands and a quick look around the playground for any sign of the nuns, she scrambled over the wall.

The baker's wife who served behind the counter looked as if she'd eaten a plate full of smiles. She welcomed Netta into the shop and wasn't the least bit concerned about why this schoolgirl was not in school. I'd be as happy and kind as her, thought Netta as she left the shop with a bag full of doughnuts, if I worked in there all the time – I bet she can have as many cakes as she wants and she doesn't even have to pay for them, she marvelled as she blinked in the September sun and focused on the sight of Schwester Hildegarda and Schwester Anna marching towards her.

She shrank back instantly into the shop, reassuring herself that since they were deep in conversation neither nun had noticed her, but Hildegarda's gobbling reached her ears long before the teachers reached the shop and the sweet aroma in there suddenly turned sickly when Netta heard her say, 'Well, I don't think the Lord would condemn us for indulgence if we were to have just one more, do you? No one makes almond slices quite like this baker.'

Netta scrunched the bag tightly in her hands and spun round to face the baker's wife, looking for a back door. The lady smiled – she'd never stopped – and asked Netta if she had forgotten something. There was surely a back door beyond the counter where the baker worked, but she couldn't very well bolt through without permission; that might even be enough to wipe the smile from the baker's wife's face. And if she did ask for permission, the lady would know she was doing something naughty and would probably feel it was *her duty*, or some other strange thing like that which adults say when they get children into trouble, to hand Netta over to the nuns, who were now looking longingly in the window at the almond slices, as yet oblivious of their wayward student just beyond their focus.

Netta heard Schwester Anna say with a quivering voice, 'Oh, well, all right then. Come on!'

She looked with eyes fit to burst at the shopkeeper.

The shopkeeper's smile stayed on, but her brow furrowed a little, anxious to hear what it was Netta had forgotten.

Netta opened her mouth to speak. But she had no idea what it was she wanted to say. She took a step towards the counter. Flicked her eyes at the doorway to the back room. Heard the clip-clop of two pairs of sensible shoes in the doorway behind her and thought she was going to vomit.

'**H**ildegarda! Anna!'
The clip-clop of the shoes came to an abrupt halt just inside the door and Netta saw the shop-keeper's attention was now on the nuns, who she could tell from the sound of their voices had turned in the doorway to face the woman who had called their names.

'Mother Joseph,' Anna said, her voice quivering more than ever.

'Well, don't look so surprised to see me,' said the head-mistress of the school. 'It is I who should be surprised to find two of my staff indulging in cake just minutes before they are due to be in class teaching, standing up in front of young impressionable minds as fine examples of temperance and observance.'

'Y—y—yes, Mother,' Anna spluttered, 'but, you see, Schwester Hildegarda said—'

'I said no such thing!' Hildegarda gobbled more than ever, 'I was merely attempting to counsel Anna in the dangers of indulgence and get us both back to school as quickly as possible.'

Netta heard Anna gasp and Mother Joseph say, 'Well, despite your impressive prescience when it comes to what Anna is going to say, it seems, Hildegarda, you have failed to counsel well, as now you are both stood inside the baker's shop.'

An awful silence followed in which Netta was convinced all the nuns had turned to look at her, until Mother Joseph spoke again. 'Perhaps I can offer some more effective counsel to you both in my study later, but first I suggest you hurry along to your respective classes before you not only fail to be fine examples of temperance and observance, but of punctuality too.'

'Yes, Mother,' the nuns murmured and Netta heard the sensible shoes scurrying out of the shop.

She remained as still as a statue until she heard the third pair of shoes clip-clop away, then she felt as if her body was melting with relief.

'Was there anything else?' the baker's wife said, her permanent smile now seriously at odds with the rest of her face.

'No thank you,' Netta said and darted out of the shop and back over the wall, tossing the bag of bounty into Peter's waiting hands first.

'About time!' said the other boy.

'Oh shush!' Netta said, brushing off her uniform. 'You wouldn't dare do it.'

'Nice job, Netta,' said one of the girls.

'Yes, nice job,' Peter said, tucking into his doughnut and handing Netta's reward to her.

'Excellent!' said someone else.

'Netta's the best!' said another and, to Netta, the praise and attention tasted as good as the doughnut.

'They reckon the Allies are preparing to leave,' Karl said, tapping at the newspaper and looking over at his son in the other armchair. But Max had fallen asleep so Karl looked for someone else to tell the news to. 'They predict they'll be out of the country by the end of the year,' he said in Erika's direction, who sat at the table finishing up her notes.

'I'll believe it when I see it,' she said.

'If they do, it says, we'll have the right to rearm and become a fully-fledged member of the western alliance against the Soviet Union. Apparently the plan is that we'll be able to establish a military force of up to half a million men.' Karl's voiced trailed off and his gaze drifted over to his son again.

Erika followed his gaze and shared his fears, until Netta stomped into the room and plonked herself on the piano stool.

'Here she is!' Karl beamed. 'Big girl Netta from big school. How is it over there, my dear?'

'Rubbish,' Netta said, finding the darkest sounding chord she could on the keyboard.

'Shh!' her mother said, nodding at her sleeping father.

Netta huffed and stopped playing.

'What's so rubbish about it?' Karl folded the paper into his lap.

'Schwester Hildegarda, that's what.'

'One of your teachers?'

'If you can call her that. One of my *torturers,* more like.'

Erika scoffed at her daughter's histrionics, but Karl was intrigued.

'Why do you think she's a torturer, darling?'

'Because she *hurts* me.'

Erika kept her eyes on her notes, but her maternal ears were now trained on Netta.

'How?'

'She *wallops* me on the head with her pen when I can't get the answer to her stupid sums.'

In the armchair Max twitched in his sleep.

'With a pen?' Karl said doubtfully. 'Can you really wallop someone with a pen?'

'She can. She must have been practising for years. It really hurts, Opa. She *whacks* me all the time. I don't think she likes me. I'm sure the other kids don't get hit as much.'

Unnoticed, Max's head rolled to one side, then snapped back to the other. His hands jumped up from the arms of the chair, then settled uneasily back again.

'And most of the time she gets it all caught up in my hair and then *rips* it out.'

Netta's words were pouring into her father's ears and dyeing his dreams the colour of pain.

He is back in the office in Gegesha, having been dragged out of his bunk in the early hours by two guards as Edgar shouted after them, 'Where are you taking him? What are you doing, you bastards!' He is choking on the floor from the way they've used his shirt as a leash and a Lieutenant is firing questions at him about his father-in-law, a Captain of the Border Guard. Then Volkov's hands are round his neck and Max's blood boils at the filthy touch of the man that murdered his brother Horst. He tries to resist, but the sergeant brings his knee up into Max's face. Max shrieks with the pain and collapses to the floor. There's a jangling and scraping above as a huge bunch of keys on the desk is grabbed and brought down on his head.

'Tell us the truth!'

Ch-mp.

'Tell us the truth!'

Ch-mp.

'Tell us!'

Ch-mp, 'Tell us!' *Ch-mp, ch-mp.* The keys bite into the ball of human on the ground.

Max puts his hands over his head until they curl up, bruised and bleeding. Then only his skull is left to protect him from death as the keys thump into him again and again. The barracks key, the office key, the solitary key, the kitchen key, the key to the storerooms, the key to the locksmith's workshop, the key to the armoured car, the key to the main gate, the key to freedom – that's what each and every one of them is. Where once he thought the guards brandished them to keep him captive, now he knows that all together and wielded like a multi-headed mace, rapped over his head until his skull caves in, they are in fact the keys to freedom, because death is the only road to freedom now.

'Look!' cried Netta and leant forward to show Karl and Erika her sore scalp and the clump missing from her hair.

Erika gasped at the sight of her daughter's vandalised body.

Max gasped as he tried to break the surface of his nightmare, but still being beaten by the demons there he lashed out at them in one last desperate attempt to free himself and miraculously sent Volkov flying across the office.

'Max!'

He woke to find Erika kneeling beside him, cuts in his knuckles and his mother's favourite vase in pieces on the living room floor.

Nearly every morning break time it was the same routine: Netta would collect up everyone's money, slip over the wall, buy a bag full of doughnuts from the smileful shopkeeper and reap the rewards, both in sugar and in attention, back in the playground. The only thing that was thankfully never the same as the first time was the arrival of those two nuns.

The whacks on the head from Schwester Hildegarda's pen became a routine too and, although the pain never ceased to shock Netta, she began in a strange way to enjoy the attention that this brought her from the other kids as well. She was admired for the beatings she took and the way she never cried, no matter how much she felt like she wanted to inside sometimes, which clearly annoyed Schwester Hildegarda, who would then try and think of more and more callous ways for Netta to earn a beating sooner.

'Anetta, if x equals 3y minus z, what is the value of x when y is 4 and z is 1?'

Netta's eyes bulged as her brain tried to cope with all the information the Schwester fired at her. 'Pardon, Schwester Hildegarda?'

The nun sighed dramatically then gobbled out the question again, but much faster this time. 'If x equals 3y minus z, what is the value of x when y is 4 and z is 1?'

Netta grabbed her pencil and began to try and write down the question.

'Do not write it down! If your big head cannot handle a simple little question like this perhaps you are in the wrong school. Now for the final time...' And as Hildegarda rattled off the question once more, Netta looked around for inspiration and saw Peter mouthing something to her from his desk at the front of the class. She missed it so he began again with a wide mouth, not unlike the baker's wife's smile, but, whether by accident or design, her teacher's big black plumage swished in the way and blocked the rest of Peter's answer.

What number begins with a smile, Netta thought frantically, one, two, three, four? No, they're all pursed lips and tongues. Five, six, seven. Hildegarda raised her pen. Eight! Eight begins with a smile, she thought jubilantly, and since she didn't have the time to explore any further numbers, she blurted out quickly, 'Eight. The answer's eight.'

'Idiot!' the nun spat and the pen whipped at Netta's scalp. 'Mary?'

'Eleven,' Mary answered in a flash and Netta winced both with the pain and the realisation that eleven begins with a smile too and it was only three away from eight. If only she'd had a little more time!

That break time Netta was still so furious with her Maths teacher that she didn't eat her doughnut as usual.

'Not hungry?' Peter's words were muffled, his mouth stuffed with warm dough, but Netta understood him.

'Yeah,' Netta said, 'but I'm going to eat mine in class.'

'What?' Mary squeaked through lips ringed with sugar.

Netta was sick of Hildegarda showing her up in front of the class. It was time for her to up the ante even more – show the stupid nun she wasn't afraid of her, and wring even more admiration and attention from her classmates.

The air in the next Maths class was fizzing with the anticipation of Netta's latest dare. Everyone had heard about it and they could barely sit still in their seats or concentrate on their sums. Even her brightest students were making silly mistakes and Schwester Hildegarda could sense the atmosphere; sense there was something she didn't know, but ought to.

She stopped attacking the blackboard with chalk and spun round to face the class. Some of the students at the front snapped their heads back to the blackboard so she knew the font of this disorder was somewhere near the back. She eyed the far rows, but there was no sign of trouble, even from Anetta Portner, so she went back to scribbling out equations.

That was when Netta eased the slightly squashed doughnut from her pocket and, when enough kids had turned to look at her again, took a big, pantomime bite from it. With her nose in the air she chewed it slowly like a cow, savouring every moment and sending electric shocks of fearful thrills through her classmates. Some of that electricity reached the teacher and she turned to find out where it was coming from. But by this time, of course, Netta's doughnut was back in her pocket and her jaw still.

'Copy the equations into your books,' Hildegarda said suspiciously. 'Then get on with solving them. You have ten minutes,' she said as she sat, opened a Bible at Deuteronomy and read:

If a man has a stubborn and rebellious son who will not obey the voice of his father or the voice of his mother, and, though they discipline him, will not listen to them, then his father and his mother shall take hold of him and bring him out to the elders of his city at the gate of the place where he lives, and they shall say to the elders of his city, 'This our son is stubborn and rebellious; he will not obey our voice; he is a glutton and a drunkard.' Then all the men of the city shall stone him to death with stones. So you shall purge the evil from your midst...

She stopped and looked up as that spark of rebellion reached her again. This time she spotted a blur of movement at the back somewhere around Anetta. She stood up and silently stepped between the desks where everyone was busy scribbling into their books, even Anetta. She stopped at Mary's desk. Mary looked up briefly, then carried on solving equations. The nun moved on to Boris's desk. Boris didn't even acknowledge her presence; he was far too busy trying to finish on time. She moved on to Anetta's desk and felt the entire class behind her turning to watch. Hildegarda examined the girl's exercise book. Anetta, of course, had barely begun to solve the first equation, but what intrigued her teacher was the glistening of her fingers holding the pencil. The nun stood there for a while until Netta looked up at the giant turkey towering over her and smiled utterly insincerely and with what appeared to be swollen cheeks.

'Everything all right, Anetta?' Hildegarda asked with unusual concern for her student.

Netta nodded, her lips tightly sealed; lips, Hildegarda observed, which sparkled with sugar.

'I asked you a question, Anetta. At least have the courtesy to answer me.'

Hildegarda heard a collective intake of breath from the children who thought she was unaware of them and saw Netta move her jaw slowly and awkwardly, her tongue shifting the pulpy contents of her mouth out of the way so she could mumble, 'I. Am. Fine. Thank—'

Schwester Hildegarda grabbed Netta's mouth between her claws, prising it open and displaying the evidence for all to see. Netta nearly choked and inadvertently spat pieces of chewed up doughnut in her teacher's direction. Hildegarda stepped back to avoid the offending mess, releasing Netta from her grasp, who then swallowed and, incredibly to both her teacher and her classmates, giggled as she licked her lips.

'You repulsive little creature,' the nun cried, 'I have never known such wicked behaviour from a pupil of mine.'

Netta was ready for the wallop, but it was a small price to pay, she felt, for such a wonderful scene.

However, Schwester Hildegarda was not brandishing her pen, nor did she return to the desk to retrieve it. She just stood quietly for a moment then said something which pulled the rug out, quite violently, from underneath any sense of triumph Netta was feeling right then. 'Let's see what your father has to say about this behaviour then, shall we?' And as she walked to the classroom door on her way to make the telephone call, she was heard by some of the gobsmacked children to be muttering, 'So you shall purge the evil from your midst.'

Max was furious. He was just about to leave the surgery to spend the afternoon doing house calls; house calls that would now be delayed and add hours onto his working day, not to mention indignation onto already impatient patients. Erika had a full appointment book for the surgery so couldn't do any of the home visits for him. All she could offer were pleas to drive safely as he yanked the motorbike from the shed and made the engine roar on his behalf. At least going on the bike he would be able to cut through the traffic and get to the school and back a lot quicker than if he went in the car.

As he zoomed over the bridge, a memory raced through him on the wind bawling in his ears. It was of another bridge and another motorbike.

The bridge is over the river Oder in Breslau. And the motorbike has been abandoned among the bodies and debris of a fierce battle which took place there before he and the rest of the prisoners were herded there by their Russian captors.

The prisoners have all been stripped of their overcoats, watches and laces, and Max is shaking with fear, assuming they are all about to be executed. But then the trucks arrive and he sees the prisoners at the front being ordered to climb into them, and he knows it is not his time to die. Not yet. He sees that some of his comrades ahead of him have realised this too; realised they will be needing something to replace the stuff Ivan has just taken from them, so they crouch down and strip the coats from the corpses, pulling off boots from stiff-ankled feet. Max spots the motorbike lying in the dirt with a leather jacket still wrapped around the handle bars where the owner had hung it just before they were attacked. He was glad he didn't have to take it from a dead man. Looking at the rest of his unit stripping the bodies, they seem to him to have acquired his detached clinical attitude to cadavers, an attitude he is quickly losing.

One of the trucks honks its horn.

But it wasn't a truck; it was a car on the bridge in Mengede. Max had drifted across the road and was heading straight for it. The car honked its horn again and brought Max back to the present just in time for him to swerve out of the way and he skidded to a halt by the side of the road.

His heart was racing. He shook the past from his head, slapped his own face in anger and an effort to keep himself alert, and set off again more furious than ever now that this interruption to his day nearly cost him his life.

He was shown to Netta's Maths classroom by a young nun, who hung around in the doorway after, eager to watch the fireworks, no doubt, until an older nun, who introduced herself to him as Schwester Hildegarda, barked at her to run along.

Netta sat behind a desk at the front, her head drooping, wringing her hands in a way which worried Max; worried him because she was clearly frightened of one of the two adults in this room, if not both, and he didn't want it to be him.

'Dr Portner,' he said, shaking the nun's icy hand.

'Well, Dr Portner, I am very sorry to have dragged you all the way over here in the middle of the day...'

Dragged? Max thought this was an interesting choice of words. There was no way this woman could have dragged him anywhere, but he had a feeling she liked to believe she could, and that she liked to practise on little girls.

'...But I think you would want to know just what your daughter has been up to.'

'I would like to know that, yes,' he said to the top of Netta's bowed head, 'as it must be very serious for you not to be able to tell me over the phone.'

The nun's perennially red face blanched and rippled ever so slightly at this, but she soon regained her composure and announced, 'Anetta is not the brightest student in my class, to put it mildly, Doctor, and yet she thinks she can afford to daydream and misbehave instead of applying herself.'

'Hmm.'

'Today in class I'm afraid this insolence of hers reached its zenith when she thought it appropriate to eat this.' She produced exhibit A from the drawer in her desk.

Max examined the half-eaten doughnut then his daughter. He had to smother a grin, not just at the absurd histrionics with which the nun had produced such an inoffensive article, but at the thought of Netta enjoying food at last.

Schwester Hildegarda crashed on. 'For the drunkard and the glutton will come to poverty,' she said in Netta's direction, 'and slumber will clothe them with rags. Proverbs, twenty-three.'

Max was not impressed. Hildegarda noticed from the corner of her eye so tried something else, which, when Mother Joseph quoted it to her the other day after their run-in in the baker's, impressed her deeply. 'For many, of whom I have often told you and now tell you even with tears, walk as enemies of the cross of Christ. Their end is destruction, their god is their belly,' she said, grabbing the doughnut and waving it in Netta's face, 'and they glory in their shame, with minds set on earthly things.'

'I am not sure Netta's god has ever been her belly, Schwester Hildegarda,' Max began with a smirk.

'Well, she did indeed glory in her shame, Doctor Portner. She laughed at me, would you believe, in front of the whole class when I caught her in this gluttonous act.'

Max *could* believe it. He found her laughable too.

'Is not life more than food?' she quoted.

'Not when you're starving,' Max mumbled as he crossed his arms.

'Food will not commend us to God,' she said, still brandishing the squashed half-doughnut.

He was thinking of Gegesha. God, food, God, food. I know which one I would have chosen on those dark famished days, he said to himself.

'But I say, walk by the Spirit,' she continued, pacing up and down in front of Max and Netta, 'and you will not gratify the desires of the flesh. For the desires of the flesh are against the Spirit, and the desires of the Spirit are against the flesh, for these are opposed to each other, to keep you from doing the things you want to do. But if you are led by the Spirit, you are not under the law. Now the works of the flesh are evident: sexual immorality, impurity, sensuality, idolatry, sorcery, enmity, strife, jealousy, fits of anger, rivalries, dissensions, divisions, envy, drunkenness, orgies, and things like these...'

Max flinched with every word in her list, not just because they were so irrelevant to Netta's predicament, but because some of them touched a nerve in him and made him wonder if the nun had not really brought him here to chastise him rather than his daughter.

'...I warn you, as I warned you before, that those who do such things will not inherit the kingdom of God. Galatians five, sixteen to twenty-six, Doctor.'

Max was speechless, but that was fine by Hildegarda because she hadn't finished.

'Did you or your wife supply Netta with such an... indulgence?' She probed the thick air between them with the doughnut.

Max suddenly felt what it was like for the children in her class to be on the receiving end of this teacher's temper and answered swiftly, 'No, we did not.'

'No, I thought not. It looks like something that is made in the baker's shop next door, so I am reliably informed, which tells me that Netta must have left the school grounds today without permission to obtain it. Yet another misdemeanour to add to the catalogue. So, what do you have to say for yourself, Anetta? What do you have to say to me and your father who has had to take time out of his busy day healing the sick to come and witness this?'

I'm not sure I *had* to take time out of my busy day healing the sick to come and witness this, Max grumbled inwardly.

'Sorry,' Netta mumbled and began to quietly cry.

Hildegarda inflated herself triumphantly at the sight of the little girl's tears, as if they were *her* food. Max observed all this clearly. He observed the way she softened her approach, now she felt she had won, and cooed at Netta, 'What does Proverbs twenty-eight tell us, mmm? The one who keeps the law is a son with understanding, but a companion of gluttons shames his father.'

'Well, I don't think we need to go that far,' Max interjected, 'I am certainly not ashamed of my daughter.'

Netta looked up at him for the first time and he gave her a comforting wink, but the nun carried on utterly oblivious of his words. 'Do you not know that you are God's temple, Anetta, and that God's Spirit dwells in you? If anyone destroys God's temple,' she said, waving the doughnut in the girl's face again, 'God will destroy him. For God's temple is holy, and you are that temple. One Corinthians, chapter three, verses sixteen to seventeen.'

Max had heard enough. 'Indeed she is God's temple,' he said calmly, but firmly, 'so who in their right mind would dare to think of destroying it in this way?' He stepped towards his daughter and separated her hair where the scalp was still sore from Hildegarda's pen and a clump of hair clearly missing. He stared at the nun waiting for an answer. The teacher was suddenly struck dumb. Her great inflated plumage wilted. Her red face paled. She tried to say something, but only the weak gobbling of a disorientated turkey came out of her mouth, and he quickly silenced that with his final words to her:

'Not many of you should become teachers, my brothers, for you know that we who teach will be judged with greater strictness. James, chapter three, verse one.'

He held out his hand to Netta. She grasped it in both of hers and they left the nun alone with the half-eaten doughnut, which she stared at in great dread for a minute or so before devouring it with a libidinous moan.

'Papa, where are we going? School's not finished yet.' Max looked down at his daughter as they stood hand in hand on the front steps of the school and smiled. 'It is for today.' Then his face dropped in mock dejection. 'Unless you'd rather spend the afternoon with Schwester Whatshername instead of your papa?'

Netta giggled and squeezed his hand to show where her preference lay. 'But what about you? Don't you have to go to work?'

Max took a sharp breath in as the thought of his normal routine threatened to mar his effort at spontaneity. He looked up at the sky, as if the weather had the answer to this dilemma. The sun was slicing through the clouds invitingly. 'Well, I think Frau Beltz and the rest of them will survive if they have to wait until tomorrow to see me, don't you? I don't know about you but I'd rather go for a spin on the bike.'

Netta stood on tip-toe as her body stretched full of excitement. She hugged his arm and cheered, 'Yes!'

They scampered down the steps together and hopped on, Netta in front of her father, encased in his arms as he steered out of the school grounds and hurtled off through the streets of Dortmund, going recklessly fast on purpose every so often because it made Netta squeal with joy every time he accelerated. The sound of her elation was intoxicating, even more so knowing it was he who was responsible for it.

After half an hour of riding, with Erika's pleas to drive safely still ringing in his ears, Max thought he should quit while they were both still in one piece and he stopped, with a little skid as a final gift to Netta, much to the disgust of a middle aged lady with a bag full of shopping who was walking on the pavement nearby.

'Where are we?' Netta asked, reluctant to get off.

'Well, I thought since you didn't get to finish all of your doughnut you might like some more here,' and he gestured to the ice cream parlour behind them as a ring master does to his circus acts.

Netta looked stunned. Max felt a tide of anxiety wash over him. She doesn't want to, he thought. She's not interested in food after all. Not even ice cream. I've ruined our afternoon already. Or perhaps it's me. She never seems to be comfortable eating around—

Netta's eyes bulged. 'Yes please!' She licked her lips theatrically and skipped off ahead of Max, who shook his head at his own neurosis and at this little wonder he had played a part in creating, but who was so much more than the sum of him and Erika.

He continued to marvel at her as they devoured cake and ice cream together. He marvelled at the white moustache which soon formed over her lip and how acceptable it was, if not beautiful. He chuckled at the thought of himself sitting here in the café with an ice cream moustache and wondered at what age it became unacceptable to have one.

'Schwester Hildegarda *is* horrible to me, but I did eat the doughnut in her class on purpose, to be naughty.' Netta's tongue was loosened by the flood of sugar through her veins and the renewed affection in her father's manner toward her.

'And where did you get the doughnut from?' Max asked, trying to keep a straight face – not wanting to appear angry and destroy the bridges they were building, nor too amused by her antics, as any responsible father shouldn't be, although he was.

'I climb over the wall at break time and buy doughnuts from the baker's for lots of the kids.'

'Ah.'

'And they buy me one as a reward for daring to do it,' she added quickly in an effort to impress her father with her bravery and her thrift.

He shovelled some ice cream into his mouth to smother a smirk. 'Well,' he said, 'thank you for being honest with me about it, Netta. And although you must stop being naughty in school, you also need to know that there is no excuse for that teacher to harm you like she does. And if she does it again, you come and tell me and I'll be over to that school like a shot.'

'OK.' Netta nodded at her cake, trying to hide the sparkle in her eyes at the thought of her papa going to tell Schwester Hildegarda off again.

'Do you find Maths very hard?' Max asked softly.

'Yeah, I really do.' Netta kept her eyes shamefully on her bowl.

'Well, perhaps I can ask Opa to give you some extra help sometimes, and then you'll be so clever your teacher will have no excuse to be horrible to you, what about that? Eh?'

Netta looked up to answer her father and was stunned to see him sitting back in his chair with ice cream smeared all around his mouth and a silly grin on his face.

'Papa!'

'What?' he said, relishing her amused embarrassment.

She picked a napkin from the holder and stretched across to wipe his mouth for him. He leaned back further out of reach. 'What are you doing? I'm fine,' he laughed, 'I don't need a napkin.'

'Papa!' She giggled and jiggled about.

Max caught the eye of a young couple watching him. They exchanged smiles and on this abnormal afternoon, he felt more normal, more stable, more at home than he ever had since he'd come back from Siberia.

'Come on!' he said, wiping his mouth. 'I know where we can go next.'

Netta was so beguiled by her father's new energy now she even left some ice cream in the bottom of her bowl in order to keep up with him. They crossed the busy street eventually and headed towards an enormous building which loomed over an intersection. It reminded Netta of their own home, but an upside-down version: the long, severe, dour looking windows made up most of its façade, but the ground floor was where its version of the Tiffany window was – rows and rows of brightly lit windows, in fact, which stretched down the street, but instead of stained glass Netta could see straight through to the fashionably dressed mannequins and the mountains of cakes inside.

Max furtively examined Netta's reaction as they approached the entrance of the Karstadt department store. She looked excited and yet a little unsure whether she was really invited to the party which surely waited for them beyond the double doors.

'Mama hates shopping,' Max informed her, 'and since we don't have anyone to help us these days I reckon it should be you and I that do that job from now on, eh? Don't you?'

Netta nodded frantically, lest any other reaction stop her papa from carrying on through the doors. He grinned and ushered her through, out of the sunlight and into the artificial glow of an Aladdin's cave. Both father and daughter stood there agape for a moment. For Max, it was by no means the first time he had been here, but the presence of his overwhelmed little girl next to him seemed to give him permission for the first time to be overwhelmed too, by the sheer abundance of stuff, of clothes, of food – and the utter cruelty of the imbalance of things in the world almost sent him running back out into the street. More people came through the doors behind them and a sharp tut at this inconsiderate man and his little girl standing in the way pierced any images of skeletal men dressed in rags which threatened to fog this golden moment for him.

'Come on,' he whispered, as he tended to in church, and led her towards the grocery.

Netta stepped carefully among the towers of tins and the pyramids of fruit. Glass cases shone with the treasures inside – mountains of butter and more cheeses than Netta knew existed.

'What do you think we should get?' Max asked her. With

his own Biblical warning to Schwester Hildegarda ringing in his ears still, he was trying to involve her, empower her as he taught her, and therefore make food something she had some control over, not something that was merely forced on her.

'Is that butter?' Netta asked, not wanting to appear foolish, but doubtful that something so big could be just butter.

'It is. Should we get some?'

She nodded and just as she was wondering how they would transport such a heap home, with a word from her papa, the man behind the counter scooped off a small section of it and began to beat it with a wooden paddle, which would have filled Netta with fear and visions of the crow lady on the Isle of Sylt, had the shopkeeper not carried out his work with an amused squint and a wink at Netta. She watched in awe as this shapeless blob was transformed by the harshest of experiences into a perfectly solid and sturdy form.

'Some cheese?' Max asked Netta as he took the kilo of butter from the shopkeeper.

She could only nod again. Some cheese would be great, she thought, but which one? There were too many to choose from.

'What about some quark?' her papa said, pointing at a glass bowl full of wet white lumps which reminded Netta of the congealed edges of the glass of double cream Frau Auttenberg used to set before her every breakfast time.

'Hmm,' she said politely before allowing herself to be distracted by a more attractive looking slab of yellow cheese encased in a dark, rich looking rind. 'What about this one?'

'The Rauchkäse?' the shopkeeper asked Max.

'OK,' Max murmured doubtfully.

'Perhaps the young lady would like to try some first?' And the shopkeeper cut a slither from the block and handed it to Netta, who felt very important, not just because she was called a young lady, but because she didn't see anyone else being allowed to try the cheeses before they'd even bought some!

Luckily for Netta, the cheese reminded her of sausages and bacon, so she could tell the shopkeeper with all the authority of a young lady that the cheese was good and they took a kilo of that too.

They bought bread and fruit and vegetables, and since Max had come without a shopping bag, they even bought two new bags to carry it all in – one each. As they finally came back out onto the street, Max looked down at Netta doing her best to look unruffled by the load she was carrying. 'You wait here with both the bags,' he said, relieved to be putting the heaviest one down, 'and I'll bring the bike to you. That way we don't have to carry these all the way down the street, OK?'

'OK,' she echoed.

'I'll be very quick. Don't move.'

Netta watched him run and weave his way through the crowds. He was so fast! She watched him cross the busy street where cars and lorries zoomed towards him. He was so brave! She could just about see him still when he reached the bike outside the ice cream parlour and she thought she heard it roar into life, but there were so many other vehicles going by it could have been one of them.

He sat on his bike, revving the engine and waiting for a rare gap in the traffic flowing away from the Karstadt so he could pull out across to the other side of the road and drive up to where Netta stood. He could just about make out her blonde hair reflecting the sun. Blonde hair like his. Nothing like her mother's raven hair. He found himself drawing breath deeply at the thought of Erika, as if he had just injected himself with an opiate. He could see Erika, nearly a decade before, on a street on the other end of the country, a cobbled street with a little brook running through it, waiting for him to come out of the bar where they had just heard his favourite poet reading. He had thought she was feeling sick and had left to get some fresh air, but it turned out that she, still flailing about in formative doubt, felt like he was forcing this poet's anti-establishment words down her throat and was sulking outside in the street. When he found her outside, they had argued about religion and the Nazis and it was like a knife in his guts.

'Bloody Hell!' she'd mumbled. 'Trust me to fall in love with a...' She'd stopped herself from spitting on his religion then. She'd waited for his question: *With a what? With a what?* But it never came. Because all he had heard was the notion that she had fallen in love with him. He had taken off his glasses then, instinctively because he was finding it hard to see, his eyes were so full of tears and his heart felt so big that he didn't know if he could carry it all the way home. Their friendship and their differences had kept them skipping through the streets and hopping over the brooks since they had met and yet now they had introduced love into the equation, actually articulated it and let it hang in the air between them, everything felt so much heavier and serious, as if the skipping and the hopping were done. The differences now seemed like ravines that needed to be negotiated, not things to laugh at and celebrate.

And yet here he was looking at the fruit of their negotiations, standing patiently for him outside the department store and his heart swelled so much it seemed to restrict his windpipe. He couldn't wait to get home and embrace Erika. He knew she would be surprised, after his recent behaviour, but he had an overwhelming desire to just lie on their bed, wrap himself around her and kiss that raven hair again and again.

He saw his moment and pulled out across the traffic, keeping his eye on the beacon of his daughter's hair. And in doing so, neglected to judge the distance between him and the lorry eager to make its delivery at the Karstadt. As he tried to accelerate away from it, the lorry ploughed into the back wheel of Max's bike.

Netta watched as the lorry seemed to bite down on the bike, rip at it with its metal teeth for a moment before it and her papa were swallowed by the beast. There was a great groaning sound from the road and screaming from some shoppers, then Netta saw her papa being dragged along the road under this awful monster's belly. The great metal brute lurched about like a ship on rough seas and eventually came to a halt right outside the Karstadt vomiting out its human meal, which went hurtling across the pavement and slamming into the wall of the store where it finally came to rest.

Netta felt her body empty of everything – blood, breath, even piss. She stood completely still as the world rushed around her, elbows and hips bumped her as adults ran to help the man who'd been mown down by the lorry, whose driver climbed from his cab on jelly legs, tugging at his hair and shrugging at the few people who were looking his way.

All eyes were on Netta's papa. She shifted her gaze to him too, or rather the mush of man on the pavement like a bloody pile of quark. Why didn't he get up and brush off his trousers and come over to make sure she was all right? He had told her not to move, told her he'd be right back. She had all the shopping with her and they had to get it home soon before the butter went too soft.

Someone was taking charge. It wasn't a policeman. The man was dressed in normal clothes. He was ordering people about and telling them to get out of the way. It reminded Netta of what Uncle Edgar had said the first time he came for a dinner party – that when her papa was a boy of sixteen he was at the theatre with Tante Bertel when a tram collided with a beer lorry in the street outside. Tante Bertel was the first to get out there and start helping the injured. She told her papa to grab a ladder from beside one of the shops and to help carry the injured up to the Klinik. The man was taking charge just like Tante Bertel did. Uncle Edgar said that Bertel was her papa's inspiration. That she made him want to become a doctor.

Netta picked up her bag and dragged the heavier one across the pavement to get closer to her papa and the crowd which was beginning to swallow him up. He was a doctor. His job was to make sick people better. He couldn't get hurt himself, Netta reasoned, because who could fix the doctor if the doctor was broken? She looked about her for a ladder that she could use as a stretcher to take her papa to hospital, but there was none. She started to panic as the wail of an ambulance echoed down the street. Uncle Edgar worked at the hospital, didn't he? He was a doctor too. Perhaps he could help her papa, she thought, then panicked even more because she didn't know where the hospital was and what part of the hospital Uncle Edgar worked in. Her mama was a doctor too, she remembered. Surely she could help him, but she was at home and home was so far away and how could she let her mama know that Papa was... she peered through the legs at the face of her father, bloody, slashed, eyes closed, mouth open, looking as if he was... Netta began to weep, but the cry of the approaching ambulance drowned her out. Two men in white suits hurried from the van and set about transferring her papa to a stretcher. They seemed to be careful but every movement caused her papa to scream with a gurgly voice. The first scream from him told Netta that he was alive and this hushed her sobs for a moment, but every awful groan of pain from him thereafter set her off again, her bawling mounting until she felt a big soft hand on her shoulder.

'Hey, my dear,' the owner of the hand said, a smooth-skinned, round-faced old woman, 'is that your papa there?'

Netta nodded, rubbing furiously at her eyes, as the men in white suits loaded him into the van.

'Hang on!' the woman called out to the ambulance men, 'this little girl is his daughter.'

'So bring her along to the Klinik, or call her mother.'

'I have no idea who she is or where her mother is, she needs to come with you.'

'We need to work on this man. We've no room for a little girl.'

'Are you working on him in the back there?'

'Clearly,' said the impatient man in white, hanging a glass bottle from the ceiling of the little van.

'And your colleague is driving, isn't he?'

'Yes.'

'So there's room in the front for this little girl then, isn't there,' the woman said, shepherding Netta into the front seat of the ambulance next to a confused looking driver.

'There you go, darling.' The woman smiled at Netta in a way that reminded her of her Oma, as she packed the two shopping bags around her feet. 'When you get to the Klinik you can ask someone to call your mother, OK?'

'OK,' Netta mumbled, her mind a tumbling mess of faces and situations she didn't recognise, and the woman slammed the door.

'Who's there?'

'It's me, Bertel,' Martha said peering round the bedroom door, 'it's Martha.'

'Well, I can see it's you, can't I, now you're here.'

'Just making sure,' Martha sighed. 'Everything all right?'

'Prop me up, would you, I've slipped down the bed again.'

Martha approached the bed with a smile, but her silence spoke volumes to Bertel.

'I don't slip down the bed on purpose, you know.'

'I never said you did.'

'You think I like asking for help all the time?' Bertel tutted as Martha's considerable bosom was pressed in her face.

'I'm sure you don't,' Martha said, delving behind Bertel to rearrange the pillows.

'I was the one who always did the helping, now I just have to watch and listen.'

'And talk,' Martha chuckled. 'At least you can still have a good go at talking, eh?'

'My mind is clear...'

Out of sight as she hauled Bertel about, Martha raised a sarcastic eyebrow.

'...My eyes are sharp, my ears are good. The least I can ask for is to be propped up so I can see. See them watching the house.'

'Who's watching the house, Bertel?' Martha sighed as she straightened her sister's nightdress.

'Hear them crying and thumping about up there.'

'Up where?'

'How is it being on the other side of the fence?' Edgar smiled reassuringly down at Max, 'Probing thermometers, bedpans, enemas, other people's repulsive noises, and, worst of all, tepid Ovaltine?'

Max just moaned in response where he lay in bed, every inch of him covered in bandages and casts except for his eyes and lips.

'You've been keeping us busy today in orthopaedics,' Edgar joked, trying his best to keep his voice from belying his true feelings, his shock at the state of his friend, his fears for Max's future.

'Did I... was it... I think...'

'Don't try and talk, Max. You're so full of morphine, you won't make any sense anyway,' Edgar grinned. 'Just listen. The good news is we saved your leg. The bad news is the pin we used to keep your leg on with went through one of your kidneys. Well, that was Dr Müller, not me, of course. I wouldn't have been such a rubbish shot, but you know Müller, he will not be told. He's the chief, no one can do it better than him. Pah! So you might have to make do without that kidney, but the really good news is, you have another one!' Edgar laughed.

Max mumbled, 'Did I hit her?'

'What?' Edgar leant over the bed.

'I hit her.'

'No, no, you didn't. Netta's waiting outside. Shall I bring her in? She's quite safe.'

'But I'm sure—'

'Max, no one else got hurt in the accident. Don't worry. The morphine is going to jumble your thoughts and memories all over the place. You're going to hallucinate. It's all part of the process. Just relax and enjoy the ride.'

'You're home now and you're around people that care for you.' Karin looked at him, on his knees in front of her, and marvelled that there could be such a difference between mother and son.

'And don't concern yourself with work until you're ready. We'll all survive for a day or two,' Max said with a consolatory chuckle.

Martha stayed out of sight in the kitchen preparing dinner, but her ears were trained on the mutterings from the living room like a seasoned intelligence operative.

Netta sat at the piano, hands resting on the keys, but she was glaring over her shoulder at the stupid girl who had stolen her father away from her just at the moment they were finally beginning to connect.

Erika stood in the hallway, unable to enter the room or go back to the surgery, stunned by the vision of her husband on his knees in front of the bloody charwoman, holding her hands as once he did Erika's on the stairs in front of their digs after the summer ball where they first kissed.

For one who had just broken up with her gentleman friend, Karin was curiously buoyant. She busied herself with the housework and, if Netta wasn't mistaken, was doing so with a hint of a song in her throat and the smudge of a smile on her lips. But then Netta was six, going on seven, so what could she be expected to know about ladies and their gentlemen friends?

It was summer now, school was closed for the holidays, and Netta was in the dining room still trying to finish her lunch. Everyone else had gone, but she had to stay, her papa had grumbled, until she ate all her food. How could she possibly finish all that when she just wasn't even hungry? So she'd learnt by now how to secretly stuff some food into her cheeks and spit it out later when the coast was clear. Which is what she was doing when Karin bowled in with a satisfied sigh saying, 'I'm going to the bakery, Netta. Do you want to come? I'm going to buy a nice cake for your father.'

Netta was disturbed by this information, the latter statement, the kind of statement you hear from your mama, not from the housekeeper. But she disguised her perturbation as mere puzzlement, inducing Karin to elucidate.

'It's to say thank you to him, for being so understanding about... you know, when I was... upset the other day.'

Netta glanced at the clock on the wall and with a glee in her heart that almost shocked herself she announced, 'It shuts soon. You won't make it.'

'But it's only twenty to one, my love. You remember how to tell time I hope?'

I am not your love, Netta thought as she tongued the food deeper into her cheeks, and yes I know how to tell time!

'It shuts at one o'clock every Wednesday because Herr Brant goes to Essen to see his mother and buy more flour,' she said carefully so none of the food fell out of its hiding place.

'Oh. Well, I better get going then, hadn't I.' The smile was fast disappearing from Karin's face, much to Netta's delight. But Karin, in her new haste, had seemed to have forgotten all about Netta coming along with her and Netta, again surprised by her own feelings, found that to be quite irritating.

'I can show you a short cut, if you like.'

'A short cut?'

'I know around here better than anyone.'

'I'm sure you do, my love, but—'

'You won't make it otherwise,' Netta said jumping up from the stool. 'I'll just go to the toilet first.'

She hurried to the toilet, ejected each horrid bolus from her mouth, flushed and rushed out to lead the way before Karin could decide to go on her own the usual route.

S omeone was watching the house.

The terraced red brick house on three floors in the suburb of Mengede in the heart of the Ruhr district. Sulphurous clouds draped the rooftop and thick soot lined the windowsills, even on the pretty, round Tiffany window in the attic.

The watcher started as the front door opened and a boyish young woman, as gaunt as the house itself, was led out by a little girl with golden locks.

'It's quicker if you go by the canal,' the girl said.

The boyish woman looked doubtful, but followed the girl anyway.

That must be Max's daughter, Jenny, the watcher, said to herself with wonder and envy churning together in her guts. And is that his wife? Jenny asked herself. She'd expected her to look more beautiful, more feminine, someone who would be more of a rival, physically at least. Part of her was offended that Max would marry a thing like that, because perhaps he thought Jenny was in the same league – and we clearly aren't, are we, she worried. And part of her rejoiced at what she thought would be an easy war to win – if that ugly little thing is all I have to contend with, she sneered.

'Jenny, Jenny, come on,' Isabel hissed as she tottered across the street from the corner shop. 'Someone's going to call the police or something soon if you keep doing that. Can't you be more subtle about it than just standing around on the street like that?'

'I'm just looking. No crime in that, is there?' Jenny tutted but let herself be tugged by Isabel down the street.

'You need to stop mooning over that bloke and think about getting a job. If I can manage it, you certainly can.'

'I don't want to be a housekeeper. Can you see me as a housekeeper?'

'Then find something else, but make it snappy. I can't keep bailing you out forever.'

'All right,' Jenny huffed and threw one more glance over her shoulder at the little girl leading the pasty skinny woman down the towpath.

Netta stared at the cloudy water as they hurried along the path. She remembered how scared she had been when she fell in after racing down the hill from the woods; when Peter and Josef had pulled her out.

'Can you swim?' she asked Karin.

'Pardon me?' Karin was focused on getting to the bakery on time and was fast becoming anxious that this wasn't such a short cut after all.

'Can you swim?'

'No. I can't.' Then she added irritably, 'Don't tell me your short cut involves swimming to the baker's shop?'

Someone was watching the house.

The terraced red brick house on three floors in the suburb of Mengede in the heart of the Ruhr district. Sulphurous clouds draped the rooftop and thick soot lined the windowsills, even on the pretty, round Tiffany window in the attic.

Rodrick, the watcher, was drunk, but aware of his own great hulking form enough to keep himself in the shadow of the trees. There were too many people hanging around: the soldier; that blonde standing on the corner and that other woman coming out of the sweet shop.

He hadn't done a stroke of work since Karin told him she didn't want to see him anymore. He had been so elated to find himself attracted to Karin, not least because he knew at last that there was life after Erika. He thought no one would ever match Erika in his affections, but Karin had done that. And now she had dumped him, just like Erika had. It was too much to bear.

Over the last few tormented days, just when he was beginning to think about something wonderfully mundane, like finishing Herr Brant's counter, or the price of varnish, an image of Karin would sweep through him like a phantom and take his breath away, make his legs buckle. He hated this feeling. He needed to put a stop to it. He hated Karin for putting him through this, but he hated the Portners more. He had a feeling that they had somehow put Karin up to it. That that meddling mother-in-law of Erika's was responsible for all this, just as she had warned him off of Erika that day on the doorstep when he came knocking. The doorstep that little Netta was now leading his sweetheart out onto. The sight of Karin punched the air from his lungs again and he felt the need to kneel in the dirt. He slumped there among all the other detritus and fungus, the booze churning in his stomach and curdling his rage.

Through the surgery window Erika watched Netta leading Karin by the hand. She was filled with a boiling jealousy at this slip of girl acting like a mother to her daughter; just as she was the night before when she saw Max on his knees in front of Karin, comforting her, in a way he had never done to Erika since his return from Siberia; just as she was that night in the bathroom when she had seen the way Karin had peered in so sympathetically through the open door at Max hunched over in the tub. Peered in with a sympathy Erika had found it so difficult to muster for the spectre of her husband which she struggled to connect with.

She found her feet marching her out into the corridor where her next patient sat looking up expectantly.

'I'm sorry, Frau von Hagens,' Erika said, 'please give me a minute. I'll be right back.'

Frau von Hagens nodded politely and cursed internally as her doctor rushed into the street.

'**D**on't tell me your short cut involves swimming to the baker's shop?'

Netta shook her head and though she wanted so desperately to push the housekeeper into the murky water, she knew the trouble she would get into would be so great it would outweigh the glory. She couldn't bear the thought of her father shouting at her again. She was scared enough of him already. So she contented herself with leading Karin the long way to the baker's shop so that it would surely be shut by the time Karin arrived to buy her stupid cake for...

Papa!

Netta came to an abrupt stop as she saw her father sitting on the bench ahead on the towpath.

'Which way now?' Karin said.

'Erm.' Netta's voice quivered. She shuffled backwards, praying her father wouldn't notice her and ask her what she was doing here. He knew the streets as well as she did. He would surely realise she was leading Karin a merry dance and then God knows what trouble she'd be in!

'Go up through the wood there and you come out on Hirtenstrasse. That's the street the baker's shop is on, but hurry, it closes soon!' Netta whined and hurried off back down the towpath, leaving Karin perplexed and slightly miffed.

Private Gerry Carter was watching the house. The terraced red brick house on three floors in the suburb of Mengede in the heart of the Ruhr district. He'd seen the young girl with the short hair coming and going many times as he sauntered past on his pointless patrols. Deep in his subconscious, the little housekeeper reminded him of his wife back in England, but he never allowed the connection to bubble up to the grimy surface of his lonely brain. As he leant with one foot on the wall of the sweet shop he watched her being led down the towpath by the little girl and bit his lip, tightening his grip on his rifle.

Erika hurried out of the house and down to the towpath trying to catch up with Karin and Netta. What on earth was she going to say to her when she caught up with her? What on earth was she going to do with Netta standing right there too? She had no idea but she was compelled to carry on, compelled to at least smack the little bitch in the face, then without a word she could go back to Frau von Hagens and deal with her inflamed bunions with a renewed sense of satisfaction; wait for the little whore to come whining back later asking Erika why she hit her, what she had done to deserve that, and then Erika would give her what for all right!

She froze at the sight of Rodrick lolling under the trees. *The little bitch, the little whore*, she heard the breeze say.

It was a wonder the whole village wasn't saying it, Erika thought, and not about Karin, but about me, after all I'd allowed to happen with him, this pathetic excuse for a man.

She stood there for a moment slowly becoming aware of the rapidity of her breathing, the trembling of her limbs. That was anger, wasn't it, she told herself. It certainly wasn't arousal, her mind insisted, although the line between the two became increasingly difficult to distinguish as she grew older, she realised.

She heard the scuffing of heavy boots from a distance and turned to see a British soldier following two women down the street. She looked back at Rodrick.

'Go home,' she pleaded, but just who she was speaking to – him or herself – she wasn't sure.

Private Carter had forced himself onto some other German bitches in that very wood over there, he recalled as the little girl led the housekeeper past him, but even he drew the line in doing anything about it when there was a child in the picture. He'd get her, some day, he told himself, but that didn't quell the stirring in his unwashed underwear right now, did it!

A woman tottered out of the sweet shop, pulled an aniseed twist from a paper bag and sucked on it slowly. Carter's eyes bulged at the spectacle. She crossed the street, hissing at some blonde on the corner in their gobbledegook language. 'Jenny, Jenny,' was all he understood.

Carter launched himself from the wall and slouched across the street after the woman, who was now tugging the other towards the village.

'Look at 'em,' he muttered to himself, 'rough as toast.'

Just what he needed to take out his frustrations on.

Karin looked doubtfully up the bank and into the wood. That way seemed muddy and steep. She did not want to attempt it in the shoes she was wearing, but if Netta was right she would be too late to catch the baker if she didn't. She looked down the towpath in desperation for an alternative route and saw Max sitting on the bench. She'd assumed he was at work so the sight of him was surprising as well as pleasant, calming in fact. Her anxiety about getting to the baker's subsided. If she had any concerns at all now it was just to find out why Max was here and if he was all right. As she approached him she saw his eyes were closed, his head tilted back, his furrowed brow angled towards the weak sun.

She flushed with the desire to sneak up on him, surprise him, like a lover might. Her worry was how best to do it. Sneak up behind him and slam her hands onto his shoulders? Flop down next to him on the bench, perhaps, with a hand slapped on his knee? Although she still savoured the protective sensation of his rough hands around hers from the other night as she wept about Rodrick in the living room, both these options seemed a little over-familiar for a housekeeper and her employer, so she opted for standing in front of him, between his face and the sun, casting a shadow which would cause him to open his eyes in irritation, only to be, she fantasised, pleasantly surprised to see her mischievously smiling down at him.

She took her position on the towpath before him. Cast her shadow. His head twitched irritably, just as she'd hoped.

He is back in the office in Gegesha, having been dragged out of his bunk in the early hours by two guards as Edgar shouted after them, 'Where are you taking him? What are you doing, you bastards!' He is choking on the floor from the way they've used his shirt as a leash and a Lieutenant is firing questions at him about his father-in-law, a Captain of the Border Guard. Then Volkov's hands are round his neck and Max's blood boils at the filthy touch of the man that murdered his brother Horst. He tries to resist, but the sergeant brings his knee up into Max's face. Max shrieks with the pain and collapses to the floor. There's a jangling and scraping above as a huge bunch of keys on the desk is grabbed and brought down on his head.

'Tell us the truth!'

Ch-mp.

'Tell us the truth!'

Ch-mp.

'Tell us!'

Ch-mp, 'Tell us!' *Ch-mp, ch-mp.* The keys bite into the ball of human on the ground.

Max puts his hands over his head until they curl up, bruised and bleeding. Then only his skull is left to protect him from death as the keys thump into him again and again. The barracks key, the office key, the solitary key, the kitchen key, the key to the storerooms, the key to the locksmith's workshop, the key to the armoured car, the key to the main gate, the key to freedom – that's what each and every one of them is. Where once he thought the guards brandished them to keep him captive, now he knows that all together and wielded like a multi-headed mace, rapped over his head until his skull caves in, they are in fact the keys to freedom, because death is the only road to freedom now.

Max gasps as he tries to break the surface of his nightmare, but the shadow of Volkov passes into his narrowing field of view, cloudy and blurred from all the blows, darkened with blood. He lashes out at the sergeant in one last desperate attempt to free himself.

Punches him square in the face.

And finds the strength to run from the office, up a wooded bank, which he swears was never there before. The flat barren parade ground is what he expects to find between the office and the barracks, but he is just relieved to be free, so he keeps on running, whilst Karin falls back from the force of his blow, unconscious before she hits the murky water of the canal.

'I hit her,' Max spoke with more volume, more conviction. 'I couldn't see it until now. But it was me.'

Edgar deflated, a little disappointed but not surprised by his friend's lack of lucidity. 'You'll see a lot now that you've never seen before,' he laughed, remembering to present his jovial self. 'We'll try and reduce the morphine later, then things will be clearer.'

'Ed! Ed! I *am* seeing clearly now. I hit her. It was me.'

'How many times, Max! No one else was hurt in the accident.'

'Not the accident, Ed. Not the accident. Karin. I hit Karin. Our housekeeper. I was on the towpath,' he groaned, 'by the canal. But then I wasn't. I was back in Gegesha. I thought it was Volkov. And I lashed out. I think it's my fault she's dead.'

'What are you talking about?' Edgar scoffed unconvincingly. 'I love you, Max, but you're the biggest softy I know. As if you are capable of hitting anyone!'

'But I have. I've done it before. Since we got back. I've done it in my sleep. I didn't mean to, but I have.'

'Need a hand?' Erika said, peering round the bedroom door.

'Who's there?' Bertel said over Martha's shoulder.

'It's Erika. Need some help?' she smiled.

'Wouldn't say no,' Martha huffed.

'Of course,' Erika cooed, crossing the room and holding up Bertel as Martha finished rearranging the pillows.

'Bertel has just been telling me how apparently she hears punches being thrown up in your room,' Martha sighed, rolling her eyes at Erika.

'Really?' Erika laughed. 'Well, I know this old house makes some eerie sounds in the middle of the night. Perhaps you're mistaking that for—'

'Mistake! It's no mistake,' Bertel squawked, brushing Erika's fussing hands from her nightdress. 'Don't try and paint me as a fool, as a dotty old bag.'

'Bertel!'

The phone started ringing downstairs.

'You're both as bad as one another.'

'I'll get that,' Martha said quickly, relieved by the opportunity to escape, and rushed from the room.

'My mind is sharp enough,' Bertel continued, 'my ears are sharp enough. Sharp enough to hear when he gives you a wallop in the middle of the night.'

'I beg your pardon?' Erika reddened. 'What are you talking about?'

'Max. Beating you. I can hear little Netta snoring in her bed up there, so do you think I can't hear the sound of someone being punched?'

'I don't... Bertel... he's never.'

'That's what the make-up's for. Or are this silly old goat's eyes not as sharp as they used to be too? He gives you a black eye, you cover it up with make-up and we all go on as if nothing has happened. He stands out there,' she nodded towards the tall, square windows; nowhere near as pretty as the Tiffany window in Erika's room above, but much more transparent, much more revealing, 'and just stares at the house, like a zombie, like he's disgusted by it, by us, by you. And then he wanders off down the canal. I can see it all from here. All of it. I even saw...' Bertel's eyes glazed over for a moment, then she snapped her head back to face Erika. 'He can't even bear to be in here, but we all carry on like nothing's wrong.'

'He's getting better, Bertel. He is. He doesn't do it on purpose. He never laid a finger on me before.'

'I know that, you silly girl! I know it's the war that changed him. Of course it's that blasted war that changed him. But the question is, what are you going to do about it?'

'I don't—'

'You're the doctor, Erika!' Bertel cried in a confluence of anger and entreaty. 'Heal him! Can't you heal my nephew, for God's sake?'

Erika was speechless, but the excruciating silence that followed was promptly pierced by Martha rushing back into the room crying, 'Max has been in an accident!'

Edgar looked around the ward to see if anyone else had heard his friend's mumbled delirium, though he knew his friend well enough to know in fact he was anything but delirious.

'I think it was me. I'm sure it was me,' Max wept.

'Shh, shh!' Edgar said as soothingly as his shocked and panicked body would allow him to. 'Shh, shh! Now, Max, you have to listen to me, OK? You are not a killer. You are not a violent man. You did nothing to hurt anyone.' Edgar winced at his own words and his eyes filled with tears for Karin, for Max, for himself. 'I know I'm not Horst, but I love you just the same, Max. I love you, brother, and I cannot lose you. I won't lose you. You're my family,' he said, leaning in close to Max's bandaged ears. 'It's not like I'm ever going to get one of my own, is it?'

He stood upright, straightened his white coat and with a gentle squeeze of Max's shoulder he left the ward.

'And I'm not going to lose another friend,' he muttered to himself as he went to find a vial of a sedative and a needle with which to administer it – to both Max and, when no one was looking, to himself – a wonder of modern medicine that could keep their demons at bay, at least until the medicine ran out, or their bodies got used to the drug.

But as he started down the corridor he saw something that he realised would make an even better tranquiliser for his friend's turbulent mind, if not his.

'Hey, Netta. There's someone here who would love to see you.'

Netta, who had been numbing herself with the hypnotising sight of her feet dangling above the shiny floor where she sat, snapped out of her reverie and hurried towards her funny Uncle. He showed her into the small ward where a man dressed as a mummy from an Egyptian tomb was half sitting in bed, both arms hanging up from hooks in the ceiling.

'Go and say hello to your papa,' Uncle Edgar said.

'Is that my papa?' Netta whispered.

'Yes,' Edgar laughed. 'He's there under all those bandages which are helping him get better as quickly as possible. Helping him get better,' he said loudly for Max's benefit, 'so he can come home where he belongs and look after you again. That would be nice, wouldn't it?'

Netta nodded then stepped carefully across to the bed and met the moist, red, but unmistakable eyes of her father.

'Sorry, Netta,' he cried.

Netta didn't know what to do or say. She tried to remember what the adults said to her when she was hurt, what they did, but she had never been hurt as badly as this, never been covered in bandages like this. Where could she put her hands to comfort him? She couldn't remember what he said to her when she broke her nose on the ice, but she could remember seeing her mama on the beach with his head in her lap. She could remember the words she said to him then as he trembled and cried in his sleep.

'Shh, shh,' Netta said stroking his head with trembling fingers and all the tenderness she could muster. 'You're safe. You're safe here. You're safe with me. There's no war here. It's over. Shh, shh.' She imitated the sea. 'There's no more war. Shh, shh.'

Erika rushed into the ward at that moment and was arrested not only by the terrible sight of her bandaged husband but also by the sight of her daughter gently stroking Max's head and whispering the very words Erika had whispered to him on so many restless nights. It was at once the most beautiful thing she had ever seen and the most terrible, not just because of Max's injuries, but the realisation that her little girl had quietly witnessed and absorbed all those awful exchanges between her parents, and she, Erika, had spent so much time focusing on the impact Max's condition was having on herself, she hadn't given a thought to how it might be affecting Netta. Children should be seen and not heard, her own father had always professed, and Erika had vowed when she was a little girl, staring out through the locked gates of his villa, that she would never treat her own children that way; that she would always remember how children, seen and not heard, still saw things and heard things, especially the things expressed inches above their heads, which adults somehow believed were inaudible and forgettable to something as absorbent as a child. And yet, here she was, an adult herself making exactly the same mistakes as her parents. Netta shared a bedroom with her and Max, a bedroom where the air was thick with nightmares and disillusion; she tinkered away on the piano in the living room where the adults played their games of emotional chess; and yet Erika had convinced herself, like all the other amnesiac ex-children in that house, that Netta should be seen and not heard, was unseeing and unhearing.

She sat carefully next to the bed. She sat Netta on her knee.

'Shh, shh,' she said, gently stroking both her husband's bandaged head and her daughter's golden locks. 'You're safe. You're safe here. It's over. Shh, shh,' she whispered, imitating the sea.

****

Acknowledgement

Thank you again to the team for all they have done to get the book published.

Love and gratitude go to my wonderful children and grandchildren. I hope I make them as proud as they make me.

Finally, also love in abundance to my husband Jeff for always being my rock.